Asking for a Friend

Doubleday Canada and colophon are registered trademarks of Penguin Random House Canada Limited

Library and Archives Canada Cataloguing in Publication

Title: Asking for a friend / Kerry Clare.
Names: Clare, Kerry, 1979– author.
Identifiers: Canadiana (print) 20220475237 | Canadiana (ebook) 20220475253 | ISBN 9780385675642 (softcover) | ISBN 9780385675659 (EPUB)
Subjects: LCGFT: Novels.
Classification: LCC PS8605.L3605 A91 2023 | DDC C813/.6—dc23

This book is a work of fiction. Names, characters, places and incidents are products of the author's imagination or are used fictitiously. Any resemblance to actual events or locales or persons, living or dead, is entirely coincidental.

Cover design: Lisa Jager
Cover photo: Johner Images / Getty Images

Printed in Canada

Published in Canada by Doubleday Canada,
a division of Penguin Random House Canada Limited,
and distributed in the United States by Penguin Random House LLC

www.penguinrandomhouse.ca

10 9 8 7 6 5 4 3 2 1

Penguin
Random House
DOUBLEDAY CANADA

KERRY CLARE

Asking for a Friend

A NOVEL

DOUBLEDAY CANADA

For Britt, Jennie, Kate, Bex, Erin, and Katie,
because you were there, and you're still here.

"Is it too hard to write your own narrative and witness another's, simultaneously? . . . Is that why some friendships between women crash into each other, noses pressed against glass, waving with wild recognition at the person on the other side, and then recede with the same force? Too much, too close, too similar, too uncanny?"

—Erin Wunker, *Notes from a Feminist Killjoy*

What things are lost?
Many. Most. And those that make it,
spared by chance. Consider
the rune poem, only copy
of a pagan text, bound between
Lucy the martyr and the date of Easter.
What brought it here?
or brought the book
to the burning library?

—Erin Noteboom, *A knife so sharp its edge cannot be seen*

ONCE UPON A TIME

Every time Jess was pregnant, Clara had been the first to know. Which, initially, was a product of circumstance. They hadn't even been friends the first time, instead, just two women who lived in the same university residence and happened to be in the kitchen together late on a Saturday night. But what transpired between them that night, and in the months and years to follow, would stitch their stories together, a ragged patchwork, the fabric of two lives running parallel. Marked by all the usual milestones: love, loss, and heartbreak. Marriage and mobility. Motherhood and all its trials multiplied by the power of two.

Parenthood, Jess observed from her perspective smack dab in the eye of the hurricane, was—if you were lucky—like friendship, a story without end. The alternative too awful to contemplate. But what this also meant, of course, was that it never stopped, there were no breaks from the possibility of something new and worse to worry about around every single corner.

And if you only knew how low the stakes had been, Jess would mutter to her former self, that idiot woman who'd driven herself crazy serving homemade organic purées to her first baby. But not the second baby, because there hadn't been time for that, and everything poor Miles ever ate came from a pouch packed with nutrients brewed in a processing plant, which only compounded Jess's guilt when she thought about it now, considering all her youngest child had to contend with. So very stupid. Even though none of it was her fault, Jess had been assured, but so often that she'd started wondering what suspicions drove everyone to be so emphatic. Did they all know something she didn't?

These days, with her children old enough to go out into the world and be wounded in all kinds of ways that had absolutely nothing to do with her, Jess finally knew why well-meaning people implored new parents—so cruelly, it had seemed at the time— to "enjoy every minute" of the baby years. Because the baby years are really hard. But see, every minute you're enjoying your baby is a minute when you aren't fretting about orthodontia, puberty's increasingly early onset, and the risks of human trafficking, all the while trying to schedule intensive speech therapy into an already over-scheduled family life. And how do you live a coherent narrative out of that kind of chaos? Where was the through-line in the anxiety, in all the mess?

It was a question that only underlined Jess's passion for the old stories, established and contained. Archetypal. Stories that came with resolution and made sense of life's terrifyingly infinite possibilities. Imagine: *Once upon a time there were two friends who chattered, a boy who didn't speak, and a woman who grew as big as the universe.*

"Fairy tales," Jess would lecture in her work. "Some of them are older than any other cultural artifact you'll ever encounter. Crossing cultures, and passed down through the ages, and they belong to you. To all of us. The building blocks for our understanding of the world and how it works." Anyone who's ever read a Grimm story, she determined, would be able to fathom ISIS, for example. Gruesome beheadings, torture, cruelty, terrible chance and destruction. Nothing new under the sun.

There were people who had never heard these stories, though, or at least the versions that hadn't been watered down, the stories about little children lost in the woods and the birds that peck your eyes out. About wicked stepmothers who get their just deserts and witches roasting in ovens. For some readers, it was all about the gingerbread house, everything Disney and sweetened right up.

But you missed something, Jess would insist, when you skipped the tragedy, the violence, the thirst for justice, the vengeance. These stories were a way to understand the world. Curses from nefarious godmothers or a witch with an apple. The Little Mermaid, who traded her voice for a pair of legs and an earth-bound life, transactions and intentions that do not go as planned.

CLARA'S ROOM

1998–1999

Clara Summers had been poaching eggs. She was known for culinary tricks, whereas the other girls on the floor thought macaroni from a box was a special occasion. And when Jess came into the kitchen, she was hit by the smell, the suggestion of something tainted. She gagged at the eggs, and Clara saw it. Glancing up from the stove with alarm, she said, "Oh, you've been crying." Jess's first inclination was to back right out into the hall.

Jess hadn't been looking for company. The kitchen door was soundproof, mostly; smell-proof, too, apparently. She'd assumed that everybody was out for the night. There was a charity thing going on in the campus pub downstairs, and Jess could feel techno beat beneath her feet, vibrations underlining her nausea. She'd been looking for the soda crackers in her cupboard, something dry and bland, the only kind of food she'd been able to stomach all week.

"It's the smell," she said. "The eggs." But she couldn't turn and run. She'd been admiring Clara Summers from afar since the beginning of the year, her easy self-possession, her worldliness. Her other-worldliness. Clara was older, had taken two years off after high school and gone travelling with a boyfriend who was now her ex. She had stories of yurts and kibbutzes, while Jess had never been on a plane. Clara knew things. If there was a person Jess could confide in, perhaps Clara was the one.

"I'm pregnant," Jess told her, putting her unfortunate situation into words for the first time. "I think," she said. "I know." The week before she'd taken four tests, bought one at a time. Disbelieving the results of each one, the stupid stick with its glaring positive, two pink lines where there should have been one, marching straight back to the drugstore to purchase another test, the one that, she hoped, would deliver the result that she was looking for. "Honestly, I can't believe it."

Clara said, "Really?" She pointed with her spatula at the pot and said, "You want me to throw this out?" The eggs were nearly set.

"No," said Jess, who headed to the couch in the corner and knelt on its arm. She opened the window and stuck her face against the screen to breathe in the cold winter air. Outside, snowflakes were falling, illuminated by the streetlights' glow. The museum across the road was lit up for a gala that was miles away from her life. She exhaled. "That's better." Even though the screen was dusty, she could almost taste the metal, and she knew the relief of the fresh air would only last a minute.

"How far along?" Clara asked.

Jess had to think about it. "Since October," she said, removing her face from the window, turning back towards the room. "When it happened. So two months, I guess?" And she really didn't like the sound of that. Two months was such a solid block of time, whereas in the back of her mind, where all these weeks she'd been keeping track, the situation had been tenuous, mostly hypothetical. Until the nausea started, kicking her butt.

Clara turned the stove off and came over to sit by Jess on the sagging couch, her profile lit up by the small artificial Christmas tree blinking on the table beside her. "And you feel like garbage, right? Everything makes you want to puke. And you're so unbelievably tired."

What a relief it was to really be seen. "Yeah, exactly," said Jess. "I slept for eighteen hours last night. But I still keep thinking maybe it's mono."

"It's not mono."

"Maybe it could be—"

"It's not."

"How do you know?"

"I know," Clara said. Of course she did. "It happened to me."

And this was something, Clara poaching eggs on a Saturday night. That a person could go through this kind of catastrophe and come out the other side. Jess asked, "What happened?"

Clara rolled her eyes, very dramatic. "Oh, man, it was a disaster." She'd been on the pill but had been on the road so long that she'd run out, and then on a rickety bunk in a hostel in China, the condom broke. "Not long after my period—I thought we'd be all right. We decided to take our chances, and then when we were in Singapore later, I realized. And abortion is legal in Singapore but you have to be a resident, so after a while it just seemed like the only thing we could do was just go home. Which meant, yeah, that everybody knew—his parents, and our friends, which was mortifying. It all became such a big deal."

"And your parents?"

"I couldn't tell my parents," said Clara, shaking her head. "They're really religious. They only tolerated me being with Alex at all because we were travelling, which technically isn't 'living together.' Abortion would have been a step too far. But Alex's family was really good to me."

"And then it was over?" Jess wanted to know that this disaster could be contained, that it might not devour the rest of her life.

"It was the biggest relief. Everything after was a mess though, all our plans derailed. We both spent six weeks living in Alex's parents' basement, doing whatever jobs we could, saving enough money to buy two tickets back to New Zealand."

"All that," said Jess, "makes what's happening to me seem almost boring." She slipped down from the arm of the couch, away from the window, sitting properly now, her legs curled beneath her.

"Oh, no," said Clara, brow furrowed. "I didn't mean that."

"No, it's good," said Jess. "Really." She was feeling lighter now, her secret so much less anguishing now that she had someone to share it with.

Clara said, "So, what are you going to do?"

"Well, I mean, there's only the one option," said Jess. A single thing of which she was certain, which was strange; Jess had always supposed such a decision would be tortured. She said, "Listen, I'm sorry. I mean the eggs, and—" She gestured around the empty common room. "I didn't think anyone was around tonight."

But Clara didn't care about the eggs. "You really haven't told anyone else about this?" she asked. Jess shook her head. "What about—I mean. Do you have a boyfriend? Have you told him?"

Jess said, "I don't have a boyfriend. Not *here*, at least." It had not been the most fruitful season. The ratio of women to men on campus was three to one. "He was my boyfriend back home. Used to be. The last time I was home, though . . . It was stupid. We don't talk."

"And what if I hadn't been here tonight?" Clara asked.

"There's crackers in the cupboard."

"What?"

"That's what I was going to do. If you hadn't been here." Jess got up to get some, keeping her distance from the eggs. There was such little air flow in the common room, even with the window wide. Opening her cupboard, she grabbed a sleeve of crackers from their box, broke open the package and stuffed three into her mouth, focussed on the chewing, on the dry and bland relief of it all. Waiting for the churning in her gut to be gone.

Once she'd swallowed, she offered the packet to Clara, who waved it away and said, "What about your friends? They're out tonight?"

"Who?"

"All those girls. That small one with the stupid name." She didn't hold back, Clara.

"Muffy."

"That's the one."

"Her real name's Melissa." Jess sat down again and leaned back on the couch. "And she's not that bad." Muffy was Jess's roommate. "But she's not my friend, not really." None of them were, the other girls in their hall. The connections were superficial, but Jess was happy to hang out with anyone.

Clara was braver. At the beginning of the year Jess had been struck by an impression of Clara eating dinner in the dining hall, her only companion a battered copy of *Fried*

Green Tomatoes at the Whistle Stop Cafe. And Jess wondered if independence was something you had to grow into, if two years from now, when she was Clara's age, she would be substantial enough to go around without a gaggle for company.

Clara asked, "How long have you known?"

It took Jess a beat to understand what she meant. "A couple of weeks, I guess. But I kept hoping it would turn into something else, that it was all just in my head." She bit into another cracker, talking with her mouth full. "But no."

Clara slid across the couch, placing her hands on Jess's face, lifting her chin. Jess flinched, but Clara didn't let go. Her blue eyes and yellow hair; Clara was shining. Holding on the way a mother might, the grip of her eyes just as steady. She said, "You know it's going to be all right, right? You're going to be okay. I remember wishing someone had been able to promise me that." Then she let go, suddenly self-conscious, aware of a boundary she'd transgressed. She said, "I'm sorry. I just see this despair. I mean, I know it."

"No, it's fine," said Jess. The warmth from Clara's palms lingered on her face. She ate the rest of the cracker but she wanted to keep talking, to keep Clara close. "I don't really even believe it's happening, though. Because aren't you supposed to feel something? I don't feel different at all. Just terrible. Like something you'd peel off the bottom of a shoe."

"Which counts as something," Clara said.

"It's just the very worst time for all this," said Jess, casting off all composure. She'd held it together so long, but Clara was giving permission to acknowledge the reality of her situation. "Exams, and the holidays. It's all such a mess," she said. "I had to spend the whole afternoon hiding under the covers." She'd told Muffy it was cramps, her long-awaited period finally arrived.

"You could come back to my room," said Clara. Because she was older than everyone else, perhaps, she had the rare privilege of a single room, four walls to herself, a door with a lock. "We'll go get your stuff—nobody will know."

Jess's protests were half-hearted; she knew this was the answer. Clara shook her head at any hesitation anyway, saying, "Bring your crackers. Come on."

Clara had plants in her room, vines creeping along her windowsill, and pink flowering ones whose stamens were terrifyingly phallic. She'd brought furniture from home; a tall bookcase packed beyond capacity and an antique rocking chair draped in a patchwork quilt, into which she urged Jess, wrapping it around her like a cocoon. Then she pulled an electric kettle out of her desk drawer—a violation of house rules about appliances in the bedrooms, a fire hazard. Clara was a cozy kind of rebel. She said, "What you need is ginger tea."

And so Jess rocked, finally warm, while the kettle boiled, steaming up the windows and obscuring the lights outside. She could have been anywhere—in Paris, or Morocco. A colourful crochet blanket covered the bed, a deep red rug hid the industrial carpet, and Clara had plastered the cinderblock walls with antique postcards, tourist maps, and line drawings presumably done by her own hand. With the fluorescent overhead light off, Clara's desk lamp illuminated the room, casting inviting shadows around its edges. And in the centre, taking up what little space remained, was an old blue travel trunk decorated with stickers from long-ago transatlantic journeys on the Cunard Line.

"That's cool," said Jess, indicating the trunk with her foot.

"I found it on the street," Clara explained. "You can see the scratches on the bottom from where I dragged it home."

The kettle started whistling, and after rummaging through her desk-drawer pantry for two mugs, Clara unplugged it. She fetched the box of ginger tea from the shelf on her headboard and removed two teabags. She poured the water with a swish, then sat down on her bed and let it steep.

"It's a bit crowded in here," Clara said, an apology. "I'm like a turtle, going around carrying my home on my back, but I like to have all my things around me." She turned and rubbed the steamed-up window, clarifying the view. "Besides, these rooms are so ugly. I had to do something."

"How come you decided to live on campus anyway?" Jess asked. Most older students lived in draughty attics, or basement apartments with ceilings so low you had to duck to pass through the doorways.

Clara moved Jess's tea to a corner of the trunk where she could reach it. "I thought maybe I could do one normal thing in my life," she said. Raising her own mug to her face, she inhaled the aroma. "This," she said, "is better than crackers." Then she folded her legs beneath her, her hair hanging down, her face shiny. She looked younger now. "And I wanted to meet people. I wanted to make friends." Jess knew that part hadn't panned out well, because Clara was always alone.

"So what happened?" said Jess. She breathed in the flavour of the tea. It was still too hot to drink, but Clara was right, it was better than crackers. "I mean, how come you came back to school?" She couldn't imagine being launched into the world like that, then opting to compress an entire life down to class schedules, meal plans, this one tiny room.

Clara shrugged. "I was stupid. I couldn't wait to get out my hometown, and I'd hated high school, so I was finished with that. Plus, Alex, my boyfriend, he was thirteen years older, and he'd got to do all those things I'd missed out on, so when we split up, I decided to go backwards. To act my age. To go to school and learn and do ordinary things." She gestured toward her surroundings in general. "It's been hard, though. It's the girl thing."

"The girl thing?"

"I went to an all-girls high school," said Clara. "An all-girls dorm is basically my worst nightmare. Not quite what I had in mind."

Jess had actually chosen the all-girls residence, brainwashed by an adolescence spent reading British books about boarding schools, so she had nothing to say to this.

"By the time I got my application in," said Clara, "it was the only dorm left. So I decided I'd give it a try." She said, "And it's been trying for sure."

Jess didn't think this was fair. Clara never went out of her way to engage with anyone on their floor, situating herself apart from them.

Clara continued, "I mean, one-on-one, girls are fine, because one-on-one, girls are just people, but put a whole bunch of girls together and things get nasty. Just like high school."

Jess considered that she and Clara must have gone to very different high schools. "The thing that surprised me," she offered, "was I thought everyone would be smart. Or at least smarter than me. A baseline IQ requirement, you know? But—" Her voice trailed off. She sipped her drink.

Clara prompted, "But, Muffy."

Laughing, Jess nearly spit out her tea. "No," she said. But yes. "Muffy's okay—she is." Muffy self-identified as "bubbly," majored in psych because her parents insisted on a university degree, but she aspired to be a nail technician.

She was good at nails, incredible patterns she coordinated with outfits and statutory holidays, and everybody loved her, which did make Jess suspicious of the general population. Maybe Jess had more in common with Clara than she thought. "And oh, laughter," she said, clearing her throat, taking another sip. It had been a long time. "That felt weird."

"So," said Clara. "When's it happening? You've got an appointment?"

"I got a referral," said Jess, "and they booked it for Tuesday." It had been so easy, staff at the university clinic treating the whole thing as ordinary, but Jess still couldn't bring herself to say the word. *Abortion*. She just wanted everything to be over.

"And in the meantime?"

"I don't know," said Jess. "I just have to wait. And just be . . . pregnant, I guess." Another word that seemed strange, and ill-fitting. She said, "You know, I really appreciate this." She nodded, indicating the tea, the room, its warmth and comfort. Especially from someone who didn't like girls. She drained the rest of her tea and set the mug down on the desk.

Clara said, "But you don't have to go."

"No?" And for a few seconds, everything hung in awkward balance. Jess was wary of venturing too far too soon, of those missteps that could be the peril of any tentative friendship. Could such warm affection really be mutual? Could anything be as simple as that?

"I could stay? Really?" Jess needed to be sure that Clara meant it. Muffy hosted after-parties in their room, and she wouldn't be able to stand it tonight. "For a little while at least?"

But Clara was already making space, pushing her trunk up against the wall, sweeping the cushions heaped on her bed down onto the floor. "Not ideal," she said, "but it will do for the night." When Jess got up from the chair, she draped the quilt over the makeshift bed, and seemed pleased with the effect.

They dashed down the hall to Jess's room to retrieve pyjamas, a change of clothes, her basket of toiletries. A brief stop at the bathroom for tooth-brushing, and at the kitchen for more crackers, then back to Clara's room, with its soft shadows and textiles, like a hideout, a womb. They closed the door on the rest of the world, and neither of them missed it at all.

Clara never ate her eggs. They sat in their pot poached and puckered, until the skin got wrinkled and they started to smell even worse. Somebody threw them out on Tuesday, when they were no longer identifiable, but left the pot and the spatula soaking in the sink. It wasn't until Friday that the pot was washed, by one of the cleaners probably, and by then Jess wasn't pregnant anymore. She was still wrapped in Clara's quilt, though, curled up on the corner of her bed eating a pot-noodle. Clara had protested that the soup mix in its little foil envelope was probably carcinogenic, but she put the kettle on. They'd had that kettle going all week.

"Did you know," said Clara, who was highlighting paragraphs in her history textbook—when she was reading nonfiction, Clara started most of her sentences with "Did you know . . ."—"that Hitler was a made-up name?"

"What?"

"He was supposed to be a Schicklgruber. His father changed it."

That morning Jess had gone into her 20th-Century Lit exam feeling a little dozy, but she knew the material. And while her bleeding was still heavy, she was feeling better, happy to be moving forward. Three more days of exams and then the semester would be over, but she didn't even want to go home now. It seemed easier, safer, there among the pillows in Clara's room. By now they'd moved the cushions off the floor, finally just crawling into bed together. Not like *that*, but it was comforting. They were oddly compatible, both sound sleepers, and it was strange to find enough room in Clara's single bed. Although Jess kept trying to make sure, to get Clara to affirm, that she was happy, that she wasn't encroaching on anything. "Just tell me when you've had enough and I'll go," she kept saying, and then she stopped, because Clara said it was exhausting to have to keep reassuring her.

"I said I want you here, and I mean it." Clara put her hand on her heart, "I solemnly swear to never tell you anything that I don't mean. Will you believe me?"

There was trouble, though. Muffy had cornered Jess in the bathroom. "Where have you been? Are you sick?"

Jess said, "I wanted to give you space." Their room was small. Although Clara's was smaller, and Muffy wasn't so dumb that she wouldn't see through this excuse.

She said, "I just miss you," the words dripping. Muffy didn't like being left out. "And you guys could come out sometimes. It's like she's stolen you."

"Clara?"

"Who else?"

"But I'm right here," said Jess.

"I'm concerned," said Muffy. "I mean, you're carrying around a bag of overnight pads in the mid-afternoon."

"It's these exams," Jess explained. "My hours are all mixed up." She was afraid for a moment that Muffy might figure out the truth about her pregnancy.

But Muffy was coming at her from a whole other angle. "That girl has bewitched you," she said. "You smell like patchouli."

"But what does patchouli smell like?"

Muffy whispered, "Like lesbians."

Everybody went home for the holidays—Jess to her small hometown two hours north of the city, and Clara to the rural county where she'd been raised and from which she'd managed to spring herself at the earliest opportunity. They spent the next three weeks on the phone, Jess stretching the cord tight across the hall so she could shut her door and have some privacy, and Clara complaining, "I hate it here. They make me go to church on weeknights, and there's nobody to talk to."

"It *must* be a boy," Jess's mom kept muttering to herself. Friends from high school were phoning too, but Jess ignored the Call Waiting—those friends seemed far away now, and she couldn't take the chance of meeting up with them and running into her old boyfriend—choosing instead to talk to Clara late into the night. The holidays disappeared in a haze, and then finally it was the new year and time to go back, school seeming more like home than away by now, rather than the other way around.

There was snow, the campus transformed into winter, and Jess wheeled her suitcase up from the bus station because the subway was two whole dollars, and she wanted to breathe the fresh air after her bus ride. Clara wasn't back yet, so Jess went to her own room, where Muffy greeted her with a squeal. She was listening to *Big Shiny Tunes 2* again. "This semester," she said, as she blue-tacked a brand-new poster of Eagle-Eye Cherry up above her bed, "is going to be wild."

Jess sat down on her own bed for the first time in weeks, taking in the view, Muffy and Eagle-Eye. She pulled an envelope out of her bag, one of the letters Clara had sent her, a card with a map drawn inside, the campus imagined as a universe. The dining hall, the library. The ice cream place on Yorkville Avenue, where you could order a sundae as big as your head—Clara had promised to take her there. Jess stared at the map, tracing the trail her boots had just crunched in the snow, imagining Clara's feet on the same route, anticipating the sound of her steps in the corridor. She was worried that Clara wouldn't come back at all, that maybe she had only dreamed her, or that what had transpired between them had been some kind of spell.

But the card in her hand was real, her own name, "Jess Weir," carefully inscribed upon the envelope, and Clara was real too, appearing later that afternoon. Her long hair was chopped shorter—"My mom cut it"—but everything else was the same, her wide shoulders, her smell that reminded Jess of tea and blankets, the glow of candlelight.

"I brought you a present," Clara said, unfurling something from her bag, a scarf so long that Jess could wrap it around her neck five times and it would still trail on the floor. Clara picked up an end, then pronounced, "What I Did on My Christmas Vacation. If I'd cast off sooner, there would have been nothing left to do."

Muffy watched them as Jess told Clara, "I've got something for you too," though it was nothing so grand or homespun. A gift for Clara had been a fraught proposition; her things were so curated, and it seemed presumptuous for Jess to add to the collection, or to hope to. But during a morning of wandering through the shops that remained of her hometown's downtown, she came across a butterfly-shaped amber pendant on a silver chain—it seemed like something Clara owned already. "Not until now," said Clara, fastening the clasp. "It's perfect."

"Now isn't that adorable," said Muffy, perched on her own bed. "Something else to wrap around the neck. You two have got yourselves fully yoked."

That winter smelled like brownies, with Clara baking endless batches from a recipe torn out of *Homemakers Magazine*, the page yellowed and brittle, Scotch-taped up the middle. Jess kept trying to help her in the kitchen, until the time they decided to bake a cake after imbibing two bottles of wine and she lost control of the hand mixer, splattering batter all over the cupboards and the ceiling, and it was confetti cake batter, so it looked like a unicorn had just exploded, and neither of them could stop laughing, or shrieking "Jackson!" and "Pollock!" at each other in a hysterical misconstrued version of the Marco Polo game. In the morning they were reprimanded by their RA for both the noise and the mess, so Clara baked another cake as penance (Jess did her a favour and sat on the sidelines), but when they offered slices around, everyone else on the floor claimed to be limiting carbs—Clara rolled her eyes. Not long after that, Jess volunteered a culinary trick of her own, a recipe for cake in a mug from her microwave cookbook, and while Clara was initially suspicious, she was fast converted by the lack of dishwashing required and Jess was pleased to be making a contribution to their domestic arrangement.

Baked goods were necessary, sweetness and warmth with the outside world so harsh and so cold. It was January, and then February, and no matter how tightly Jess wrapped her new scarf around her neck, her head, a chill crept in, except for when she was curled up in Clara's bed, which was most of the time; Jess was not doing well. The day she got her period again—a return to business as usual—she burst into tears at the stain on her underwear, an emotional reaction she didn't fully understand. And lately these disconnects were everywhere, like shallow holes she kept stumbling into. She'd started skipping classes, and meals, finding herself detached from the pattern of hours and days that tethered normal people to reality.

Clara tried to minimize the drama: "It's February. Everybody's sad in February. You've been through a lot." She gently suggested Jess might feel better if she stopped playing "Torn" by Natalie Imbruglia on repeat—Clara didn't think it was useful to dwell.

But Jess wanted to dwell, to talk as though words were a spiral through which she might make her way to the essence of her experience. "It's grief, I think. But I'm so confused. Because what am I grieving? How can you grieve a thing you never wanted? Or at least I didn't want it now. Not like this."

And Clara understood this part. Not the lyrics about being naked on the floor—she'd finally turned off the CD player—but about what Jess was going through, the seeming contradiction that wasn't. "No, I know," she said. "I mean, I want to have kids one day."

"Me too," said Jess.

"Like, I'm as certain about that as I was that I didn't want to have a baby then."

"Because two things can be true at once," said Jess.

"Which is what a lot of people don't seem to understand. They think it's simple. And it makes them crazy." Clara told Jess about the clinic just a block from their campus that had been firebombed in 1992.

Just seven years ago. "I had no idea," said Jess.

They were lying in bed. The sky had no colour, and Jess watched dull pigeons on the roof of the dining hall through the window. She was wondering how the birds could stand the cold. "But doesn't that almost make it worse," she asked, "that I'm feeling bad right now, because isn't it kind of anti-feminist to feel sad . . . after . . . *you know?*" She still couldn't say the word. Everything Jess knew about feminism she had read in a book, but she was beginning to understand that real life was less straightforward. "And I also keep thinking, what if this was my only chance, and I threw it all away?" This was an idea she only dared to put into words because of the comfort of Clara's room, her bed, Clara's arms around her as she started crying again.

"You're going to get other chances," Clara promised. "Chances for everything. Life is long, and you're going to change your mind a million times. You have no idea. *I* have no idea. But I hope. The only thing I know is that nobody has to have it all figured out and settled when she's my age, and I really didn't know that when I was *your* age. I mean, Alex and I were practically common law. It was madness. Jess, you're going to want so many things." Clara was holding her even tighter, and Jess buried her face in Clara's neck, wondering if this could be enough, the obvious thing in front of her.

Years later, Jess would reflect on these moments. The line they never crossed but they could have. She would have, she thought, if Clara had made a gesture, a particular touch, her hand on her shoulder and drifting. There was something about Clara's body that invited such thoughts, her sumptuousness, the ease with which she carried herself. Jess had never been so aware of another woman's physicality, outside of all the usual comparisons to her own.

Someone had scrawled "Rape all Dykes" on the sign outside their building with a Sharpie, and Muffy and the others stopped asking Jess and Clara to join them on nights out, had stopped paying them attention altogether. Jess, who wasn't sorry, confided to Clara, "They think we're lesbians," and Clara raised her chin, defiant: "What if we were?" Jess aspiring to be as brave as that, even pretending she was. But this was as far as it went. A yearning was missing, Jess would have admitted, to have one thing lead to another. She knew too that if the line was crossed they could never go back, and so here they were in the moment, bodies entwined, but for comfort instead of desire, and Jess was starting to think maybe comfort was enough. It could be everything. She and Clara were going to move off-campus and get a place together next year, which made the future seem fixed and limitless at once.

Except they hadn't signed a lease, and Clara wouldn't confirm that she'd be in the city for the summer, so their plans were still up in the air with just eight weeks left before the end of term. And Jess had to keep a lid on her anxiety, on all her spiralling, because she didn't want to wear on Clara's patience. Clara had her own struggles. The weather was bad, her classes were difficult, and she hadn't stayed this long in one place since moving out of her parents' house years ago. Even if Jess hadn't been wrapped in blankets and listening to depressing music on repeat, Clara would have gone looking for a diversion.

"I'm auditioning for the Drama Society," she announced on the Monday before Valentine's Day, coming into her room, her winter coat sopping from rain.

Jess sat up in bed for the first time that day, unwrapping Clara's scarf a few times, the beginning of her sloughing off her cocoon. "Auditioning for what?" The first she'd heard of such a plan. Up until now, Clara had shunned campus life entirely. And this was what Jess had been dreading since the evening she'd found her way into Clara's regard: the moment when it would become clear that everything between them had been a misunderstanding. She'd always suspected that Clara would wake up one day and wonder what Jess was doing in her life, never mind her room, her bed.

"The director's in my philosophy tutorial. I thought it might be fun," Clara was saying. "A way to meet people. You could come too."

"You want to meet people?" Jess's voice sounded feeble to her own ears.

"Well, surely some of them are worth meeting," said Clara. "Isn't this the kind of thing that you're supposed to do in university?"

"It's not the kind of thing *you* do."

"It would be if I did it," Clara said. Her urges were expansive, which is why Jess wanted something in writing, a contract, an apartment lease, to confirm their future together. All Jess ever wanted, in addition to everything, was to know that she and Clara would always be friends.

The play was an original production called *A Blandishment of Porcupines*, written by Brett Bickford, this guy from Clara's class who was older than even Clara.

"He seems interesting," Clara told Jess. She was more tolerant of men than she was of women. Poor Muffy had received no clemency, but Brett Bickford got to be *interesting*.

"The script doesn't make any sense," said Jess, who had followed along to audition because she was afraid that, otherwise, Clara might fly away.

Clara dismissed her concerns. "It's abstract. The story will look different on the stage." She was determined to believe in the show. And then she won a leading role, so it was imperative she believe, even though her love interest would be played by Brett, a man as oily as he was arrogant.

"And how are you going to pull that off?" Jess asked.

Clara said, "That's why they call it acting."

Jess ended up in the chorus—a blessing, she thought, because then she would have to take no responsibility for the play being so bad. As rehearsals began, however, she was surprised to be actually having fun. It felt good to be in the world, to be part of something larger than herself, larger than her and Clara—even if being in the chorus entailed standing on risers that flanked the stage and watching Clara in the spotlight.

It helped too that now it was March, and spring was beginning to emerge. And while Brett Bickford was indeed a pretentious lech, and the entire production was his vanity project, the others were okay, worlds away from Muffy. More like what Jess had imagined when she'd pictured being away at school: fun, smart and creative people who made her want to belong. And sometimes she felt she did, like when she was standing in the back row beside Clayton Kerr, whispering snarky comments about Brett, his inability to move on from undergraduate productions.

"I heard he once auditioned for an off-campus play," Clayton muttered at rehearsal one afternoon, talking out of the side of his mouth. Clayton was an incorrigible gossip. "And he didn't even get in the chorus. They offered to make him stage manager."

"Stage manager is a very important job," Jess replied out of the other side of her mouth. All the Drama Society's shows were stage-managed by Emily Holt, who was in love with Brett Bickford and had sex with him twice a year at the closing night cast parties. It was a Society tradition.

The conversation paused. Their part was coming up, where they had to warn Lord Tortoiseshell (Brett) that Lady Jocelyn (Clara) had lost her maidenhead, and cheer when he vowed to avenge her honour. And at the end of the scene, the chorus took a break and everyone headed outside to smoke. Jess carried a pack of cigarettes in her bag now and borrowed Clayton's lighter. "It's just social," she'd explain when Clara pointed out that Jess's smoky coat made their room smell. But at that moment Clara was somewhere else, going through her lines with Brett, so Jess didn't have to deal with her expression of mild disdain.

Outside, Jess took her place in the group of cast members, smoking and getting wet in the drizzle, and she leaned in close to Clayton, who would sometimes put his arm around her if she was cold. Everybody was dressed in the same vintage uniform, flared jeans with soggy hems, second-hand suede and leather jackets, and that smell of wet coats mixed with cigarettes would, for Jess, ever after be a time machine.

"Let's sleep outside tonight," Clara suggested the following week. They could bring their mattress out to the balcony. "We'll be able to see the stars," she said.

It was the kind of March that could go either way, with crocus shoots and a chill in the breeze, but that day smelled like spring, like mud and grass and a hint of garbage with the melted snow. Jess had walked back to the dorm in short sleeves, the sun on her arms for the first time in months, passing the frat boys up and down St. George Street who'd dragged their crappy couches onto the lawns.

"Sounds good," she said to Clara. By now, Jess had learned not to question Clara's impulses, to just follow along and reap the rewards.

And that night, snug on the mattress under piles of blankets, Jess asked her, "Have you done something like this before?" They were lying even closer than usual to stay warm, the evening chillier since sundown, which made it more important to follow through with the plan, fond as Clara was of incongruity. If the night had been milder, she might have lost interest and headed inside.

Clara said, "I mean, I've been camping."

"But not like this," said Jess. Not beneath the lights of the city, surrounded by its sounds, traffic and sirens. Jess thought about how, from Clara, she'd learned how you could build your own little world. You could bring home a trunk from the sidewalk, or move your bed out under the stars.

Clara agreed. "No, not like this." They lay in silence for a while, and then Clara said, "You know, every time I've been close to anyone—friends, boyfriends—they've been so much older. And I don't even know why. Maybe because my sisters were teenagers when I came along? So I've always been the one running behind, trying to catch up, trying to be faster, to be more. And with you, it feels like the first time ever that I don't have to do that."

She added, "I've never had a best friend before. Honestly, I thought I wasn't the type."

Which was ridiculous. Clara Summers could draw other people with the force of a magnet when she turned her attention on them—the guy who'd fixed the oven on their floor had sent her flowers. Clara could be friends with anyone if she just bothered to give them a chance, but she almost never did. So how exactly had it transpired that Jess, of all people, would finally end up here at the centre of the world with Clara beside her, the entire night sky above them? What did Clara see in Jess that made her so different from everyone else that Clara never had any time for?

But she couldn't ask a question like that, especially not to Clara, whose self-assurance Jess had been trying to mirror all along. Jess was scared that if she spoke at all, the spell would be broken. Because, even though the usual inclination between girls she knew was always to relate, to say, "Me too! Same, same," Jess had had strings of best friends for as long as she could remember, often changing with the seasons. But her connection with Clara went deeper than any of those, it was true. She said, in all honesty, "I don't know if I've had a real one in my life."

Little by little, Jess and Clara started to broaden their world, to prop the door open and let other people inside. Something had shifted and Jess felt confident enough in their connection to trust it, and even to turn her mind to other things, such as the endearingly dorky boy beside her in the chorus. Clayton, with whom she shared all kinds of inside jokes now after weeks of standing by his side in rehearsals, and who didn't seem to mind that she'd stolen his yellow bucket hat. Who already had his own favourite mug from Clara's collection, the cracked one with the hippo, since he'd started turning up on their doorstep all the time, although Jess couldn't tell if he *like* liked her, or if they were only friends. The other week at the campus open mic, he'd dedicated a song to her, but it was "MMMBop," which didn't clarify things. She tried to engage Clara on the topic, but Clara was noncommittal, insisting that she mainly regarded Clayton as a pet, scruffy and lovable, and that she was incapable of thinking of him in any other way.

But Jess was thinking of him now on the afternoon before opening night. She was putting up promotional posters downstairs at the entrance to their building, but really, she was waiting for Clayton. They were going to help Clara run her lines. The play was still terrible, but they were buzzing with the prospect of finally performing it, the culmination of so much work. The theatre would be full no matter what, the campus being its own universe with nothing else going on so close to exams.

When Jess saw him approaching, she threw open the door. "I was just postering," she explained, hoping not to seem too eager, spinning the roll of tape on her wrist. Clayton hugged her back the way he always did, hard and close, and then she scrambled up the stairs behind him and down the hall to Clara's room, which was empty.

Clayton stopped. "Where is she?"

"Clara?" Jess asked. "She's around. Probably in the kitchen." He popped into the hall to look again. "Or the bathroom." Jess sat down on edge of the bed. "What's going on?"

"She didn't tell you?" He came back in and started rummaging around for the hippo mug. "How our man Brett made a move?"

"A move on Clara?" Jess pointed to the shelf where he'd left the mug the last time he was over.

"She shot him down, obviously, but I guess he found her acting skills quite convincing."

"Whose acting skills?" asked Clara, arriving in her oven mitts, carrying a loaf of banana bread fresh from the oven.

"Yours," said Jess. "Apparently."

"A woman of many talents," said Clayton, leaning close to breathe in the baking. "I can't believe you actually made this," he said, which was what he said every time Clara made anything, as though she'd performed a miracle instead of merely reading a recipe. "The poor guy, I heard you broke his heart."

"But you never said a thing," Jess said to Clara. They'd been together all day. If anyone had ever made a move on her, she would have had Clara analyzing it from every angle for hours. Clayton hadn't made a move yet, and she'd been going on about it for weeks.

"Because there was nothing to say," said Clara, plugging in the kettle. And here was the distance between them. Jess wondered what it must be like to be the kind of woman who found it literally unremarkable when men, even awful ones, fell at their feet.

The show opened and, of course, Clara stole it, reading lines from Brett Bickford's awful script like they were satire, highlighting their absurdity, which made the bad play almost make sense. That week the campus paper published a positive theatre review for the first time in its history.

And then it was over, this huge, amazing part of their life collapsed like a fan. To aid with the transition, they drank until they were stupid at the cast party backstage, Brett Bickford with Emily Holt in the props cupboard as usual, apparently over his heartbreak at Clara's rejection. Everyone else was out in the corridor drinking warm beer out of red plastic cups, debauchery flowing like the booze was. The costumes room had been raided and people were already taking off their clothes, putting on wigs.

"Where's Clara?" Clayton asked, appearing with two drinks and handing one to Jess. He was wearing an oversized Viking hat with horns. Jess had no idea where Clara was, having last seen her in a pink wig arguing about cultural appropriation with some jerk in a feather headdress, but that was ages ago. Someone else said that Clara had left. Jess sipped her drink, no longer able to properly string a sentence together. She reached up and fondled Clayton's right horn. "Really, are Vikings culturally appropriate either?"

"Listen, I gotta talk to you," he told her. Finally, Jess was thinking. "Not here," he said, leading her along the corridor, around the corner to the lounge, where two people were already sucking each other's faces, setting the tone.

Jess and Clayton sat down on the other couch, Clayton looking nervous. Somewhere along the way, Jess realized, she'd shed that drink, or perhaps she'd finished it. Clayton had taken her hands in his, and what was he waiting for? A kiss was the threshold they could finally cross and everything would happen.

But his hands were sweaty. "It's about Clara," he said, not meeting her eyes. "I mean, does she mention me?" He looked up, felt the need to clarify. "Like, what has she said about what I said? About her feelings."

"Her feelings," Jess repeated. And she knew; on some level she'd always known, yet she hoped that she could bend reality to her will anyway, that maybe fate could be so malleable. She felt small and stupid, sitting before this besotted boy, for imagining she could possess that much power.

Clayton wouldn't shut up. "I'm crazy about her. It's very uncool. Just, like, watching her on stage, the way she shimmers. I can't turn it off." He laughed, but it sounded more like a honk. "And, I mean, has she ever said anything that would make you think . . . that maybe there's a chance?"

Jess said, "No." She could be definitive about this thing, the only ground she had to stand on.

But Clayton wasn't having it. "And I know that. She told me it was never going to happen, but I thought—"

"She said that?" They'd talked about this? The betrayal cut deep, because Jess hadn't known, would never have suspected. All those conversations with Clara listening to her blathering about Clayton, and she'd never said a word.

"I didn't believe it," said Clayton. "Or maybe I just didn't want to." He was still holding her hands, but she realized it was to keep her in place. She pulled away. "She said she didn't want to wreck our friendship."

"Your friendship?"

"Me and her," he said, "and I just really wanted to ask you, um, what she'd said about it all. If you think I have a chance anyway."

Jess said, "No." Her tiny desert island.

"No, what—" he said.

She said, "No, *everything*."

"Clara said that?"

"Clara never said anything."

"I thought you guys were so close," he said, "like two sides of a coin."

So she kissed him. Because he was right there, and there could be no way to make the situation worse than it was, a kiss the best strategy she could think of to blow this moment into an oblivion. And Clayton must have been as drunk as she was, or else they wouldn't be here at all, and maybe this was why he was kissing her back, kissing her hard, his hands all over her body. Kissing her with his eyes closed, which could even mean passion, something real. Instead of the idea that occurred to Jess immediately—sometimes she was too smart for her own good—that he was imagining Clara in his arms.

They went back to his room, and it was difficult to remember exactly what happened, except that everything did, in a drunk and fumbling fashion. And when it was over, Clayton slept, softly snoring, his arm slung around Jess. She could have stayed there, fitting the part exactly, except he hadn't asked her to and his roommate might be returning any moment. Unwinding her body from Clayton's leaden limbs, she retrieved her clothes from the floor and got dressed again. She made her way across campus, her stomach full of butterflies, partly because she was nervous about what was going to happen when she saw Clara.

But also—and mostly—the butterflies were because something had happened. Finally. Exhilarating. And this—walking home in the night feeling shameless, bold and desired—was like something Jess had imagined, a scene recognizable from a movie or a book. The spotlight was shining on her, for once. And for the first time with abject certainty, she was glad that she wasn't going to have a baby, no ambivalence left from the choice she'd made in December. Because she'd have a baby someday, she knew she would, when the time was right, but in the meantime there could be so much more. Those butterflies, and parties, too much to drink, and mistakes that would be inconsequential—because she was still so young, just like Clara had promised, which felt like a revelation after a season of feeling broken and sad.

And Jess was reflecting on the season as she made her way up the steps to their building and inside, heading up to

Clara's room, which had always been Clara's, never properly *theirs*. Jess didn't even have a key, which meant they had to leave the door open with the bolt on to stop it from locking automatically. Would the door be open now? In leaving with Clayton, had Jess betrayed her friend? And why did such a prospect seem so awful? Because hadn't Clara betrayed her too? Seemingly thoroughly absorbed in the open book that was Jess's heart, but all the while holding herself at a remove, keeping secrets, these parts of her that Jess could never reach or know.

A crack of light shone out into the hall from where the door was ajar; Jess felt relief at the sight of it and nudged the door open. Clara was in her stage makeup, curled in a corner of her bed by the window, a book on her lap, the one about the Ya-Ya Sisterhood, but she wasn't reading. The room felt all wrong, bright and garish, Jess taking a moment to realize what the difference was, that the overhead light was on, which it never was, fluorescent, not a hint of a shadow so there was no place to hide, and everything so quiet she could hear it buzzing.

"Somebody told me you'd gone," said Jess, breaking the silence. Clara hadn't looked at her, was gazing out the window, though Jess could see her own image reflected there. "I couldn't find you. And then we left. I went—"

"I know where you went," said Clara, looking over finally, her expression hardened. Sounding bored, annoyed and tired at once, she spoke as though Jess were a child, a tone that Jess had never heard from Clara before, not even in the depths of February when she'd been at her most frustrating. All the distance between them, actual years and life experience, opened up like a chasm, and Jess found herself wanting to retreat, but Clara wouldn't let her. "Come in and shut the door, all the way," she commanded. Jess did what she said, secured the bolt. Clara asked her, "So, what happened?"

Jess sat down beside her on the bed. "I guess you know."

"And it's what you wanted?" This was a rhetorical question, delivered with a patronizing kind of patience.

Jess said, "What's wrong with that?"

"I didn't say anything was."

"You didn't have to," said Jess. Would anyone ever be good enough for Clara, she wondered? "People are allowed to want ordinary things."

Clara conceded, "Well, he *is* ordinary."

"So what?" said Jess. "And he isn't." He wasn't. Clara folded her arms and met her stare. Jess said, "Why are things only okay when they happen to you?"

Clara started speaking, "Jess—"

She cut her off. "You knew I liked Clayton. You could have anyone you wanted, and you could have left him alone—"

"He was literally over here all the time."

"And *you made him like you*."

"I didn't make him do anything," said Clara.

"You didn't have to," said Jess. "That's the thing." She flopped back onto the bed. "You should have told me."

"Told you?"

"That he had feelings for you. That he'd told you he did."

"He told you *that*?" asked Clara.

"Somebody had to."

"And that made you want to *sleep with him?*"

"Well, no," said Jess. "I slept with him anyway."

"But, why?" asked Clara.

"Because I wanted something to happen," Jess sputtered. Surely it wasn't so hard to understand. She took a breath. "This whole year has felt like waiting."

"The whole year?" Clara sounded sad.

"Well, not entirely," said Jess. "Not the parts that were you." Was Clara jealous? Was this even possible? "But those parts can't be everything," she continued. "You know that. You *showed me* that." She tried to imagine how she'd feel in Clara's place and didn't have to reach very far.

After a while, Clara said, very slowly, "I could be happy for you. I could. If Clayton was what you wanted. If you've really thought it through."

"But I haven't thought anything through." For all Jess knew, Clayton thought he'd gone to bed with Clara. "It might just be a one-off thing." It might be a disaster.

"How did you leave it?" Clara asked.

"We didn't. He was asleep." Clara said nothing, so Jess continued, "I guess we'll see."

"But *Clayton*? Really?" Clara said, but there was warmth in her tone now. "He didn't sleep through everything, right?" Jess started to answer, but Clara put her hand up. "Nope," she said. "Actually, I really don't want to know anything at all." She got up to turn the overhead light out, returning the room to the desk lamp's soft glow.

Jess wiggled around to lie the right way on the bed, to place her head on the pillow now, staring up at the ceiling as Clara lay down beside her and nudged her head against her shoulder. "I want good things for you," Clara said. "That's all. The things I want for you are better than ordinary."

"But I'm going to be living with you," said Jess. "So I think better than ordinary is all locked up." She paused, then added, "If that's really going to happen, I mean." She was kidding, but not entirely.

Clara got up again. "I've got to wash this stuff off my face," she said, waiting for Jess to come along, to wash off her own makeup, brush her teeth, but Jess was too exhausted to move. That night she would fall asleep in her clothes, waking in the morning with that delicious kind of ache and regret that affirms that, while your life might be ridiculous, at least you're actually alive.

THE APARTMENT

2001–2002

Clara spent the summer after her third year at university assisting in the excavation of a 400,000-year-old firepit in the south of England, analyzing the soil to determine its sediments and that the pit had been a hearth and not a less deliberate burn. No, none of it had been an accident: for hundreds of thousands of years, people had been settling down in spaces with fire at the centre.

And unlike so much of what Clara was learning at school, this wasn't merely theory, as evidenced by the apartment she'd shared with Jess for the last two years, a tiny place up a narrow flight of stairs above a Chinese herb shop, where there wasn't an actual hearth—the closest thing was an old electric oven where only two of the stove elements functioned, and the oven handle kept falling off. But their kitchen always felt warm, with the window facing south so the light was usually golden.

Clara loved that kitchen, even with the oven's faults, and the family of mice that lived under the fridge. It was the first kitchen she'd ever had that was properly hers, a basil plant on the windowsill, spice jars lined up along the counter. Jess

didn't cook enough to be territorial and was happy enough
to sit at the oak table, a relic from Clara's parents' basement,
eating whatever was being served. Just being there pleased all
the senses: candlelight, the warmth, the flavours, and the
conversations that continued long past the time the candles
had dripped down to nothing.

Growing up, dinners at Clara's home had been different. Her father at the table's head, delivering grace before
anyone was permitted to eat, and her mother not relaxing
until he'd started eating and declared the meal to his liking,
and even when it was, their conversation usually wasn't.
Clara's sisters had moved out, married with families of their
own, by the time Clara was old enough to have opinions,
which meant it was just Clara and her opinions at the table
with her parents. Three weeks after her sixteenth birthday,
cracking under the weight of their disapproval, Clara fled to
the home of her boyfriend-at-the-time, whose understanding family sheltered her in their spare room for six months,
even after the relationship had ended. Clara then rented a
room in a house with a shared kitchen, where nobody paid
proper attention to the stove and the smoke alarm was
pretty much a constant, her fellow tenants burning the bottoms off pot after pot. With the help of some very good
teachers, she'd finished high school while working part-time
at a health food store, which is where she'd met Alex, and by
the time her classmates were framing their grad portraits,
Clara was far away with him, embarking on a round-the-
world adventure. Properly outfitted kitchens, for a long
time, were few and far between.

Who knew Clara would turn out to have such a weak-
ness for basil on the windowsill, a green thing to gaze upon
as she washed her dishes? Clara had thought she made a

respectable nomad during all those years, but it turned out she could also stay put, and not merely to defy her father either, who'd always maintained Clara was too flighty, unable to follow through with anything because, after all, she'd fled his house. But now here she was, most of the way through her university degree, and she'd managed to make a cozy home in this place with Jess, in their kitchen with all that incredible light.

Clara's room was upstairs, tucked under the eaves, the walls so poorly insulated that the wind blew in. The solution, Clara learned their first winter there, was layers of rugs on the floor and quilts and blankets on the bed, which made the climate bearable, and she could remind herself that at least the rent was cheap.

Jess's room downstairs was warmer, but smaller. Decorated with a frog motif, a preoccupation that started with a weird batik bedspread and a poster from *The Frog Prince,* and grew from there. She collected frog figurines, and then people started giving them to her, ceramic ones and a few carved from wood, and one with ridges on its back that you ran up and down with a small stick, producing a croaking sound. Which Jess would do intermittently, startling Clara, who would hear the sound in the attic and start wondering about wild creatures in the walls.

Wild creatures in addition to the family of squirrels who'd built their nest in that narrow space between the ceiling and the roof above Clara's bed, a roof that was barely there in places and not only welcomed the wind but let in the rain sometimes. Clara caught the rain in a bucket, falling into sleep those nights lulled by the drip and the pounding on the roof outside, which sometimes drowned out the skittering of paws overhead.

One night late in the autumn, the skittering turned to scratching and the squirrels broke through. Clara was getting ready for bed when it happened, the scuffling, the crackle, and then a cloud of dust. Rats, she thought at first when she saw the beady eyes, recoiling further as she took in the entire creature. She was so much bigger than the squirrel, but it didn't matter. That squirrel wasn't afraid of her, or maybe it was afraid of everything, mad, literally bouncing off the walls, and joined by three companions, each one's emergence making the hole in the ceiling even bigger. Before the fourth had made it all the way through, Clara was out on the stairs with the door slammed shut, the squirrels slapping, thumping and hissing on the other side.

Clara realized she'd been screaming like a woman in a horror movie, useless and distressed, her screeches summoning Jess and Clayton, who thundered up the stairs. All of them peered around the door at the black shapes tearing the air like bats, Clara screaming still, only stopping when Jess clamped a hand over her mouth. Clayton ran back downstairs, returning with a broom. Then he charged inside, kicking the door shut behind him in a beautiful choreography, as if a whole life spent watching action movies had been preparation for this.

Jess and Clara stood in the dark listening to Clayton swearing and the thumps continued, but there were more of them now, presumably from the broom. They heard the strain of the window being wrenched up, and Jess let go of Clara's mouth.

"Oh my god," Clara said, when she could find the breath to talk, and she even laughed as she heard Clayton exclaim, "Fuck YOU!" from behind the door and then a triumphant crash. Another bang, the window slammed, and Clayton opened the door, letting the light into the stairway.

"Clayton, you're a hero!" Jess exploded, enfolding him in her arms.

But he shook her off. "There's squirrel piss everywhere." And there was, all over Clara's desk and her bed and the floor, and the ceiling had been ripped to pieces, along with the Bob Dylan poster Clara had taped up there, the one of him walking down the street with his hands in his pockets, a girl in a green coat clutching his arm, all gone to confetti.

"A knight in shining armour," said Clara, watching Clayton and considering the way he'd wielded his broomstick. "Who'd have thought we still needed one?"

"Or that he'd have to fight a squirrel," said Jess.

"Maybe all the dragons have been slain." Clayton didn't have a shirt on. They'd been in bed, Clara realized. "I'm so sorry, guys."

"We're going to have to call Ferber," said Jess. Ferber was their landlord's nephew, a dubious handyman at best who'd show up to repair a leaky faucet and end up drinking all their beer, which was why they put up with things like leaks in the roof for as long as they did.

"We could patch the wall with duct tape," said Clayton. Living in that place, they had a lot of the stuff on hand. The seal on the fridge door had gone; tape was how they kept it closed, and it also held up the shower head.

Jess went downstairs and came back with some tape, as well as a dustpan and paper towels. They piled up Clara's rugs and blankets for the laundromat tomorrow, along with Clayton's track pants. Jess taped the hole in the ceiling, although they could already hear the squirrels back skittering about, while Clara swept up the mess on the floor and got on the phone to Ferber, who said he'd be over in the morning. And when all that was finished it was after eleven and they tramped downstairs exhausted.

"You'll have to bunk with us," said Jess, because it was either that or sleep in the kitchen. Their apartment came so cheap because it lacked other common space, and linoleum would make for a terrible place to slumber.

So that was how Clara ended up on Jess's floor, uncomfortable on the foam mattress they kept rolled up for guests, listening to Jess and Clayton's respiratory harmony and surrounded by the frogs.

The frogs had started a couple of years ago, when Jess was taking a course in myths and fairy tales and became preoccupied with the frog in "Sleeping Beauty." "What the frog foretold came true" was the line that haunted her. No one ever remembered the frog.

Clara was sure there hadn't been a frog.

"You don't know the frog because it was the easiest part of the story to cut," said Jess. "The frog is incongruous, discomfiting. Without the frog, it's simple—relatively speaking, as fairy tales go."

The fairy tales we know, Jess loved to explain—emphatically, and this was what Clara loved about Jess, how her obsessions ran away with her, and everybody got to come along and learn about "Sleeping Beauty," "Snow White and Rose Red," "Hans My Hedgehog," "Iron Heinrich"—have been watered down, sanitized. Disney and Little Golden Books have made us think that we know these tales, that they're stories we can hold in our hands. Stories meant to be told to *children*, no less.

"The frog in 'Sleeping Beauty,'" she said, "was in the mother's bathtub."

"A frog in a tub?" She and Clara were sitting in the kitchen talking about this and everything. They could never get to bed at a reasonable hour. "And what was the mother doing in the tub?" Clara asked.

"Contemplating her fertility," said Jess. "A man and a wife who waited for a child, and they waited and the seasons changed and they began to grow old, and then . . ."

"And then?"

"The frog," said Jess. "'And what the frog foretold came true.'"

"Which was what?"

"That there was going to be a baby."

"And isn't that weird?" asked Clara.

Jess said, "Totally."

Clara wasn't sure how Clayton put up with the frogs. And the jokes people made about Jess kissing frogs, which Clayton tolerated too in his easygoing fashion. He was easygoing about most things, which was fortunate because he was always over. Technically he had his own place, a basement room in a house of friends a few blocks away, but he was never there. After nearly three years as a couple, he and Jess were nearly inseparable, and they were good together— although this brought its own complications.

"Sometimes I think it's anticlimactic knowing your happily-ever-after at the age of twenty-two," Jess had confessed not long ago. It was three o'clock in the morning, she and Clara the only ones still awake, still buzzing after a night of drinking and fun. Their apartment had been full of people that night, still scattered throughout—Lori passed out with her head on the kitchen table; somebody asleep in the bathtub; and Clayton was in Jess's bed, where he belonged. It was

near the beginning of their final year at school, it felt like
they were at the centre of the world, sitting on Clara's windowsill, dizzy and overlooking the rooftops. They'd been
singing "Landslide" at the top of their lungs until someone
from a neighbouring building had screamed out of the
window for them to please shut up.

Jess was smoking, which was mostly an affectation, but
Clara didn't call her on it because friends forgave each
other these things, the same way Jess never said a word
when Clara sang the wrong words to the songs on the CDs
they played in the kitchen: *We sit here in our store and drink
some toast . . .*

Jess exhaled, and they breathed in the night, city lights
shining beyond chimneys and power lines, the air filled with
the drone of exhaust fans from the restaurant next door.
Clara was relieved to hear Jess say what she did, about the
anticlimax, because that was it exactly, and Clara understood
better than anyone. She knew what it was like to try to arrive
at the centre of your life years too early, the way she'd hitched
herself to men a decade older when she was still in high
school, eschewing the trappings of adolescence, missing out
on so much that mattered.

Clayton had come on to her once, years ago, before he
was with Jess, and she'd had no qualms about rejecting his
advances because Clayton was just such a *boy*, and after all
this time he still was. Ending up with Clayton would be like
spending your life in the town where you were born. This
was a thought she found herself saying aloud.

Jess said, "Plenty of people are born in nice towns."

"But that's not the point," said Clara.

"And you like Clayton," Jess reminded her.

Which was true, but this should not be the point that it all came down to. Clara liked a lot of things, but that wasn't reason enough to carry them forever. Here they were, about to leap into unknowns. Graduation was in June. They were thinking about grad school but had yet to apply, Clara trying not to focus too much on what was coming next, to just live in the moment, although her experience in the field the summer before had awakened a passion and given her an inkling as to the direction her life was moving. Change was inevitable—after grad, Jess's parents would stop paying her rent, which meant she'd have to get a job, but also that she and Clayton could finally move in together. Once Jess was on her own, they said, she could do what she liked. Which meant that Clara, who had been paying her own rent all along, would probably have to give up her basil on the windowsill and find someplace else to live, begin again. Somewhere on the horizon she'd also have to start paying back student loans that added up to a figure she didn't like to contemplate.

"But life is long," she'd reminded Jess, and the curious nature of time was what Clara was contemplating now all these weeks later, lying awake on Jess's floor remembering the night of the party. She hadn't been kind about Clayton during the discussion on the roof, but what would she have done if he hadn't been there to fight off the squirrels tonight?

It had been a strange, surreal kind of autumn, just a handful of weeks since the Twin Towers had fallen. The school year was rushing by—a blur of essays and deadlines, pub crawls, all-nighters, long stretches in the library, hands forever stamped with faded ink from admission to one event or another—but right now the minutes themselves seemed endless, each one ticking Clara no closer to slumber. What if everything was a paradox? Clara was in a room with two people but totally alone. And if she lay awake long enough, could those minutes stretch into infinity, warding off the future—and all its questions—forever?

Every evening, like a ritual, Jess and Clayton retired together to bed to read. Clara wondered if their sex life had been diminished by so much cold and slimy symbolism—how could sex itself not be a casualty when writing a thesis on the theme of frogs and sexuality in fairy tales? Surely it would seem more salubrious just to fall into bed with a book?

Clara herself had not had sex in seven months, since she went out to a dingy bar with cheap sangria and brought home a pyrotechnician who attracted her attention by lighting his wrist on fire. This appeared to be the extent of his marvels, however, plus he had a swastika tattooed on his shoulder, and even though he insisted it was from another time, she called him a cab, and had been celibate ever since.

"You can't write off everybody because of one bad guy," Jess insisted. "He looked like a toad. He smelled like baloney. Red flags were everywhere."

"You're the one who's always saying that I need to give people a chance."

"Normal people," said Jess. "Not someone who's singed off all his arm hair."

All of it was just so complicated and mired with pitfalls that it just seemed easier not to bother, so Clara decided she wouldn't, consigning herself to a lifetime of spinsterhood—imagining how much simpler everything could be. Clara had a very good vibrator, and some days she thought she had it all figured it out. But then there were other days, days when she looked up to find another hole in her ceiling—which sounded like a bad thing, but this hole was letting in light. Illumination. *And why the hell not?* was the thought on her mind when she decided to sleep with Ferber.

So that was the road to here, lying in bed with the ceiling intact, finally, and Ferber snoring beside her, a few months into something vaguely resembling a relationship. The surprise of his body had been that it smelled really good, because Ferber seemed kind of greasy, sweaty. But his skin turned out to be so smooth, and his shower-gel scent turned her on more than he did; it was the chief part of his appeal.

Of course, Jess was skeptical, even though Clara was only doing what she'd told her to do, but Jess thought all the guys Clara gave chances to were the wrong ones. She didn't think Clara had good instincts. And even Clayton had opinions on the matter, which was annoying, because none of it was his business.

"You don't even live here," she told him, when he suggested Clara might be better suited to someone whose respect for women was demonstrated beyond his open admiration for boobs and butts that were "more than a handful." But frankly, men had said less respectful things to Clara, and what Ferber lacked in decorum he made up for in other ways.

However, this wasn't something she could explain to Clayton. And any time Ferber tried to reach out to Jess and Clayton, to let them get to know him better, they would get up and leave the table, so it ended up being him and Clara alone again, and they didn't have a lot to say. But in bed together they were great, and she even liked lying beside him afterwards. He was the kind of guy she'd never end up going to bed to read with, and not just because Ferber didn't read.

"I'm not into the book thing," he said the first time he was presented with her bookshelves, long before she'd ever contemplated sleeping with him, years ago when he was up in her room shoddily repairing a window screen. Clara couldn't say she hadn't known what she was getting into. None of it was complicated.

She breathed Ferber in, wondering what he smelled like underneath. His bodywash scent was a kind of veneer, and for the rest of her life, whenever she smelled anything like it, she was transported back to the simple comfort of his presence, which was always more comfortable when he wasn't conscious.

But he was conscious now, one eye open. "Hey, babe," he said. She knew that everything he said was a line he'd heard in a movie, but she was willing to play her part. Ferber was shockingly attractive without his shirt on. She knew this already from the time he'd installed crooked kitchen shelves during a heat wave and it had factored into her decision to pursue this avenue.

"It's just casual," she promised Jess. "No strings."

But Ferber kept coming back to her until strings were undeniable, and now Clara was tied up like cat's cradle, and no, it wasn't bad at all.

She kissed his shoulder. It was Saturday and she had to work, and Ferber would be heading out to do whatever Ferbers do. His uncle owned dilapidated buildings all over downtown, including their own, and the lack of precision that Jess and Clara had come to know as Ferber's professional signature only furthered the decay—although they had to admit that their place had been in better repair since he'd started coming around more often. In addition to the ceiling in Clara's room, Ferber had fixed the lock on the back door and repaired Clara's rain-damaged drywall. He had even been talking about pulling up the linoleum in the hallway to reveal the hardwood. Truth be told, Clara figured, Ferber was more useful than Clayton, whose most substantial contribution to the household (aside from battling squirrels—and it was only that one time) was eating all their bread.

"You want coffee?" she asked, and Ferber nodded. He was slow to rouse. Even when he hadn't been drinking, he woke up with a hangover.

She left him nearly asleep as she plodded out of bed, tugged on a hoodie and pyjama bottoms and made her way down the dark stairwell to the light at the bottom. She found Clayton already up and dressed in the hall, zipping up his jacket, which was strange because he was never out of bed this early.

He said, "Hey." His voice sounded off. He wouldn't look at her.

She asked, "Where are you going?" but he was already halfway down the stairs to the street.

"See you later, 'kay?" he called back. Clara heard the front door slam behind him and paused. Clayton was gone; Clayton was never gone.

She knocked on Jess's door but got no answer. She opened it and peered inside at the lump on the bed. "What's going on?"

Jess sat up, pulling the covers off her head. "He broke up with me." She sounded incredulous. She looked terrible.

Clara was also confused. "No," she said.

"Last night," said Jess through tears. Her nose was running. When Jess submitted to her sadness, she went all-in. "And I told him to wait until morning. I said everything would make more sense then. And then when we woke up, he said I was right. Now he knew that he was definitely sure, and he really had to go."

"I saw him," said Clara.

"He wouldn't talk about it." Clara perched on the edge of the bed and handed Jess a tissue from the box on her bedside. Jess blew her nose and continued. "Last night he comes over and he said something's been off for a long time, but how come I didn't know? I really didn't see it coming."

"Oh, Jess." Clara was fishing under the covers for a part of her to hold, her hand. "But it's all going to be okay."

"No," said Jess. "I think he really means it."

"But, I mean, *you're* going to be okay," said Clara. "Even without him."

"How?" said Jess.

And Clara wanted to say, "What are you even talking about?" This had always been the problem. Clayton was a stand-in, a blank space that Jess could fill with something wonderful or even nothing, but you couldn't tell someone that about their boyfriend. Maybe Jess would finally figure it out.

But not now. "I love him," she said, collapsing onto Clara, resting her head on her shoulder. "So much. And now what am I meant to do with that?" The sun was pouring through the window, such golden light on the tangle of sheets on the bed. She sat up suddenly. "Clara, you've got to catch him."

"Catch him?"

"I mean, he's probably gone too far by now. He's a really fast walker." She got up from the bed to look out the window.

"Jess—"

"You need to find him." She spun back around. "We don't even know what's going on here. He could have a brain tumour. He's acting erratic. You need to check on him, to talk to him." She was shaking.

Clara spoke calmly, "I think if anyone needs to talk to him, it's you."

"But I tried that. It didn't work." She sounded desperate again. And then they both turned at the sound of someone in the hall, another layer of confusion. It was Ferber, whom they'd forgotten, in his underwear and nothing else. Madeleine—his ex-wife's name—was tattooed across his bicep, the letters expanding and contracting as he stretched, revealing the expanse of his body, his hairless chest (he waxed). Oh, Ferber, thought Clara, and she got up from the bed, calculating how to contain this moment. Ferber was clueless, smiling like nothing was happening. "Hey, ladies," he said.

Jess threw herself face-down on the bed as Clara ushered Ferber back out to the hall, closing the door behind her. "You should go. It's Clayton, and she—I don't know what's up."

"But what about my coffee?"

"There's coffee on every corner, Ferber. Why don't you go and get one there?"

Clara didn't want to leave Jess alone, but her shift started at eleven. She convinced her to take a shower, at least, and tidied up her bed, opening the window to fresh air.

"You'll be all right until I'm home?" Clara asked, once Jess was lying on the bed in clean pyjamas, wrapped in a towel and staring at the ceiling. But Jess just shrugged in response, and all Clara could do was promise to bring dinner when she returned.

She had just ten minutes to get to work, hustling along and across busy streets, cutting through the hospital parking lot and nearly getting hit by a streetcar on College Street. She arrived just as the kiosk was scheduled to open, already in trouble because she was working with Connie, who greeted her with a grunt, brewing resentment along with the coffee she'd had to get started alone.

"I'll make it up to you," Clara promised, tying on her apron and pulling her hair into a ponytail. When the caterer showed up, Clara made a point of accepting the order, loading scones and muffins into the display case. They weren't busy, so Connie could have given her a break, but she didn't.

Once customers started arriving, Clara didn't have time to think about Connie, focusing instead on the steady line-up of students. She was busy steaming milk, filling cups, bagging muffins, crowning an extra-large hot chocolate with a blast of whipped cream, and then suddenly Lori and Holly were at the front of the line—her friends, but really Jess's.

"How *is* she?" Lori asked, before Clara could take her order. This was no simple inquiry, as her tone made clear. Lori lived in Clayton's house, but it had only been a couple of hours since the breakup, so how did she already know?

Clara could feel Connie watching her, so she didn't waste time. She took Lori and Holly's orders, poured their coffees, and asked, "Jess, you mean?"

"Well, at least it's all out in the open," Holly said with a sigh as Clara knelt down to get two low-fat bran muffins from the case below her till.

"And honestly, she's nice," Lori called over the counter. "You really can't blame her."

"Who—?" said Clara, standing up as the muffin in her serving tongs tumbled to the floor. Stepping back, she felt it squish beneath her shoe.

"You're going to have to mark that down!" Connie called over the racket of the steam wand.

The girl's name was Natasha, from Clayton's Soviet history course. She and Clayton had tried to ignore their attraction until it became impossible.

"They were friends," said Lori. "And then . . ."

"I don't know her," said Clara. How could Clayton have a friend she didn't know?

Holly said, "It's complicated."

Lori said, "And there's two sides to every story."

Holly added, "Or three."

"Less chatting, Clara," called Connie. "Keep moving."

Holly said, "This is kind of awkward. Sorry!" Her final syllable was a trill ringing over her shoulder as they hurried away, leaving room for the next in line: a kid who paid for his order in nickels, which took forever, followed by a woman who changed her mind seven times before settling on an Americano. Clara kept expecting Lori and Holly to come back for refills, to help her make sense of what they'd told her, but they'd scuttled off somewhere else.

Oh, this was going to be bad. Jess was already a mess, and she didn't know the half of it. Would Clara have to be the one to tell her, launching her further into a tailspin of despair? Jess would start listening to Fiona Apple again. Clara knocked a cappuccino, which spilled all over the counter. "Seriously," Connie muttered as she wiped it up. "What's with you today?"

And then a half hour before the end of her shift—so busy she'd missed her break—there was Ferber, towering over everybody else in line.

"You're here," she said, when he finally got to the front.

He said, "I like to watch you work."

"What are you having?"

"The girl behind the counter, I hope."

She said, "You've got to order something or Connie is going to kill me."

He said, "A coffee?" Finally. And then he waited over on the benches, rifling through a stack of campus papers. Ferber reading—Clara could have died, it was so incongruous. And kind of sexy.

They closed at four, and Clara washed out the urns while Connie wiped down the counters. There were muffins left over, but Connie had bagged them and thrown them out before Clara had a chance to grab them.

"You're in a hurry," Connie said, gesturing toward Ferber, who'd abandoned the paper and was drumming on his knees.

So Clara made a point of finishing everything as thoroughly as Connie would and telling her, "Thanks for picking up my slack today," as she put on her coat and they locked up the stand.

And then finally she found herself in Ferber's arms, against that chest. *Inhale.*

He said, "I finished early today. Thought I'd drive you home and we could hang out."

It was all she wanted. But reality persisted. "I can't."

"Why not?"

She explained about Clayton, what had happened that morning. How she'd told Jess she'd get pizza.

"I'll drop you off," he said. "I really only wanted to see you. We can get the pizza on the way."

He brought her to the door, where he kissed her obscenely, and it took all her good sense not to bring him inside, or to get back in his car and head over to his place. Because that would just be so easy, unlike everything else that lay before her now: breaking the news to Jess about Natasha and then enduring the weeks—or more—that lay ahead, waiting for her to get over Clayton. *Clayton.* But duty called, and Jess had been alone all day, so Clara told Ferber she'd call him tomorrow.

The apartment was quiet and Jess exactly where Clara had left her, in bed under her covers, although a mountain of used tissue was now piled on her bedside table.

"I've got pizza," said Clara, settling down on the edge of the bed, flipping back the duvet to reveal her friend's dull eyes.

Jess said, "I thought you might be him."

"Clayton."

"Do you think he's okay?"

"I'm sure he's fine." These were the conversations they were going to be having. Clara decided she wouldn't say anything about Natasha right away. Instead, she and Jess would eat the large meat-lover's pizza, whose grease had already soaked through the bottom of the box.

Later the phone rang and it was Ferber, "Just calling to say good night, babe." When Clara got off the phone, Jess looked disgusted. She said, "I guess you can break up with him now."

Clara tolerated this with silence and three whole days when Ferber stayed away, only coming over again on Tuesday, once Jess had resumed the rituals of basic grooming, the tissues thrown out. News of Natasha had thrown an additional wrench into things, but Jess seemed numb to it. "I've met her," she said, "and she's not even pretty."

Clara knew there would be trouble when Ferber reappeared, which was why she hadn't told Jess he was coming over. Instead, she spent the evening listening for his footsteps at the door and flew downstairs to meet him when he finally arrived.

When Jess asked who it was, Clara replied that it was nothing, because if Ferber and "nothing" were synonymous maybe it was fine. On the doorstep, Clara let him take her into his arms and into a devastating kiss that sent her spinning. Jess was peering over the banister as they came up the stairs. "Oh," she said. She had been expecting better news. She was still waiting for the phone to ring, for the doorbell to sound, for the message to arrive that Clayton had changed his mind.

But Ferber wasn't paying attention to Jess. He drifted Clara up to her room to do what he had come to do, for the reason she wanted him. It was nice for Clara not to think about anything for a little while but her body and his, the remarkable ease with which they came together.

And then in the morning came the knock at her door. Clara's bedroom door had never been closed until she started seeing Ferber, who was softly snoring beside her now. Clara traced her finger along Madeleine's name, then hauled herself out of bed and threw on a T-shirt and pyjama bottoms.

She encountered her best friend's face with a start, so white and desperate-looking. It was dark in the stairwell and when the light hit Jess she recoiled, unsteady on the top step. Clara put out her hand, but Jess pushed it away.

"What's *he* doing here?" she asked Clara, gesturing into the room, at Ferber. He had shaken off the covers and looked like the kind of person you'd want to sculpt. The fact of his body was undeniable. All the other guys Clara had been with were skinny, tortured, stretched out in ways that looked painful, with ribs you could count one after another. Before Ferber, she hadn't known what a body could be.

But this was the problem. Jess didn't want to see that. Jess didn't want Ferber to be here at all, which had been the case from the moment he started coming around, but now, in her broken-hearted state, she had no qualms about expressing everything on her mind.

Clara squeezed out onto the landing and shut the door behind her. "Let's go downstairs."

Jess sat at the table while Clara filled the kettle. The oak table was covered with a yellow cloth they never laundered, so now it was splattered with tiny islands, stains from red wine and spaghetti sauce. Jess traced her finger around their coasts. "I don't know what you're trying to prove here."

Clara put the kettle on.

Jess said, "When he's over here, you disappear." She waited another moment. "You're not saying anything."

"Would it help if I did?" Clara kept her back to the room, her hand on the kettle lid as the burner started turning red. Outside the window were treetops and rooftops; Clara pretended to be absorbed in these.

Jess said, "What do you mean?"

Clara turned. "I'm not trying to prove anything. I'm on your side."

"Then would it hurt you to show it?"

"This is exhausting." Clara fell into the seat across from her.

"What?"

"I know you're hurting, and I get it. But this isn't fair."

"Because I'm not celebrating you parading your boy-friend past my door?"

"He's not my boyfriend." Silence. "And it was hardly a parade."

The kettle was beginning to whirr.

"It just seems unnecessary, is what I mean," said Jess. "You bringing him here."

"Honestly, it's got nothing to do with you."

"But it does, because I live here," said Jess.

"Did everything about you and Clayton relate to me?" asked Clara.

"It's not the same," said Jess. "And we included you. We always did."

She has a short memory, Clara thought, remembering all those nights in her room trying not to listen to the muted noise downstairs. She asked, "Do you want to be included?" She wasn't sure if she could include Jess in her relations with Ferber in a way that wasn't mainly pornographic.

"Of course not," Jess said, as grossed out as Clara would be if Jess had ever proposed a threesome with Clayton. Yuck. "I would just appreciate a little consideration. It's been four days."

Clara said, "Jess, I'm here for you. I'll be here for you. He's going soon. This is not a big deal."

"But you don't even like him," said Jess. She paused. "The kettle's boiling."

Clara got up to turn off the burner. "I do like him." Which was difficult for her to say, to admit to being soft or tender. Jess was the only person she could do this with, and sometimes even that was hard.

Jess asked, "Why?"

"Why did you like Clayton?"

"I told you, that's different. I mean, we were together three years. A seventh of my life."

"Who measures out life in sevenths?" Clara said, filling the teapot.

"But you're screwing Ferber," said Jess. "The handyman. Who isn't even handy!"

Clara got two mugs out of the cupboard and put them on the table. Then she brought the teapot over, holding the spout to balance the weight. "Let it brew."

The two of them sat across from each other at the table, cross-pyjama-legged. "What the frog foretold came true," said Jess.

"What?"

"No one ever breaks up in fairy tales," Jess told her. "Have you noticed that?"

"As fates go, getting dumped isn't very fateful."

"In fairy tales," said Jess, "love isn't so disposable. People are fated and they stay that way."

"Do you really think that you and Clayton were fated?" Jess made a face at her. "Life's not a fairy tale."

"No shit," Jess said. She poured her tea, warming her hands on the mug, then took a sip. "And what about Ferber?"

"I never said that was *fate*," said Clara. "I like him, but that's not fate."

"Well, what is it then?"

"Why does it have to be anything?" Jess shrugged. "And wasn't it you who told me anyway?" Clara asked. "*What the frog foretold came true*? It was only ever about sex."

"I just don't understand," said Jess, "how you can love somebody and just quit. And the worst thing," she said, "is just knowing that I got it all so wrong."

"But there's nothing wrong with being wrong," said Clara. "As long as you finally figure it out." There wasn't even anything wrong with being wrong but going along with it anyway. She thought of Ferber asleep upstairs. She poured her own cup of tea and it was almost clear. Peering inside the teapot, she said, "I forgot the teabag."

Jess said, "I thought something was off."

"You should have said."

Jess said, "Everything's off. How am I supposed to know the difference?"

"Anybody who deserves to love you," said Clara, "is going to know better than to quit. I'm not going to quit."

"Even though I'm making it tempting."

"A little bit," said Clara.

She got up from her chair and got the tea box down from the cupboard. She tossed four bags into the pot and put the lid back on.

"That's going to be strong," said Jess.

"Well," said Clara. "If it has to be one or the other . . ."

It was not to be a spring like either of them had planned, or a summer for that matter. Three weeks later, Jess learned that Clayton's girlfriend had moved in with him, which seemed like the end of the world, until two days later when Clara's father died, a drunk driver sailing through the stop sign at the top of their country road and T-boning his truck. The accident had happened at ten thirty in the morning, but Clara got the call around noon, while she was still in bed, reading *A Heartbreaking Work of Staggering Genius*. Ferber had left three hours earlier to go to work, but she was meant to be studying for her exams. Textbooks were stacked beside her; she'd had to dig the phone out from underneath them.

After she hung up, having given her sister ample time to take back her words, to preserve life as it had been for just a little while longer, Clara went down to the kitchen to tell Jess, but she couldn't.

"What?" Jess kept asking, and even once Clara could get words out, the only ones she could manage were, "My dad," so that Jess had to extrapolate. The details really didn't matter anyway. Clara felt the strength in her legs dissolve, and she slid down to the floor.

TEMPING

2 0 0 2 – 2 0 0 4

In the beginning, Clara had drawn Jess a map of the universe, *their* universe, the campus and a few streets beyond, which was as far afield as they got back then. And in their second year when they moved just beyond the margin, off-campus into their apartment above the herb shop, there had been room for Clara to add a line for the street and a small square topped by a triangle standing in for their home. A home that was theirs no longer, because Clara's dad was dead and she'd gone back to be with her mother. They'd given up their lease and at the beginning of May, Jess moved into Clayton's old basement room at Lori's, which was a less-than-ideal arrangement.

Jess had spent a night there years ago, right after Clayton moved in, and it had been so cold and damp that she'd never done it again. The room was dingy and low-ceilinged with just one tiny window sunlight never reached. The laundry room was right next door, where the ancient washing machine creaked and jumped across the floor anytime anyone used it, and somebody was always using it, because six other people lived upstairs.

Clayton had gone up north for another summer of tree planting, taking his new girlfriend with him, and too many of their friends seemed to think that Jess getting his room made up for what he'd done to her, that somehow they could call it even. Jess definitely couldn't, but one good thing was that Clayton had spent so little time in the room that Jess wasn't surrounded by memories of him now. Instead it was Clara she missed. Clara, whose friendship Jess had taken for granted, all the while staking her future on Clayton, naively imagining the life they'd build together. But it had turned out that Clayton was inconsequential, and Clara was the key to home.

And now Jess was supposed to learn to get along without her, which, in practical terms, was like learning how to walk on one leg or how to carry home the groceries with your hands tied behind your back. It was like arriving at a party unable to speak, but having to make oneself known all the same. And how could anybody know who Jess was without Clara? She didn't know how to get along without her.

But she did get along—albeit awkwardly. Everything felt like the first few weeks at a new school; and it kind of was, the school of hard knocks, as though four years of education had prepared Jess for nothing.

She did her best to settle in, buying a lamp, trying to make the place familiar. She started unpacking her box of frogs—the posters, the figurines in pewter and wood—but the room was too subterranean for the effect to be charming. Plus, outside of her academic work the frogs made no sense, or at least not the sense she was aspiring to, so she put the frogs back in the box and left it in a corner with all the other things she didn't have a place for—mismatched dishes, the dirty yellow tablecloth, her Norton anthology, and a collection of hooded sweatshirts with collegiate crests.

She found Clara's map, however, and hung it up, bolstering the tattered edges with masking tape, but she didn't bother to mark her new place because it didn't matter, especially with Clara so far away. Jess traced a line with her finger, visualizing the highway ribboning far across the room, down the wall, and arriving in the corner where the plaster was cracked. A different universe altogether.

At first Clara's return home was temporary, understandable. She had to be with her mother, she was home for the funeral. But then Clara's mother wasn't doing well. Her sisters were busy with their children and someone needed to stay with their mom, who'd never lived alone before. She'd had to be prescribed sedatives.

"Things aren't good here," Clara emailed after a couple of weeks. She came back to the city and wrote her final exams while they packed up their apartment. In a few short weeks Jess had lost everything—her boyfriend, her home, her best friend. But Clara had lost her dad, which trumped it all, even though she and her father had been estranged and he had been a tyrant. In fact, this only made it worse; it made his death a relief in some ways, and Clara felt guilty about that. She had to make it up to her mother, who had been devastated when Clara left home while still in high school.

"I'm going to be taking care of her for a while," Clara wrote near the end of June. She also found a job in a flower shop, she told Jess. And Jess couldn't imagine any of it, Clara a florist or Clara living with her mother. When friends asked her how Clara was doing, she didn't feel qualified to answer.

Jess had spent the last three summers working at the university library, a position she was no longer eligible for as a graduate. And so, into the actual working world she was flung, equipped with a degree in English literature and library shelving her only work experience since McDonald's in high school, which meant there were no responses to any of her job applications. Her parents had stepped in to pay the rent on her terrible basement room, but they weren't willing to do it two months in a row.

Lori worked at a temp agency and seemed almost like an actual adult as she moved between admin jobs. "You could try it too, she said. "I could get you in at my agency." She encouraged Jess to enliven her resumé by translating her library duties into office skills, put down her own name as a reference, and promised to pass along Jess's application when she dropped off her timesheet that week.

Within days Jess was a temp as well, acing the typing test because she'd spent the last four years writing essays; it turned out her education had been good for something. Lori took her shopping for skirts and blouses, which they charged to Jess's mother's credit card, and Jess promised to pay her back once her first paycheque came through.

She was overdressed for her first assignment: stuffing 2500 envelopes in the storeroom at a driving school.

"No typing?" she asked, confused. She'd been prepared to wow them with her prowess and be offered a permanent job by lunchtime. Stuffing envelopes was far too rudimentary to lead to such results.

When she returned the following morning—hands adorned in Band-Aids from papercuts—nobody could believe it. "How could you stand two days of this?" asked the receptionist. It hadn't occurred to Jess that she had a choice—but of course she didn't, with only sixty-seven dollars in the bank.

When she came out of the storeroom on the third day, all the envelopes stuffed, her fingers were shredded and the office was empty. Everyone had gone out for drinks, but no one had thought to invite the temp. There was a hierarchy at play, she was starting to understand.

She would have liked to make sense of it all by talking to Clara at night, sitting at the kitchen table with lighted candles, something delicious cooking in the oven. But she didn't share a kitchen with Clara anymore, and the kitchen in her new house didn't have a table, because the table had belonged to a girl who moved out in May, and nobody else had one. After her third day of work when Jess arrived home, the kitchen was crowded with hippies in a drum circle.

So she went down to her room, closing the door to shut out the tribal beats, and dialled Clara's number. She was prepared to relay the whole sorry story, but when she heard Clara's voice, she couldn't do it.

Instead, she adopted a different tone, blasé and tired. She had no idea where it came from. "The commute is long," she was willing to admit, the subway and then a bus out to the suburbs where nothing was more than two stories high. "But I can read on the bus. And the people are nice—they'll be talking to the agency about getting me back for another contract." The supply closet was crowded with boxes containing a four-year backlog of instructor timesheets that needed to be entered into the computer, but the work had always been considered too tedious for anyone to manage. "You, though," said the receptionist, "You just might have the capacity."

"Well, I'm glad," said Clara, sounding buoyant. Jess could picture her sprawled on her parents' bed (now just her mother's) because Clara didn't have a telephone extension in her own room. "I knew you'd be okay," she said.

"For sure," said Jess, perpetuating this fantasy. "And me and Lori are going out on Saturday. Some club on King Street. With people she knows from work, and some others."

"You and Lori, huh?" said Clara. "You guys sound pretty tight."

"I guess," said Jess. She knew she was laying it on thick. "How's your mom doing?" And then someone in the house picked up the phone on another extension and set it back down with a crash, and she missed most of what Clara said.

"—and the doctor's hoping the new meds will help. Alleviate some symptoms, at least. I mean, they're not going to take care of everything. My dad's still going to be dead. There's no medicine for that."

Jess said, "I'm sorry."

Clara said, "It's all right. I'm just glad that I'm here."

"Me too," said Jess. A lie. "I just miss you."

"I miss you too."

Jess got the contract for the timesheets, but after four weeks she felt she'd made little progress, carbon paper being so fine. The weather was beautiful that summer, but she was spending most of her time in a closet or a basement, so she didn't appreciate it much. She stayed up too late at night, either just not sleeping or sitting on the porch listening to one guy or another playing "Wonderwall" on his acoustic guitar, and the next day, in the dim light of the supply closet, she'd be exhausted.

"So you like the work?" Clara asked during another call. "It's engaging?" She'd been talking about her own job, fascinated by so much botanical knowledge. "Did you know," she said, "that tulip bulbs are totally edible and can even be substituted for onions in a recipe?" Clara was excited about the art and science of flower arrangement, the ways in which the craft was an inversion of archeology, which had been all about death and digging. She said, "I'm learning I have an affinity for living things."

And Jess let Clara have that, an affinity for living things. Never mind that cut flowers were dead, or on their way to being dead, surely Clara knew that. But as long as Clara was rhapsodizing about her job, she wasn't asking about Jess's. She wasn't asking probing questions about *engagement*, even though engagement was a lot to ask of temp work. Mould was growing on the walls of the supply closet, black spores that Jess imagined leaching into her lungs, shortening her life with every breath. Plus, the mountain of boxes full of timesheets never seemed to get any smaller, and she suspected someone on staff was adding to the pile—probably the smug receptionist. She'd been a temp once too, before they'd made her permanent.

"Sometimes it happens," Lori told her. They were sitting on the porch, where, mercifully for once, they were alone. It was strange being with Lori without any of the intermediaries who'd connected them before. Clara had never liked Lori much—she thought she was two-faced and shallow—but Clara was hard on people, and if it weren't for Lori, Jess would be homeless and unemployed.

"Going permanent isn't always the best choice," Lori said. "Sometimes temping is better. Do you really want to be locked in?"

A bit of permanence might be welcome, though. The last six months had been a lesson in upheaval, a necessary education, Jess kept telling herself. Permanence was illusory anyway. She hoped she would turn out to be stronger than she imagined.

But eventually the timesheets proved to be too much. The texture of the carbon paper made her feel like throwing up, and when she looked at the grids of days and numbers they refused to make any sense. Finally, one day she called in sick and went downtown to her agency to ask for another position.

"But you already have a contract," said Graham, so self-satisfied in his shirt and tie and stylish glasses, with his human resources diploma. Graham's entire identity was a façade of professionalism, and Jess envied the power he got to wield. "Plus, it wouldn't be fair to Gary"—Gary, the owner of the driving school. Jess had never met Gary, and possibly Graham hadn't either, but this was part of his HR schtick, pretending these transactions were genuine human relationships. As though Gary weren't the type of person who'd send you to work in a closet with spores.

Jess phoned Clara and said, "I have some time off next week. It would do me good to come and see you." She was tired of pretending that everything was fine, and she'd managed to save enough money for bus fare and to tide her over until she found another position. She had admin experience now—"filing" was just a fancy word for envelope stuffing, anyway—which would make it easier to get her next job.

But Clara wasn't sure if her mom would be up for it. Then she told Jess about a date she'd gone on the week before, with her boss's nephew, a guy called Jake. After hearing Clara's story—a movie, then a drink, and a kiss on her mother's doorstep—Jess hung up the phone and lay on her bed, crying, staring at the wall, at the map without Clara on it, at its sad and shabby taped-up edges. Clara was gone and Clara didn't even seem sorry.

But she must have been a little sorry, because she called back and determined that a visit would be feasible after all. And the following Monday at the bus depot, after a long and winding journey, Jess watched Clara climbing out of a dirty white pick-up truck, so much thinner than in the spring, thinner than Jess had ever seen her. But everything else was the same, and the moment she wrapped her arms around Jess, Jess was home again, Clara's hold so strong and fast that all her doubts about their friendship disappeared.

On the way down the highway, yellow fields spread out all around them, Jess, unable to keep up the easygoing act, finally admitted the truth. She told Clara about the drum circle in her kitchen, her damp and terrible room, the long bus rides to work, and the carbon paper. About how lonely she had been. She said those words.

"I really thought," said Clara, not looking away from the road, "you'd barely noticed I was gone."

"How could you think that?"

"With Lori, and your job, and the King Street clubs." Clara didn't sound bitter, just tired. "You made it all sound pretty sweet."

"I don't know," said Jess. "I was just trying to make it all okay. I could hardly start complaining, after what you've been through." There was also the preservation of her dignity. Surely a person could be permitted such a thing.

"I still would have listened," said Clara. "I'm not so delicate. You can be real with me."

Maybe, thought Jess. But had Clara ever truly been real in return? There was always a part of her she kept for herself, so that she remained a mystery, a puzzle, even to Jess—maybe *especially* to Jess, who was supposed to know her better than anyone.

Jess told her, "I wasn't sure you'd noticed I was gone either. You walked away like it was easy."

"It wasn't easy," said Clara, signalling then speeding up to pass a slow-moving sedan. "Nothing's been easy." She pulled back into her lane. "But I just didn't have much of a say. You really think I would have chosen moving back in with my mother?"

Jess thought about "Snow White and Rose Red," a fairy tale that was rare in that it featured two girls, a pair of sisters who'd promised never to leave each other as long as they lived—although what happened next involved an evil gnome, a talking bear, and a double wedding to a pair of princes, so perhaps everything about it was unlikely.

She said, "Sometimes it just seems like . . ." She was choosing her words carefully, daring to articulate what had been on the tip of her tongue in every telephone call, deleted from every email she'd written to Clara in the last couple of months. ". . . you're not planning on coming back. Not anytime soon. And it makes me wonder if you even want to." She looked to see Clara's expression as she considered what Jess had said. Maybe it wasn't that Clara was a puzzle, but there were these parts of her that Jess couldn't bear to know, all those parts that insisted on freedom.

"I guess," Clara finally responded, "it's just that I've got to keep facing forward right now. So much is going on, and my mom needs me. And here I've got a place to live. I've found a job."

"And Jake."

"Jake," said Clara, "is definitely not a factor in my life choices."

"Not yet."

"Not ever," said Clara. And Jess believed her. Clara could be cold. After her dad died, she never saw Ferber again.

Clara put on her signal and turned into the long driveway to her family's house. Jess had never been here. The funeral had been just family. She'd seen photos, she'd heard stories. She knew Clara's family from their trips to the city when her mother would drop off baking tins stocked with squares and cookies, but never stay for long.

"Here we are," said Clara, pulling up to the house. "Ready or not." She turned off the engine. "I'm glad you're here. It's been so quiet. I'm hoping you can help us fill in the space."

And after just a few minutes, Jess understood a whole lot more about what Clara had been going through. The house was silent, their voices echoing through the empty rooms. Jess immediately started speaking in low tones, the way Clara's mother did—when she spoke at all. She seemed so slight, but she'd taken Jess in her arms with such a crushing force.

"She's a bit intense," Clara explained later. "These days she's only got two gears, and it's either that or catatonic."

Sound travelled through the house in a strange way, so they stayed outside a lot that week. It was easier to escape on walks down gravel roads and then the hot black highway, taking shelter on the dusty shoulder when big trucks came barrelling by. Sometimes they wandered through fields or rambled in the woods. But no matter the route, there came a point when they had to turn around and come back, too far away from anything for there to be destinations.

"I don't know how you can stand it," Jess said on their second trip to the pond in a single day. At least there was birdsong and breeze, sunshine. The heat felt good on their skin, and at the pond they could go swimming. They discovered something new together after all these years: they were both amphibious. This hadn't come up when they lived in the city beside a lake that seemed so far away.

"Well, you can imagine what growing up here was like then," said Clara as they made their way through the meadow. "And it's not so different now. When I go out, she has to know where I'm going. She doesn't like me being on the roads—she never did, and now . . ."

"But you can't stay forever," said Jess.

"Of course not," said Clara, as though the statement were ridiculous. But that she was here at all was no more absurd. Then she added, "I don't want you waiting for me."

Jess stopped walking, confused.

Clara continued making her way down the path. "I don't even know what I'm doing these days. And the strange thing is that I don't think I want to know. But I don't want to be the one that holds you back." She turned around so Jess could catch up.

Jess was trying to work out whether Clara was giving her something now or taking it away. "But when have we *ever* known what we were doing?" she asked. "It never stopped us before." None of that mattered if they were doing it together. "And I don't think you can take all the credit for the fact I'm going nowhere."

"You haven't gone anywhere *yet*," Clara corrected. "And that's not even true." They started walking again. "I *want* to come back," said Clara. "But my mother needs me; my sisters can't manage it. But there's all these other places too— maybe teaching in China? I don't know. And I was so anxious about the end of school, about what was going to happen next. But then the world blew up, and I'm still standing. And don't you think that's kind of miraculous? Don't you feel it too? I just don't know where all the pieces are going to land yet. And I'm really not in a rush to find out."

They'd arrived at the pond and Jess could hear the deep tones of the bullfrogs. Their first time here, Clara had delighted in showing her the actual frogs and even managed to catch a tiny leopard frog in her hands. She chased Jess around the perimeter of the pond as she ran away shrieking. Jess was a folklorist, not a biologist. Frogs were all about symbolism, and she'd never realized how little that meant until she was confronted with flesh-and-blood frogs, so cold and slimy. How little she'd been trained for the actual world.

"All I'm saying," Clara continued, "is that there are other possibilities. There always have been, but I just couldn't see it. And you were going to be living with Clayton anyway, so what was I supposed to do?"

"But that was never going to happen," said Jess finally. "You always knew. Even when I didn't, you did." She ventured out onto the rotten dock, once used to tie up a rowboat that was now sunk, the wood soft and yielding beneath her feet, her arms outstretched for balance. Then she whipped off her shirt and bra, scrambled out of her shorts, and jumped into the water. She surfaced with weeds in her teeth. She pulled them out of her mouth, flinging them over her shoulder. "So I don't know that you're being entirely genuine. You're the one who said we need to be real with each other."

Clara sat down at the end of the dock, her legs dangling in the water, the silver band around her ankle adorned with the butterfly charm from a necklace Jess had given her years ago, the chain long since broken, now lost. "It's just that I have to be here now. And I'm as surprised by that as you are. And if I have to be here, maybe I could end up having to be anywhere. I just don't know anymore. Where I'm going—"

"So you're not coming back." It was easier just to say it, Jess thought, easier than hearing it or leaving it unsaid, hanging in the air above them.

Clara said, "I need to be looking forward now. You do too." Her voice was calm, as though this were a fact, and perhaps it was. She peeled off her clothes and slipped into the water. "It's cold," she said, and for a moment the frogs were quiet. "It was always going to be one of us," she said. "Not because of Clayton, but eventually. You're going to want things. The world is so large."

"But I want you," said Jess. While the water was murky, she'd never been so naked.

Clara was already drifting away. "You've got me," she said, floating on her back, offering her brilliant body to the sun. "Forever and ever. But now you've got to come up with the rest."

Everything started to happen in September, when Jess moved out of the basement into one of the bedrooms upstairs. She was moving on up in all the ways because she had a new, long-term assignment as a receptionist for a cancer-research charity on the seventeenth floor of a building midtown, and now each evening as she made her way to the elevator she'd catch a glimpse of the sun going down on the western horizon, and she'd think about Clara somewhere out there.

She didn't hang the map on the wall of her new room, though. She slipped it inside the pages of *Summer Sisters* by Judy Blume instead. She was taking Clara's advice, expanding her horizons beyond the confines of the picture drawn so long ago. She left her new walls blank—not only because they'd just been repainted, but because she was trying to embrace possibility rather than kicking against her fate.

Clara flew to Korea in November with the slightest lead on a job opportunity there. She didn't even have a visa, but she knew a guy, and she wanted to see what would happen. Her mother was supportive of the endeavour, admitting she was looking forward to having her house to herself again. The night Clara flew out, Jess went to see her at the airport. They didn't have long because it was rush hour and Jess had been stuck on the subway, and when she finally got there it was forty minutes before boarding.

But Clara was waiting, sitting on her enormous backpack. "I was worried you weren't going to make it," she said, jumping up to greet Jess. Her hair was long and tangled, and she bubbled with nerves and excitement. There wasn't time for a cup of coffee, or even to sit. "I can't believe this is really happening."

"I can't either," said Jess, who had been hoping Clara might still turn around and decide to come home with her, but she could see that wasn't going to happen.

"You could come too," said Clara, tilting her head, biting her lip. And for a moment Jess considered it, recalling how Clara had always led her to places she'd never have gone on her own. But then Clara's expression changed as she shifted her heavy pack, and Jess knew she could never carry such a load.

"But I couldn't," Jess replied. "I don't even have a passport." She wanted Clara to stay, and that was different from wanting to go with her. She wrapped her arms around Clara and the bulk of her backpack. "You don't need me anyway. You're going to be fine."

And they stood like that, Clara's arms around her too, this old familiar place that was them, hugging until the last possible second, and maybe longer—Clara was cutting it close. Then she joined the snaking security lines and soon was lost in the crowd, everybody in their sock feet because it hadn't been so long since the Shoe Bomber. Jess boarded the bus back downtown and watched Clara's plane taking off out the window, a tiny speck in an enormous sky. It didn't matter that it probably wasn't Clara's plane—she was likely still in her socks in line for security—because it was all the same, and Clara was gone. And it was now the sky Jess looked to each evening when she made her way to the elevators, instead of the horizon.

Clara was working under the table in Seoul and sleeping on somebody's floor—she sent frequent dispatches from internet cafés. Jess finally had the internet at work, and she could reply right away. Sometimes their messages back-and-forthed to create an actual conversation.

She'd write to Clara, "*What are you doing up in the middle of the night?*"

Clara would respond, explaining it was a matter of economy. The rates for the internet café decreased as the hours crept by till morning, resulting in an infinite session, so it was hard to know when to go home.

Hearing footsteps behind her, Jess reflexively minimized Internet Explorer, spinning around in her chair, but her furtiveness proved unnecessary, because it was only Bronwyn, another admin, in search of the key to the stationery cupboard. Jess's job was to greet visitors at the National Society for Childhood Cancers, which was never really a happy place to turn up at. It was usually quiet, so most of the time she was answering the phone, directing calls, and sending emails to Clara and other friends less far afield who were as under-stimulated in their post-graduate employment as she was.

The internet was wondrous, though. In the past, Jess had to check her email at the library, but now at work she could surf the web for hours, keeping one hand on the mouse, prepared to minimize as necessary. She read newspapers from all over the world, researched graduate programs, looked for deals on cheap flights—to Korea, even—and read online diaries written by interesting people who lived in New York City. While the work continued to be dull, it beat stuffing envelopes, and because of the time she had on the internet, Jess could leave work feeling as though she'd used her brain that day.

She also got home by six, which meant that she could socialize with her housemates or head out for a drink. Her pay was better too, so she could even buy a round sometimes.

Which was not to say that calamity didn't still periodi-cally rear its head. Like the time she clicked on something accidentally, and suddenly every cursor on every computer on the office network was transformed into a purple magic wand that scattered pixels of fairy dust as it moved across the screen.

"What the hell?" she heard someone exclaim from a cubicle. For a few minutes Jess entertained the possibility that she was a victim in this whole twisted scenario, taking care to use her magic wand to close all her browser windows just in case.

She got up from her desk. "What's going on?" she asked her colleague, who shrugged. People were coming out of their offices to congregate. They'd tried turning off their computers and turning them back on, to no avail.

"They think it's a virus," somebody said, and anyone still at their desk started inching away from their monitors.

So Jess and Bronwyn went down to the food court, and when they returned, everything had calmed down. Jess booted up her computer to find a cursor where a cursor should be. And then Andy from IT crept up behind her, so stealthily he might have been reading over her shoulder about Tom Cruise's struggle with childhood dyslexia on *People.com*. His breath was on her neck. She'd been caught, but she closed the window anyway before turning around to address him.

"Anything you want to tell me?" he asked, looking amused rather than angry. Andy from IT had a square head and wore a T-shirt with Shaggy from Scooby-Doo on it at least three days a week. He wasn't even cute, but Jess tended to develop a crush on anyone close enough to touch. Cute was relative.

Andy said, "It was you, the cursor thing. You downloaded something."

"I didn't download anything," she protested.

He shrugged. "You did." Like he was omniscient, which was weird for a guy in a Scooby-Doo T-shirt.

"*He told me not to do it again*," she emailed Clara later. "*And I told him there were no guarantees, seeing as I didn't even know how I'd done it in the first place.*"

Clara wrote back saying, "*Don't do it. I know what you're thinking.*"

"*I'm sure he's not even single.*"

"*Andy from IT in the Scooby-Doo T-shirt?*" Clara responded. "*Trust me: he's single.*"

They dated for five and a half months, and for a while Jess was worried because the arrangement had the potential to putter along forever. What if she ended up going out with Andy for the rest of her life?

"*You might as well be dating Clayton,*" wrote Clara before she left her job in Korea and her all-night internet connection. She became much less in touch in a yurt in Mongolia learning to herd cattle, honest to god. They didn't have computers there, so Jess received a letter from Clara every couple of months, but her words kept echoing in Jess's brain.

Then out of nowhere, Andy broke up with her, and mostly Jess was relieved. When she realized this, she was horrified. Surely it was time she became the pilot of her life?

It was even a possibility now. Her pay was decent and she could put money aside for first and last months' rent on a one-bedroom apartment, a cozy place that was hers alone in an up-and-coming neighbourhood. She got rid of her futon and bought an actual couch. And she decided to apply for teachers' college, something sure and stable that would lead to an actual job instead of a vague and distant future. She contacted an old English prof, her thesis advisor, asking if she'd provide a reference, and was surprised to hear back right away.

"*So strange to get your message just now*, the email read, *because I've been thinking of you. Can you make some time to meet? I might have a little opportunity . . .*"

"*I've got a new job*," Jess wrote in a letter to Clara, even though she knew her news might seem humdrum compared to Clara's adventures in various sites across Africa digging for hearths and unearthing ancient artifacts. "*Turns out it's the end of me and childhood cancers—and Andy. I'm starting as office administrator at the Nordstrom Institute—do you remember it? At the library? It's the special collection of folk and fairy tales, and it's magical. It's a three-month contract, but it's up for renewal.*

Their last office administrator died; she was seventy-seven. They haven't hired anybody new there in twenty-three years."

The letter was sent in care of some person or another affiliated with the archeology department at the university where Clara's boyfriend, Tom, was employed as a professor. Through these circuitous means it would make its way into Clara's hands.

Clara's responses arrived in creased and battered envelopes bearing postmarks from Nepal, Namibia, Tunisia, Jess fishing them from the mailbox as she left for work in the morning. She received emails from Clara, but not often—it was tricky for her to access a computer. And even when Clara did email, she never had much time to write, or privacy to do so in a meaningful way. Her letters said so much more, clearly conveying Clara's voice—she was much more pen-and-paper than keyboard. Jess also liked the idea that she was carrying a little bit of Clara with her as she made her way through the streets, through the rhythms and routines of this brand-new life she'd created all by herself.

After six months, Jess's position at the Nordstrom Institute had been made permanent, with benefits, and she went to the dentist for the first time in years. She got eight cavities filled and vowed to take better care of herself from this point onward. These days she was feeling impressively responsible, having put a down payment on a condo to be built on what was still a parking lot that she walked by every morning. She was proud of how far she'd come in the last two years, even if her progress seemed conventional compared to Clara's. But this had always been the way between them. That distinction had been part of what attracted Jess to Clara in the first place, that she was going places. Jess reminded herself that they were two people who had made different choices, that none of those choices invalidated the other's, and most of the time she actually believed this. Though she was still stuck on a comment Clara once made about people who spend their whole lives in the towns they were born in. While Jess might have left her town, she was still in the same time zone. How far did a person need to travel to know they'd arrived?

The library where Jess worked was designed like a castle. The entrance was a Romanesque arch flanked by large bronze sculptures of a griffin and a winged lion, references to the folk and fairy-tale collections on the fourth floor. The Nordstrom Institute was named after Charlotte Nordstrom, a children's librarian who had inherited her family fortune and had no children. When she died she endowed the institute with her inheritance, put towards a book collection that attracted the attention of scholars from all over the world. Decades later, as an undergraduate, Jess was lucky to have access to the collection, rare books that required gloves for handling. Now, to spend every day in such a sanctified space was like winning the professional lottery, particularly after her year in the temping trenches.

In many ways, however, the Charlotte Nordstrom Institute for Folk and Fairy Tales was a workplace like any other, just one that featured vintage pop-up books, a cabinet full of book-branded board games, and special exhibits on picture-book portrayals of circuses and the history of paper dolls. There was still filing, of course; the photocopier often jammed; and the fax machine was usually out of paper. There was speculation among staff about who was responsible for neglecting to refill it, and the team had divided into factions. Discord also persisted about other matters, such as failure to remove food containers from the refrigerator, the right not to be overwhelmed by perfume, and the perfidy of computers.

There was certainly technological savvy among the staff, but nobody was sure yet about the internet. Digitizing the collections? Yes, without question, so that all that history could be more accessible. But beyond that, Jess's librarian colleagues didn't understand: what exactly was the internet for? The library was insisting the Institute required a homepage, and Jess was put in charge of this, her first major initiative beyond unjamming the photocopier and fetching everybody cups of tea.

She was still a receptionist, but this was different than her previous job. She was more like a gatekeeper charged with operating the drawbridge. Ordinary people never showed up at the Charlotte Nordstrom Institute for Folk and Fairy Tales. When things were slow, Jess would be tasked with dusting the collection of ships in bottles that had once belonged to Charlotte Nordstrom's father and were now housed in a glass case that ran along the wall in the reading room.

It was the most incredible mix of the mundane and the extraordinary, and she loved the balance, the way every day of her professional life was analogous to a cabinet of curiosities. This meant that when she sat down at her desk that morning and removed Clara's latest letter from its envelope, she didn't have to feel her view from here was so inferior to Clara's adventures in the wider world. It was easy to be happy for her friend when she was happy with herself.

But when Jess opened the letter and read its contents, she felt guilty for entertaining these thoughts. They seemed petty now, and her stomach sank as her eyes moved down the page.

Dear Jess,

I've been sicker than I've ever been—which is saying something after a year and a half dealing with rashes, gastrointestinal explosions from eating lettuce washed in unfiltered water, and bad reactions to anti-malaria drugs. Then I got pregnant, and everything's gone wrong. Getting pregnant on anti-malarial drugs is a disaster, never mind that I had no business being pregnant in the first place. But the way things work here—living in our encampment, sleeping under canvas, being hot and sweaty and dirty all the time—the usual rules don't apply. You can do stupid things, but it's okay, because it's temporary, plus we need a diversion from the minute focus we devote to our working days, the details in the grains of a handful of sand. So when the work is done, we do what we like, which for me—since Tom and I broke up—has been a guy from Burkina Faso. Tom claimed not to care, but he did. And then after I was so sick, and at around eight weeks I began to miscarry, which I'd been expecting, but the surprise was that I was devastated. Partly because the experience was so physically brutal, but it was more than that. Maybe I'd wanted this baby? I haven't even begun to unpack what I mean by that, because in practical terms it makes no sense, but I'm old enough now that I could imagine making it work, being somebody's mother. This baby wasn't a baby, but instead a mess of blood and tissue, hope and possibility, gushing out of me as I crouched over a squatting toilet trying not to die.

It was the worst pain I've ever experienced. We were out in the field and there are no comforts there, no place to go and rest and be alone, and everybody knew. Some people were supportive, but most of them thought I'd got what was coming to me. There are plenty of guys who think a girl has no business being out in the field in the first place, and there I was proving them right as I miscarried for three days, leaving a literal trail of blood behind me.

That was about six weeks ago, and since then I've been getting ready to leave, to go someplace else, but I don't know where yet. Ever since Nepal, I've been following Tom, and I really don't know how to do this without him. But it's time for me to go it alone, so I have to figure something out. He says maybe he could finagle something and find me a job back at his university in England, but I don't want to continue in his debt. There's also the option of coming home, but I'm not ready yet.

So what next? I don't know. But I wanted to write down what happened to process it all, and I need you to know because you'll be the one who understands.

Jess checked the date at the top of the letter—Clara had started it a month ago, which meant that she could be anywhere now. Jess realized she hadn't actually heard from Clara in weeks. Her computer took far too long to boot up, but as soon as it did, she logged on to her email, opened a new message, and typed in Clara's address.

"I got your letter," she wrote. *"And I'm here for you—in every way and for whatever you need."*

THE MIDLANDS

2004

For almost two years, Clara dragged her backpack across Asia and then Africa, patching the holes with duct tape, believing there was truly no limit to how much she could stuff inside . . . until the zipper broke on an airport carousel and the pack exploded, leaving everything she owned strewn about for anyone to trod on. Once she'd rescued her things, she had to tie the whole bundle together with yellow twine. She got the zipper repaired by a tailor in Botswana, but nothing was ever the same after that because now she knew what could happen.

She did her best to pack lighter from then on, and the backpack never exploded again; it only got dirtier, marked by mud and rain and sludge picked up on trains and planes the world over, slung up onto various luggage compartments. Its journeys were marked by pins and badges she found along the way, stickers she'd slap across its surface that would eventually peel off, leaving a shadow of adhesive. Clara's backpack was like her body, mapped with scars and bruises, a survivor of conditions rife with discomfort—mosquitos, heat, and typhoons, not to mention dodgy moments when she'd been decidedly unsafe. But she'd made it through, and though far from unscathed, she was basically intact—the backpack too, both of them patched and repaired, totally filthy. And then the bag was stolen from King's Cross station shortly after her arrival in London.

She reported the theft to a police officer patrolling the platform. "But you're not to leave bags unattended," said the officer, far more concerned that the wayward backpack would be dumped and then reported as a suspicious package than that all of Clara's worldly possessions were gone.

The station police began preparing for the report of an imminent bomb threat rather than trying to track down the thief. And what kind of thief would steal a disgusting bag that contained nothing of value and weighed a ton? Twenty minutes earlier, Clara had left the backpack under the table in a café where she'd just had a cup of tea and a stale scone. She realized she might prefer that the bag be stolen rather than having to drag it into a tiny toilet stall one more time. Her first response when she returned to find it gone had actually been relief . . . and then panic. Those were her books, her clothes, her only footwear other than the filthy rubber boots she was wearing.

"But really nothing of value at all," Clara tried to explain to the officers who were even more hysterical in their funny hats, as they considered the practicality of pre-emptively evacuating the station to get ahead of the chaos that would ensue when the bag was found. "Mainly sentimental," she said. None of them were listening and she didn't blame them. Who carries sixty pounds of sentimental halfway across the world? She'd nearly broken her back doing so and now, thanks to the thief, she was free.

Clara ended up filing a lost-property report and left the station three hours later unencumbered, save for the clothes she was wearing and a tiny cross-body bag stuffed with the essentials that hadn't been in the backpack: her passport (working-holiday visa stapled inside); her wallet; an almost empty tube of lip balm; an assemblage of hair ties, and small change in various currencies. When she took stock of what she'd miss, it was mainly her correspondence from Jess. Clara had printed her emails whenever she had the opportunity, rereading the messages until the papers were ragged. They were at the bottom of the bag, bound with the same yellow twine that, for a time, had held her life together.

Jess had written actual letters sometimes too, but her handwriting was small and tentative, her ideas constrained by the exercise, formal and awkward. Jess's letters didn't sound the way her emails did: easy, conversational, and present. But Clara loved all of it, and she saved the letters along with the emails because she missed her friend with a force that surprised her once she was so far from home. She'd come to depend on Jess during their years together, a fact that drove her to put distance between them just to prove that she could. Clara knew it was bloody-minded, how she did everything the hard way. It was a remnant of her religious upbringing, which had drilled into her the belief that there was virtue to be found in suffering.

And so she'd suffered, but the emails and letters from Jess had been a balm. Now that they were gone, it was the digital that would endure. While Clara ran out of inbox storage on a regular basis, Jess's messages were never deleted.

It was impossible to know what would last and what wouldn't. Clara was aware of this from her work, seeing the unlikely objects that had come down through history, the wonders that could be discovered in a hearth or a latrine. It was extraordinary that anything lasted at all when you considered that most things eventually crumbled and disappeared. And yet you could walk around a museum imagining that the process of preservation was nothing special, that it happened all the time, that objects that had lasted through the ages represented the big picture in a meaningful way.

Clara spent the next few days in London with a couple she'd crossed paths with in Korea two years earlier. Both had got their MBAs and worked fourteen-hour days doing something called management consulting, so Clara barely saw them. Her days, on the other hand, were wide open, apart from calls to Lost Articles to see if her backpack had been found. Clara eventually gave up on seeing her bag again; it was really just a bundle of clothing intended for another climate.

Her friends had high-speed internet in the flat—they had high-speed everything, stainless-steel kitchen appliances, their life a vision of the future—and Clara was free to log on to their computer and go through her old messages, rereading Jess's emails. Clara wrote new messages too, their connection enduring, ever-unfolding, with Jess responding in real time, sending commiserations for the lost bag and trying to be diplomatic when inquiring about Clara's state of mind. *"You know, you can always come home. You have so much support here."*

But Clara couldn't. She was still on the run from all she'd been through in Tunisia. Going home would mean she'd have to process it, finally coming face to face with herself, all the while trying to avoid getting tangled up in the usual familial drama. She wasn't ready for any of that. So instead she applied, via Tom, for a position in the department of archeology and ancient history at his university in a small city in the Midlands. Tom was also concerned about Clara's well-being, and while she would have preferred to stride off into the unknown untethered from such connections, she was beginning to realize that there were only so many times a person could begin again. Adult life was meant to be cumulative, and she was already twenty-seven. It was time to start building on her foundations.

She had sent Jess an update on her lost bag, and she waited for the unread message indicator to appear on her inbox now. Email was faster than it had ever been, but Jess was busy managing projects, putting on exhibits, and studying part-time for her Masters in information science. She had actually found a job in the fairy-tale industry, working at the library with the bronze statues of a lion and a griffin at the door, studying those mythical frogs that had been her preoccupation years ago. This, Clara supposed, was the kind of thing that might happen to a person who didn't treat continents like stepping stones, stupidly jumping from one to another. A person for whom happily-ever-after might be possible.

Jess's message appeared. *"Keep me in the loop, okay? I want to hear how the job works out. And I'll repay the favour by keeping you abreast of the online dating chronicles. Having a third date this weekend with a fellow who seems promising . . ."*

As had always been the case, Jess's dating life was cribbed from Jane Austen, all misunderstandings and protocols, everything complicated. Over the years, observing Jess from both near and far, Clara had learned that she enjoyed the drama. Clara's own romantic life was not without its troubles, of course, but communication tended to be straightforward—no one had ever accused her of behaving like a nineteenth-century

heroine. Whereas Jess's forays into online dating had exacer-
bated her tendency to view the world as a setting for her love
plots. She came up with rules, like no kissing on the first date
and no sex until the fifth. Such an insistence on formality—
Clara saw nothing wrong with rolling into bed with whom-
ever she saw fit.

But maybe this was part of the problem. This was why
Clara was sitting here today in someone else's flat, without a
backpack. She was in England now, a land of decorum,
restraint, of Jane Austen herself, and she wondered if it might
rub off. Could she be a heroine after all? She could look at it
all as an adventure, discovering what could happen when a
person exercises prudence. She would not have sex with her
boss, for example, assuming that Tom's academic supervisor
could set her up with a position. Tom's supervisor was about
ninety-seven years old, so this was a goal that Clara had an
actual chance of achieving. And there could be other rules,
she supposed, arbitrary as they might seem. Save money,
drink less. Exercise, don't sleep in. Go to bed on time, and so
on—what kind of a life was that? But what kind of a life was
this? Something had to give.

By the time Jess had her third date with the promising fellow—he was some kind of consultant too; it was an epidemic—
Clara had left London, her meagre belongings packed in a
suitcase she'd bought at Woolworths, a suitcase with wheels
that she pulled behind her to a train that took her all the way
up to the Midlands, where she disembarked, booked into a
backpackers' hostel, and called Tom's supervisor from a pay-
phone to confirm their meeting.

Oh yes, he'd been expecting her, he said. Tom had filled
him in—and Clara wondered what exactly he'd told him. It

might have been most convenient for Tom to attach a note to her duffle coat:

> *Please look after this woman. She has spent the last six*
> *months drunk, depressed, and/or hemorrhaging. I tried to*
> *save her, but she thwarted my efforts, and I'm tired. I enclose*
> *this note in the hope that my care absolves me of any guilt,*
> *and in the future I promise not to pursue relationships with*
> *employees who are most likely insane.*

It was a long note. She'd need a big duffle coat.

The situation was indeed a little bit irregular, admitted Dr. Quincy Falstaff-Beddington, Tom's supervisor, when they met the following week. Usually research assistant positions were reserved for graduate students, but he could make an arrangement for Clara, since she came highly recommended . . . although, he warned, if this was going to be a serious pursuit, she'd need to get her Masters. He could offer her a six-month contract, part-time. Some fieldwork.

And Clara took it, because he was doing her a favour, and she had no other option except to take a job in a sandwich shop, which they seemed to have on every corner here. She might end up working at one anyway if she didn't get enough hours at the university.

There were two computer terminals in the common room of the hostel. Clara dropped a line to her mother confirming that she was still alive, and even employed again. After she sent that note, she read the latest email from Jess about the promising fellow, who had a name now: Adam. Jess wrote, "*It's possible that this might be the real thing.*

"*But how am I supposed to trust my instincts?*" she continued. "*I think of all the times I've been in love, or thought I was. All the times I was sure that* this time *it was different, and it turned out to be the same. With Adam, it feels so right, but what if I'm fooling myself? Is it strange to be having doubts about the absence of doubts? Does everybody feel like this?*

"*It just seems unbelievable that things could work out, that I could find 'the one' via a computer program. Adam is really good, not ordinary, I promise—this is the part that makes me think you're going to like him. I never understood what you meant by 'ordinary,' but now I do. Or I think I do. How does a person ever know?*"

"*Stop overthinking,*" Clara typed in response. "*Let it happen!*" She was feeling humble enough these days to consider that leaving all her choices up to a computer might not be such a terrible idea.

But she had a job now, so that was something to share with Jess. "*I'll be spending my time in library sub-basements, and even getting a chance to do some fieldwork.*" Dr. Falstaff-Beddington was running a five-year project excavating a park not far from the city that represented one of the last remaining local examples of wet heathland.

"Heaths are my passion," he had told her, and Clara tried to summon the requisite enthusiasm for scrubby terrain. She wanted him to take her seriously, even though she lacked a graduate degree. She'd done more fieldwork than she would have accomplished had she taken a more conventional route into archeology, and it was dispiriting to realize that it didn't count for much. She'd just spent months unearthing fragments of the world's most ancient civilizations, finds with potential to change the way human beings understand themselves as a species, trying to learn where we'd come from and where we were going—though she still didn't really know. But she wasn't sure the answer would be found on a heath.

She sent the message to Jess and logged out of her email, distracted by the gaggle of girls who'd turned up in the common room to watch *Strictly Come Dancing*, all sparkles and bangles, midriffs exposed.

"You're going out tonight!" Clara exclaimed. They were drinking red wine from disposable cups—she'd forgotten about these rituals. And they assumed she was asking to join them—"You're welcome to come," one of them offered. They were all as friendly as they were noisy, but it wasn't Clara's scene. She'd thought they were all travelling together, but it turned out they'd only just met. How do people do it, Clara wondered, just create connections like that?

"*Were we ever as young as them?*" she wrote to Jess. The girls were on a gap year. Clara herself had done a gap year—or three of them—way back when, but she hadn't known the terminology. And even if she had known what the term meant, she hadn't seen the time that way, hadn't thought of those years after high school as a space to be filled. Maybe this was her gap year right now—just a decade late.

"*You were twenty-one when I met you, already a woman of the world, so no, you were never that young,*" Jess wrote back. "*Maybe I was, though. And you were patient with me.*"

But Jess was different and always had been, something Clara had noticed before they were even friends. At the beginning of their first year, all the other girls on their floor had been a pack. Jess was part of it, certainly, but she was the only one in the group who would turn around and smile at Clara, eating her lunch alone in the dining hall. Jess used to carry all her stuff in a tattered canvas cross-body bag with the lyrics to Des'ree's "You Gotta Be" inscribed across it in blue ink, which Clara found so embarrassingly earnest as to come full circle and be cool. The urgent strains of Ani DiFranco, Tracy Chapman, and the Indigo Girls poured out of Jess's room whenever her awful roommate, Muffy, was away. It made Clara wish, in the words of another singer, that she too could have "a way with women," even though most other girls just made her feel invisible. But Jess never did, and this was what Clara missed now, in the Midlands, that feeling of being recognized—and not just as she was recognized by the sparkly girls, as someone unfathomably older who owned only two pairs of jeans.

Owning just two pairs of jeans meant that when Clara finally found a flat—a room on the third floor of a shared house, although they called it the second floor here—she didn't even need to take a taxi. Instead, she folded her belongings into her Woolworths suitcase and wheeled it twenty minutes across town to her new front door. Her flatmates were graduate students, so there were fewer midriffs and disposable beer cups, and for the first time in two years she had a room of her own.

She was so skinny now, and nobody in her life—her flatmates Kathleen, Ivan, and Jeremy—realized how strange it was for her to have cheekbones. She still hadn't gotten around to replacing her one bra, which was threadbare, the cups like deflated balloons, her now-smallish breasts lost inside them. The pants she'd bought in London were a single-digit size she didn't recall wearing since she was a child, even with the disparity between Canadian and British sizing. It was odd, and she was not herself, although things were improving—the shadows under her eyes had disappeared, and colour was returning to her face.

She had a kitchen again, which helped. None of her flatmates cooked much, so it was her own terrain, and she could put together proper meals for the first time in a long time—roast chicken, chili, pasta sauces, enchiladas, souf-flés, stews. She started baking bread, and the smell would draw her flatmates out of their hidey-holes, creating a sem-blance of community. Everyone was grateful, and she also got to be well-fed, to fill the gnawing emptiness inside her. She was feeling better and stronger, and this was what she wrote to Tom: *You don't have to worry about me.* She was trying to get better mostly so she could tell herself she didn't need him and even for it to be true.

It had been a mistake, she could see this now, to hitch a ride on Tom's professional coattails. He'd been her passport to anywhere, but it meant that she gave up charting her own course. Where might she be now without him? There were so many possibilities for what a life could turn into. Jess was right: how do you ever know?

This was why it seemed especially safe and comfortable where she was now, this space between, her gap year. She'd have a new beginning, but only when she was ready, and right now she was resting and recovering, returning to her-self. The Midlands were in-between, just like she was, and the landscape, flat and unassuming, suited her needs. Low and soft, just like a heath, an ideal place for her to land.

THE WEDDING

2006–2007

When the phone rang in September, out of the blue, Jess was still holding the test in her hand. She heard Clara's voice on the other end of the line, and thought, *Of course, it's you.*

"You're never going to believe this," she started, but Clara was already speaking. "I've got news," she said.

"You?" Jess was thrown off, her narrative hijacked. "Are you okay?"

"Fine," said Clara. "Really. I've only got a bit of phone credit. We might get cut off. You're coming to my wedding."

"What?" She hadn't heard wrong. Clara was like this, capricious, impulsive, but it still made no sense. Jess had forgotten how disorienting it could be to connect the constellations of Clara's whims. What she hadn't forgotten was how much Clara had been through, how she'd been messed-up and broken. How vulnerable she was.

"I know. It's sudden," Clara continued. "But I need you to be there. That's why I'm calling, giving you lots of notice." Jess had gotten married in the spring, and Clara missed the wedding due to the excavation of an ancient harbour in

Cyprus. "It's going to be at my mom's. Not even far for you."
She paused. "I'm coming home."

It was all overwhelming, everything at once. This had
been Jess's moment, and now it wasn't, but Clara was coming
home. Getting married, but to whom? She had no idea. "Is
this Ivan . . . ?" Jess asked, that being the name of the last
boyfriend she'd heard of, but Clara said no.

"His name is Nick. And he's a good one. He—" The connection broke up.

"Clara? I can't—" This was all too much.

"He owns a bar," Clara said, speaking loudly and slowly.
"A pub. It's where we met. And I want you to be my brides-
maid. At the end of June."

"June." Jess was still holding the test stick. Finally she
said, "I'm pregnant, Clara." The two pink lines had emerged
so faintly at first, but now they were undeniable. "Just. Like,
I mean, I just found out. Right now." She was still sitting on
the toilet with her pants around her ankles. She'd brought the
phone into the bathroom so she could call Adam, but Clara
had gotten to her first.

There was silence for a moment. "Well, this is huge,"
Clara said, sounding even farther away than before.

And Jess thought about June, and then May, when the
baby would be due. *The baby.* "We were trying. I just never
imagined it would happen so fast."

"It's all happening," said Clara. There was a noise on the
line. "Credit's almost all gone," she said. "I'm thrilled for
you, Jess." She paused. "You're going to be there, right?"

Jess said, "Of course." Even though she didn't believe it,
she didn't believe any of it: the wedding, the baby. June was
another century, a different continent. "You're coming home.

And Nick." It was a lot to process. "You've got to email me a picture," she told her. They were friends on Facebook, but Clara never updated, had little truck with the online world. The only photos Clara ever posted were of the sky.

For months both things seemed impossible, that Clara was coming home, and that Jess would have a baby in her arms. The baby would be six weeks old by Clara's wedding day, transformed from post-fetal into an actual human, but small enough to still be portable, stowed under a table during the party. Jess had never actually met a baby, but she'd been reading books, feeling as though she and Adam were preparing to jump off a cliff—or maybe they'd jumped already and were flying, hands gripped tightly, feeling exhilarated and terrified to contemplate the landing.

At night they would lie awake, Adam's hands on her belly, waiting for the magic of the baby's kick. It was impossible to predict when it would happen, but when it did, Jess would lie still and wait for it again. Feeling was believing, however fleetingly, that they weren't just imagining this creature floating inside her. They tried to interpret the kicks as if they were a code, as though they could decipher their destiny.

On these nights, they were so solidly joined, a shell around her burgeoning belly—"I'm making a *person*," Jess kept repeating, marvelling at her body's bag of tricks—though things were more complicated in the daytime. Jess skimmed the books, reading the charts mostly, and she noted with relief that by six weeks babies could sleep through the night, although six sleepless weeks still sounded like torture.

But Adam considered books inadequate preparation for what lay before them. "What you've got to focus on," he told

Jess, unpacking a box that was larger than their kitchen table, "is gear."

"Gear," said Jess, as Adam pulled out a plastic seat with suction cups that doubled as a feeding chair and a bath seat. He felt confident enough to dwell in unknowns, fortified by consumer goods. He was quite sure their daughter (their daughter!) was going to sleep all night from birth because he had purchased a $300 blanket with black-and-yellow stripes called the Swaddlelullabee. He wasn't even worried about a wedding weekend with a baby just a few weeks old, because there were these portable baby travel-cots that folded up into a tiny bag you could carry over your shoulder.

"The part I really don't get, though," Adam said, "is that Clara leaves you high and dry for years, and then just summons you to her side the minute she decides to come back home."

Jess probably would have seen his point if Clara's call had come at any other time, if their lives weren't once again intersecting at a point so crucial that it was eerie. Hadn't this always been the nature of their connection, how Clara could be so close and far away at once? Clara, who by now was as much a myth as an actual person—every time Jess planned to travel to see her, she had already moved on someplace else. Clara kept in contact, but on her own terms, impossible as ever to hold, all of it difficult to explain.

Although Jess tried. "It wasn't high and dry, exactly. She stays in touch—you've seen her letters. Honestly, Clara is probably closer to me than she is to anyone. She's a wild one, like a dandelion. She doesn't do things the way everyone else does." For example, getting married: Clara's wedding, to someone she hadn't even mentioned before, was coming at the tail end of the devastating time she'd had. It had been two years since her miscarriage, and while Clara didn't mention it in her letters anymore, Jess knew how deeply she'd been affected. It wasn't the sort of hardship a person simply shakes off, and Jess was going to be at that wedding because Clara needed her, and being needed by Clara was no small thing.

Besides, it wasn't as though Jess had been sitting idly by waiting for the summons; Adam and the baby would be living proof of that.

So they were going. It wasn't even up for debate, because as long as Adam had known Jess, he'd known that Clara was somebody who mattered—which was not to say he didn't grumble about taking two days off work, but he booked them. The travel, the wedding, the hassle of it all—Jess knew none of it was rational, but she wasn't about to miss Clara's wedding to appease reason. The journey was just a few hours up the highway. Reason didn't always have to be king.

But while ignoring reason had seemed an inspired idea when Jess was growing a human being (because what was reasonable about that?), when the baby was born—Arabella Jean, the middle name for Adam's late mother, Bella for short, six pounds eleven ounces—Jess found herself clinging to any semblance of rationality, rules, and structure. It turned out that she might be a creature of reason after all, now adrift in a world upside down with sleepless nights and disappearing days, sidewalk circuits walking to nowhere, feeding a body that was never satiated, that constantly mewling, wailing, sucking mouth. Eleven hours of sitting propped up on pillows while the baby cried and refused to sleep.

What had happened to time? It was as though the baby's arrival had undone a zipper, turning the world inside out, which was almost literally what had happened to Jess's body, now mangled and destroyed. But her body was the least of her problems.

Adam tried to help, but he couldn't, and his uselessness made Jess hate him. She hadn't known it was possible to hate Adam, who bounced through life like a rubber ball. Jess loved his bounce—what a way to travel, and she got to bounce alongside him—but now they were so tired, and he had to go to work in the morning. He had clients and deadlines and managed a team. So Adam started sleeping on the couch, leaving her alone in the dark cave of their bedroom while the baby cried, and then he bought earplugs, and Jess had never felt so betrayed.

Bella cried almost constantly, refused to feed, and even in those rare moments when she did eat contentedly, Jess would stare at her ear, thinking how it resembled a gaping maw, and start anticipating the dark night ahead. It defied everything Jess understood about narrative—how stories should have a beginning, a middle, and an end—the way her baby's furious needs went on and on without ceasing.

And it was here in this broken place that everything Jess had never understood about mothers in fairy tales—"Snow White" and "Hansel and Gretel"—made sense. In the original version of the latter, there hadn't been a stepmother but a mother proper, and Jess could understand it, sending your kids out into the woods with a trail of breadcrumbs, a path that would never lead back home. She almost felt relief at the idea, and then she began crying along with Bella. She peeled off the breastfeeding pillow and got out of bed, her sore and decimated body unaccustomed to being upright. She walked around the room and the motion calmed the baby, but still Jess cried and cried, clutching her bundle to her heart, where its beating, she had read, might prove soothing.

"I'm so sorry," she kept saying to the baby through her tears. When she wasn't plotting to send the baby into the woods, her heart was breaking with the knowledge that this poor child lacked a loving mother. How did anyone do this?

Jess tried asking her own mother, who had no answers. "I don't remember feeling like that," her mother kept saying. "I think you just slept."

Apparently there were people who charged thousands of dollars to teach your baby to sleep, and Jess was willing to try it, but her mother thought it was nonsense and Adam had lost his faith in such things since the disappointment of the Swaddlelullabee.

Walking was the only thing that calmed the baby, at least until Jess stopped moving. And so she didn't, and they went around the room, around the house, and in the evenings, through the neighbourhood. It was the closest thing to good times during those terrible early days, the beginning of June so the evenings were as golden as afternoons. Adam would join them when he managed to get home on time, and he'd wear the baby on his chest, because Bella hated the stroller along with everything else in the world. Being outdoors, breathing the fresh air and feeling the sun on her skin—for Jess, this made it almost bearable. As they walked, they'd pass other couples like them, shell-shocked and shattered, bearing their own tiny bundles—a *family*—and it was like looking into a mirror. Jess wanted to tap those other new mothers on the shoulder and say, *I know, I get it, and we're going to make it,* because on those evenings she almost believed that they were.

All this was a moment that seemed like a lifetime, which it *was*: the baby's so far. It was also an eternity and so far from the comfortable and happy life she and Adam had had before, something that Jess grieved.

It was three weeks, or maybe four, before the broken pieces of Jess's universe started to assemble into something that sort of made sense, day and night nearly distinguishable. She still saw four and five o'clock in the morning as she rocked by the window, streetlights illuminating Bella's head with its dark curls. But Jess would stroke it now, thinking, sometimes, *this is love*.

There had scarcely been room in Jess's frazzled mind to think about Clara at all, much less her wedding; that is, until the baby was five and half weeks old and Jess received an email with the subject: *LANDED!* Clara was back, the two of them on the same continent again, but Jess felt so alienated from herself and the world that it meant very little. Clara wanted to see her, to come to the city, but Jess couldn't do it, set a date or make a plan. She was so exhausted—a person could be still alive after sleeping no more than scattered half hours for five weeks, something she would have never believed. There had been nights when the closest she'd come to dreaming was bizarre hallucinations of the baby grown gigantic, exploding out of her arms, out of the room, taking the roof right off the house, and threatening to crush Jess with the enormity of her life force.

It was a struggle, all of it, to string words into a sentence, to follow a conscious thought to its end, even though Jess was starting to get a handle on ordinary days, to anticipate feedings and diaper changes. She'd even made a list of meals she could cook with one hand so Adam didn't have to bring home take-out every night, and sometimes Bella fell asleep early in the evening, and Jess and Adam would have a half hour or forty-five minutes alone, and it felt like a blessing, a sliver of something recognizable.

The wedding weekend crept up on them, impossible then imminent. Clara had asked them to arrive on Thursday, when her close family would gather before the ceremony. Clara wanted Jess to be there to save her from all the sisters and cousins, she said. She wanted a chance to finally catch up after the four years they'd been apart.

So Jess and Adam packed the car, and somehow their sedan wasn't big enough to accommodate the bouncy chair, the bassinet, a box of diapers, the take-along baby swing with the plastic toucan, the breastfeeding pillow, an assortment of ordinary pillows that Jess required behind her back during nighttime feeds, and enough other items to fill up an array of tote bags.

"Are you sure we need all this?" asked Adam. The irony— he wasn't the one home all day, so he didn't understand how each of these items was essential in holding a fragile world together: the bouncy chair so Jess could put the baby down for a few minutes, and the swing to soothe her evening rages and help put her to sleep. The plastic bathtub, however, they could live without, because otherwise the trunk wouldn't close.

And with that, they were done, they were really doing this. Adam slammed the trunk shut, which woke Bella up. She started crying in her car seat while Jess was trying to buckle her in. Jess squeezed in beside the baby, fitting her legs around the swing, the plastic toucan's beak stabbing her in the thigh. The passenger seat, which used to be hers, was now a tower of bags and diapers, one she hoped would not topple. She hummed along with the calming CD, hoping to coax the baby from her fury.

The three-hour journey took six hours, with five stops: for diaper changes, feedings, coffee, and donuts, plus two more stops because the baby was covered in puke.

"Tell me again why we're doing this?" Adam asked at the rest stop as he changed Bella on a picnic table covered with graffiti. Jess was trying to rinse spit-up off her T-shirt, but mostly just succeeding in getting wet.

Adam remarked, "I can see your nipples."

"Who hasn't seen my nipples?" Jess replied, deadpan, amazed at how many strange things were unremarkable now. "But hey, we're almost there."

They rolled up the long driveway shortly before four o'clock. Jess stared at the house, thinking how much Clara had hated this place, remembering the week they'd spent together after her dad died, all the solitary parts of her friend that Jess had never got to know.

They parked around the side of the house, and Clara came outside looking like herself, exactly like the Clara Jess had last seen at the airport five minutes ago—or had it been a thousand years? Her cheeks were round and rosy, her hair long and tangled. She wore a flowing skirt and that jingly anklet, her bare feet filthy. She looked so happy, so well, which was a relief, and Jess could tell that Clara was examining her with an equally critical eye, neither of them quite believing that the other was real. Clara was a most uncanny mirror; her radiance and beauty made Jess even more conscious of her own pathetic state: her stained shirt, her stupid ponytail, her saggy abdomen, and the bags under her eyes.

But if Clara saw any of that, she didn't let on. "You're here," she said. "Sometimes I wondered if I'd ever see you again. I wondered if I'd made you up. Nick thinks I did."

They were so close Jess could have pushed the tangled hair out of Clara's face to see her more clearly, the way she would have done once upon a time without even thinking, but she was afraid to touch her now. Or maybe she didn't know how, now that their once-casual intimacy was a long-ago dream. And who was Jess now? Who was Clara?

But Clara was Clara, uninhibited as ever. She closed the distance, enveloping Jess in her arms for the first time in so long, such a stabilizing force after all these weeks with her universe in pieces. Jess could feel the tension leave her body as she let herself be held, and she returned that hug, the space between *you* and *me, here* and *there, now* and *then* obliterated.

"Well, now you can tell him," Jess said when they finally let go, stepping back, recovering her senses, still trying to straighten out her haphazard appearance, adjust her twisted skirt. "I'm really real." She looked around for Nick, but he was still inside, like the moment in a play before the curtain goes up.

Clara had moved on, embracing Adam and the baby in his arms. "Oh my god, Jess," she was saying. "Look what you made." She was crying. "Look what you made," she said again. She wanted to hold Bella, Jess could see that, and she signalled to Adam to pass her over.

"Jess, you have a *daughter*," Clara said, her hair falling over the baby's face. It was mind-bending, this was true.

"And this is Adam," Jess said, inviting him in from his awkward place outside their circle.

Clara looked up from the baby, who was gripping her index finger. She said, "Adam I know all about. This one, on the other hand—" planting a kiss on Bella's bald head (her black newborn hair had fallen away over the last six weeks when Jess wasn't looking), "is still to be discovered."

"You know all about me?" asked Adam, looking uncomfortable. He knew all about Clara, but perhaps he hadn't expected the arrangement, the scrutiny, to go both ways.

"We're Facebook friends. And I've filed away every single detail Jess has ever told me about you." Clara said, sniffing the baby.

"And it's all been good!" Jess cut in, trying to smooth things over.

Clara said, "Mostly." She planted her lips on the baby's forehead. "I would have registered objections otherwise." Finally she looked up. "You're the only reason I joined that loathsome website," she said, staring Adam in the eye. "I had to check you out." Then she handed him the baby and hugged Jess again, her wild hair everywhere.

"I never realized you were so vigilant," said Jess when they drew apart again, feeling pleased. Pleased about Adam and Facebook, pleased that she'd been on Clara's mind.

"Just keeping tabs. You're prolific." It was true. Jess had handily signed up for Facebook just three days before Adam proposed and her life ever since had been a montage of engagement, wedding, honeymoon, real estate, and baby-bump photos, right up to the birth and those precious photos of them immediately after Bella's arrival, bowled over, dumbfounded, and stunned. Though soon after, reality had set in and she was less prolific. The chaos of her life since then had been so much harder to compose, but maybe all this was difficult to tell from the outside.

Clara led the way into the house, where they were welcomed by her mom and her boyfriend, as well as Clara's sisters, Diane and Julie, whose kids were running in and out of doors in a blur as Jess sat down to feed the baby again. It was hard to imagine Bella ever turning into one of those children. And there were Clara's cousins, one whom Jess remembered and another she didn't. Then a woman with an English accent Jess had mistaken as one of Nick's relations.

But Nick didn't have any relations, or at least none who'd seen fit to make the trip. It was only him, and he was so much older than Jess had expected, older than he'd looked in the photo Clara sent. Jess didn't understand why Clara hadn't mentioned that she was basically marrying somebody's dad. Literally: he had a son, he told Jess when she introduced him to Arabella.

"I've changed my fair share of nappies," he said, averting his eyes from a particularly nasty one Jess was changing on the floor. Clara's mother was hovering at first—she'd told Jess she could change the baby upstairs; what she really meant was not to do it on the carpet. But Jess was so tired, the change-mat would suffice, and she didn't know where Adam had disappeared to. There was only Nick, who wouldn't be offering much help even with the experience he claimed.

"How old's your son?" she asked, making conversation, fastening the fresh diaper and snapping on a onesie.

"Twenty-seven," he told her. "He's got babies of his own."

Clara had mentioned none of this.

He said, "Looking forward to giving it all another round."

"Another round?"

"Clare wants it all, the baby thing."

Jess said, "Clare?"

Nick said, "My betrothed." He was trying to be cute, and here was Clara now coming into the room with Adam.

Jess got up off the floor and handed the baby to her husband. "He calls you Clare," she said to Clara accusingly. How could a person marry somebody who didn't even know their own name?

"A lot of people call me Clare. It's more common over there." Clara had grabbed Jess's hand and she drew her down the hall into the enclosed back staircase, shutting the door at the bottom. They were almost in darkness, and the sounds of the party were far away.

They sat down on a step side by side, Clara leaning in close. "Your boobs are unreal," she said. They were, but most people were polite enough not to comment. "Can I touch them?" Clara asked. "That's not weird, right? You know why I'm asking. Scientific inquiry." Clara had always been the one with the huge boobs; Jess's tended toward unremarkable.

"Of course." They were right back to the way they'd always been, like no time had passed at all.

Clara put her hand on Jess's left breast and squeezed. She was just one of the many people who'd done so in the last six weeks—midwives, lactation consultants, a public health nurse, the baby herself with her tiny, grabby fists. "They're so soft," she said.

"Because I just fed her," said Jess. "When we first got here, they felt like rocks."

"Sounds painful."

"It is."

Clara touched the other one, squeezed gently. "They're incredible." she said. She pulled away. "I can't believe you're a mom. A mom! I mean, I can't even believe you're here. It's been so long."

"We almost weren't," said Jess. "Here, I mean. The drive took forever." She paused. "He's old, Clara."

"Nick." Not a question.

"You didn't tell me."

"It didn't matter."

"It didn't?"

"You're going to like him. I promise."

And Jess thought about Ferber, their landlord's nephew, whom Clara had been with at the end of their final year at school. Clara regarded all men as curiosities, which made it hard to be selective. And it didn't help that all of them wanted to sleep with her.

"I didn't take it seriously at first, because he was so much older and I was trying to learn to be on my own," Clara said. "Honestly, I thought I was finished with relationships, but he turned out to be persistent, and we kept ending up together. I couldn't shake him. And then I realized I didn't even want to."

"You met him in a pub."

Clara heard her derision and brushed it off. "It was a nice pub. It was his place. It was doing well for a while but it's hard to make a go of it. The culture's changing. It eats your life. He wasn't sorry to let it go. He sold it and ended up with a profit, enough that we can start something here."

"So you're staying?" Jess hadn't dared to entertain this possibility. She didn't want to be disappointed, but she also didn't know what it would mean to have Clara close again.

Clara said, "I want to be home. To make my own home. It's time."

"You want to have kids. He told me that, Nick," Jess said, wanting to show she wasn't as out of the loop as Clara thought.

"He wants it too. He has a son."

"The same age as me." Not an inessential detail.

"They're estranged," Clara explained. "He's made mistakes. But who hasn't? We like the idea of a fresh start, a new leaf."

"It's just hard, having a baby," said Jess. "I really had no idea what I was in for." She hadn't properly admitted this to anybody, and she could say so now only because of the darkness.

But Clara wasn't really listening. "I know," she said, but she didn't. Clara had no idea. "I can't wait," she said. "I want it all. I honestly can't believe we did it."

"Did what?"

"Found our people. These men. Our men." It was so neat and tidy, and it had a kind of symmetry, the way Clara was putting it, but was it really the same? Clara was still flying by the seat of her pants, whereas Jess had been practical and wise, making all the sensible choices, and everything had *still* come so close to disaster once Bella arrived. And she wasn't out of the woods yet. Babies up the stakes—it's unimaginable until you get there. Clara needed to be careful.

Jess said, "Nick seems nice." And he did, but it was a weak baseline.

"He's fifty-two years old, and more self-possessed than any guy I've been with before," Clara said. "By then you've figured out what's what, right? You've gone after all the things everybody says you need to go after and discovered it's all a bit hollow."

"It's not *all* hollow."

"I mean that by then a person knows where he's going."

"He's been married before."

"Just twice."

Jess thought, *Just?*

Clara went on. "Make enough wrong choices, you'll figure out what the right ones are. Like by deduction." She shrugged. "I'm proud of him. I admire him."

"Did I tell you we ran into Clayton?" said Jess, on the topic of wrong choices. "Last year, in a bookstore." She and Adam had been browsing and she had found her ex-boyfriend in the fiction section. He seemed shorter than she remembered. When he saw her, he tried to hide by taking a book off the shelf and flipping through it. "Except that he was standing at the very beginning of the fiction section, where all the sexy books by Anonymous are shelved, so he was hiding his face behind a giant screaming vulva."

"Do vulvas scream?"

"Some do," said Jess. "Anyway, I went over and said hi. It was awkward."

"Clayton was always awkward."

"I can't believe it, really, me and him," she said. "How does anything ever happen, really? The way we jump out of one life and into another." Jess looked at Clara. "So what's your plan then? For after the wedding. Are you staying here?" At her mother's, Jess meant.

Clara said, "Hell, no. With Diane and Julie? Like a holy trinity? They both live along the concession." A funny term, the official name for the rural roads that divided the land into rectangles and squares. Bucolic yes, but to live there would be conceding something, Jess knew. "And I'd murder my mother," said Clara. "Or else she'd murder me first. I think I had to stay away so long just to make sure there was no danger of being pulled back again."

From somewhere in the house, Jess heard the baby cry and her milk let down in response, soaking the pads inside her nursing bra. Her body had become a strange machine with its own operating instructions. The cries grew louder, closer.

"The baby's amazing, Jess," said Clara. "You must be over the moon."

"Over the moon," Jess repeated, because nobody understood when she tried to explain the way it really was. She had thought Clara might, but maybe she didn't want to know. The way a person can get everything she wanted but it's too much to carry. Jess said it again, "I'm over the moon."

"What were you doing in the closet?" Adam asked when she and Clara finally opened the door and tumbled out of the stairwell, blinking as their eyes adjusted to the light. He pushed a screaming Bella into Jess's arms. "You've got to calm her down," he said. And more quietly, so only she could hear, "I don't know anyone. You left me alone."

"It wasn't a closet," said Jess, jiggling the baby out of her plum-faced indignation. All it took was a little distraction. The baby was fed, so it wasn't even about the boobs—although really, it was always about the boobs. Jess was the mother and Adam the father, and her presence always meant more. She didn't even have to do anything, just be there, but when she wasn't there all hell would break loose, much to Adam's frustration and her own. Bella was quiet now. "I wasn't gone that long."

"It was long," he said.

"We were on the stairs. Catching up," she said. She watched Clara make her way down the hall, where she couldn't hear them. "Did you meet Nick? The grey-haired guy?"

"I thought that was her dad," said Adam.

"Her dad is dead," said Jess.

"See, how was I supposed to remember that?" said Adam. "I told you you shouldn't have left me alone."

They took turns holding Bella during dinner so they both had a chance to eat, which worked all right until dessert, which was accompanied by speeches during which Bella needed to be kept quiet. Clara's mother and her uncle spoke, then her sister. Then Nick stood up.

"Clare," Nick began.

He could be talking about a stranger, thought Jess.

"The first time I met her, she told me the music in my bar was wrong. She came back behind the counter and she went through my CDs. She turned off the Happy Mondays in the middle of a song and put on Lucinda Williams. Like my place was a honky-tonk. I thought the vibe would be all off, but it wasn't. And that would be the first but not the last time that Clare would set me straight."

Nick was charming, Jess would give him that.

"Some people told us that we were a terrible match," he said. "I was too old, she was too free, but we did it anyway, in spite of ourselves. We fell in love, head over heels. She came around behind my bar, and I don't let anybody come behind my bar, but she didn't know that—or rather, she didn't care. I started to find that the nights when she wasn't there weren't very good ones. I discovered Clare can make a day complete just by walking into the room."

Bella was fussing, so Jess pulled up her shirt and unsnapped her bra. Adam whispered, "What are you doing?" Jess was going off the feeding schedule, but Bella wasn't falling asleep, and Jess needed to hear what else Nick had to say.

"Clare has turned my life into a different world," he was saying, and Jess felt a vivid and familiar stirring, the same feeling she'd had all those years ago clamouring up the stairs behind Clayton to Clara's room. Surely she wasn't jealous? But Nick seemed to know Clara so well after all, to care about her in a way it was impossible not to take seriously. All of this was surprising, because Jess had imagined this wedding business to be something of a whim.

As Bella latched on and starting gulping, Adam waited a moment before asking, "Do you think it's a good idea?"

"She'll be fine," she reassured him.

"But the routine—" Adam insisted.

"Screw the routine," whispered Jess, just as the baby coughed and spat up everything she'd just ingested.

Up at the front of the room, Nick was now singing, mostly very badly, the song by Sam Cooke about the wonderful world and all the classes he failed in high school. Clara came up to join him, not speaking, just smiling in a docile way, impossibly absorbed in his light.

Jess and Adam were to stay in the apartment above the garage, cozy with a bedroom, bathroom, and kitchenette. It was a generous arrangement, seeing as Clara's grandmother was sleeping on a pull-out couch, and Clara's cousins were all in tents on the lawn. A pair of portable toilets had been delivered, and Jess was glad to have nothing to do with them. But there was still one complication: Clara wanted Jess to bunk with her the night before the wedding.

"You can do it if you want," said Adam, mostly because he didn't believe Jess would go through with it, leaving him alone for a whole night with their six-week-old baby.

"You're really sure?" he asked her once they were up in the room, their stuff unpacked. Bella was tucked in her swing, which played a tinny version of "Frère Jacques." The plastic toucan swung back and forth like a pendulum.

"It's important to Clara," Jess emphasized, because she didn't want to tell him how much she wanted it too, a break from motherhood, an extension of the intimacy of those moments in the stairwell, the chance to be so close to Clara again with the world locked out.

Adam would be fine. Bella could take a bottle, and Jess had pumped and frozen more than enough milk, which they'd brought along in a cooler. Adam was as capable of caring for the baby as she was, if not more so, and she'd be just across the driveway. It was just one single night.

She came back to the house as Clara and Nick were hugging goodbye on the porch. He was heading into town to stay at a motel, and they wouldn't see each other until the ceremony the following afternoon, a plan Jess found surprising: since when was Clara a traditionalist? Jess remembered waking up on her wedding day with Adam beside her, bursting with joy that this would be the rest of her life. But she was beginning to see that Clara was approaching her wedding as she approached everything: all or nothing, the very same intensity with which she'd found Jess all those years ago. Maybe Nick was also an uncanny mirror, she considered, which was why he made Jess uncomfortable; he was a reflection of her most avid and earnest self.

Right now, however, Jess could also admire the way Nick was holding Clara, the way he kissed her hair. They didn't even know Jess was watching until she stepped on the creaking porch stair. Nick pulled away from Clara slightly, raising his hand in a half-hearted wave.

"Well, this is it then," he said.

"I'm getting married in the morning," Clara sang.

"Why doesn't he just stay?" Jess murmured as she watched them struggle to detach, hands held until the last second and Nick made his way to the car. Clara's arm was still extended and she was waggling her fingers. "If it's going to be that hard."

"It's not hard," said Clara, waving with more fervour. Nick was in the car now, looking at her through the window. He blew a kiss as he pulled out of the driveway. "But since we got together, we've barely spent a night apart."

"Really?"

"Eleven months ago," said Clara.

Barely a blip in the grand scheme of things, Jess thought. She'd known Clara for almost a decade, and she was still an enigma. What can you know about anyone in just eleven months?

"But it's not like it sounds," Clara said. "Everything just clicked from the start." She grabbed Jess's arm. "Let's go in now." They passed Clara's sisters in the kitchen, where they were clearing away the dinner and getting ready for the wedding the next day.

"Having your slumber party?" asked Diane.

"We would have thrown her a bachelorette," Julie told Jess, "But she said she didn't want any of that if you weren't going to be here."

"I didn't want it anyway," said Clara.

Clara's mom said, "Don't stay up late tonight." She turned to Jess. "She wouldn't let anyone come do her makeup."

"I can do my own makeup," said Clara.

Her mom said, "There'll be shadows under her eyes."

"There won't be," said Clara.

"What about me?" asked Jess. "Who's going to cover up mine?" She had a six-week-old baby. Maybe she could wear a bag over her head.

"You look fine," said Clara's mom. "The baby's gorgeous. I know everybody says it and I always do, but I even mean it. She's lovely." And Jess said thank you, even though such comments were always weird, and it seemed strange to take credit.

"We're going up," Clara called, pulling the door to the staircase shut behind them. Then it was dark, but they knew where they were going, one step at a time to the top.

They went down the hall to Clara's room and closed the door, which had a white dress hanging from a hook on the back. "This is it?" Jess asked. It was cotton, sleeveless, an A-line with a scooped neck. Orange and yellow flowers were embroidered up one side of the skirt, which was full and cut just below the knee. "It's really beautiful." Jess ran her finger along the flowers. She hadn't been expecting this. She hadn't been expecting Nick, or any of it, the way everything between him and Clara seemed so real and so heady. Jess had never seen Clara in love, she realized. She'd always assumed besottedness was something Clara didn't do, something she would spurn the way she did fast food and reality television.

"I bought it off the rack," said Clara. "Seriously, this whole thing has been just like that. I dreamed it, and there it was. On clearance. "It even fit. You know what I'm saying? How rare is it to find a beautiful dress that's also comfortable? Anyway." She shrugged. "I thought it was a sign."

"And so you decided to get married."

"We were getting married already," said Clara, shaking off Jess's sarcasm. "But the dress was like an affirmation, and there were all these other things. We both have two older sisters; our mothers have the same birthday."

"And have you met her?" said Jess. "His mother?" It had only been eleven months.

"She's dead." Clara flopped down on her bed, her patience waning. "You don't get it; I know you don't." She kicked an oversized pillow onto the floor. "You only just met him, and you're all caught up in your own thing."

"My own *thing*." Jess heard the dismissal.

"Your life," Clara acknowledged. "But you must have had your own signs, affirmations, that Adam was the one for you. Did the sun shine on your wedding day?"

Jess said, "Yes."

"Well, there you go," said Clara. "And wasn't there something to that?"

"It was the middle of a heat wave," Jess told her. "The driest May on record. It hadn't rained all spring. There were wildfires." She was still holding the dress, thumbing the flowers on the fabric. She let go and wandered over to the rocking chair that had been in Clara's dorm room when they first became friends. A photograph of mummified remains was thumb-tacked to a bulletin board that hung over a desk. The window looked out onto the sunset, or what was left of it, and the light was reflected in the windows above the garage. For a moment Jess thought she heard the baby crying, but when she listened there was no sound at all.

"You being here—it means everything," Clara said, sitting up. Jess turned around to face her. "All of this, the wedding and the family—you're the part that really matters." This was the assurance Jess hadn't even known she was waiting for, and she felt awkward now receiving it, for even needing it, although it also made her feel like someone she recognized for the first time in recent memory. She sat on the bed beside Clara, who wasn't finished. "More than anything, I was coming home to you. To have you get to know Nick. And I want to know Bella, and Adam. I've met so many people, but it was never the same."

"I know," said Jess, and there was such relief in this, in their mutual understanding, and in being able to affirm, *Yes, this is it exactly*. It was the reason Jess was here, with her husband and their tiny baby, even though the journey had been so hard. Because there were friends and there were *friends*, and in her day-to-day life she too kept waiting for the former to turn into the latter. Clara had set a bar that was high.

"And I've been drifting," Clara admitted. "I know that. For so long, it was what I had to do. After my dad, and everything—and it only got more complicated. I couldn't do it the way you did, one thing just leading to another."

"Oh, I've been drifting too," said Jess. Since the baby arrived, she'd never felt so unmoored.

"It's different, though," Clara said. "Because you've got this baby now, a tiny perfect thing who *needs* you."

And Jess wanted to tell Clara about the endless nights and that endless need, how the last thing she'd been expecting was for motherhood to knock her over like a wave that just kept coming and coming. How it wasn't different at all. "It's the hardest thing I've ever done," she said. "Sometimes it's like I'm lost in outer space."

"But you're not," Clara said. "I mean, you've got all the pieces and you're actually building something tangible, a family. A *life*."

"It's not so simple," Jess said. She wanted to say, *I'm not so simple*. "And all those pieces have to come from somewhere." It wasn't easy for anyone. Did Clara think she'd just stumbled upon the pieces, like magic?

"I just never seem to know where to find them," said Clara. "How to do all those normal things." She paused. "The way other people settle—I don't know how to do that." Jess raised an eyebrow. After all these years, she still didn't know whether these comments were deliberately cutting or if Clara was just obtuse. "I don't mean it that way," Clara said, aware enough to know something had stung. "It just felt like as long as the scenery was changing I didn't have to think." She looked at Jess. "I envy you, the way you always seemed to know where you were going, while I was spinning in circles."

She really didn't get it, Jess thought, amazed, dismayed. Although before Bella, Jess had thought having a baby would be not so different from carrying around a clutch purse, so maybe this shouldn't be surprising.

She asked Clara, "What happened? The spinning circles." She'd read Clara's letters, trying to put the pieces together and figure out what lay between the lines.

Clara put her head on Jess's shoulder and sighed. "It was all too much," she said. "I don't even want to remember, but what matters is that I got through it. And I'll take responsibility. I wasn't being careful, I got pregnant, and you can have one abortion, and you can even have two, but three just seems awfully irresponsible."

"But your situation," said Jess. "You were on malaria drugs. What else were you supposed to do?"

Clara moved around Jess to stretch out lengthwise on the bed, and Jess lay down beside her. Clara said, "I couldn't have had an abortion even if I'd wanted one. We were out there in the middle of nowhere. I didn't have the money to fly home. And then I lost it, the baby. It was honestly brutal, and I kept thinking of my dad. He used to have a 'Life Begins at Conception' sign hanging in the back of his pick-up."

"Those notions of divine justice," said Jess. "They're hard to shake, you know, even for those of us who weren't brought up fundamentalist."

Clara said, "Really?"

"I never even think about it much, what happened to me. My abortion." It had taken years, but Jess had finally learned to say the word, although she would always have to lower her voice in order to do so. "But when Adam and I decided to get pregnant, there was a part of me that was so scared I wouldn't be able to get away with it, that surely there'd be a price to pay."

"Because we're just steeped in it, in our culture," said Clara. "There's the stigma and shame."

"There's an abortion in 'Rapunzel,'" said Jess, unearthing this detail from the scholarly part of her mind that had lain dormant since her baby arrived.

"The Grimms took it out of their version," she continued. "Which is crazy when you think about all the things they didn't censor—those stories are brutal. But in the early versions of 'Rapunzel,' the ones in French and Italian, it was *parsley* the woman was craving at the beginning of her pregnancy, and parsley is one of the herbs that people have always used to induce abortions. Like, nothing about this is out of the ordinary. When I told my OB-GYN about mine—I had to, it's part of my medical record for the rest of my life—he didn't even flinch. And if I hadn't had an abortion, Bella wouldn't even be here."

"I think the children you have," said Clara, "make the idea of any other world impossible. And honestly, the miscarriage was such a turning point. Everything was such a mess, and I finally asked myself, 'What are you doing with your life?' I didn't even want a baby, not then, and the guy was all wrong—it would have been terrible."

"Who was he?" This was the longest uninterrupted conversation Jess had had with anyone since Arabella was born.

"He was no one. It was brutal. I drank too much, before and after. So yes, it probably happened the way it was supposed to—even though anytime someone told me that, it only made me angry." Clara paused. "But I'm finally looking forward now. And I'm happy that you're here, I'm happy about tomorrow, about Nick, and everything. When I met him I was so broken, and he put me back together again. I don't even know how he puts up with me sometimes."

"It might be because you're wonderful," said Jess. She was thinking of the way he sang to Clara that evening, how he kissed her on the porch. "Because you are beautiful, brilliant, *and* fabulous, and now he's the one who gets to live with you for the rest of his life."

Clara lifted her head up on one arm, smiling. "Well, he did mention something like that." Jess had never seen her so open-hearted, so comfortable with being soft and feeling. "He's terrific, and he really loves me. You'll see it when you get to know him."

"I think I already do."

Clara beamed. "For the first time, I knew that everyone—and really, I mean *you*—was going to say, Yes, she's making a wise choice. I mean, there's his age and everything, but you stop noticing that once you really get to know who he is. He's so good. There is no compromise. I don't even wish he was younger, because he wouldn't be him. And I love him. I even *like* him. That, I've got to tell you, was some kind of revelation."

"Oh my god," said Jess. "Remember Ferber?"

Clara groaned. "Do I have to?" They were lying on their sides, facing each other. She started laughing. "He was a startlingly magnificent fuck, though."

"I figured," said Jess. Clara's laughter was contagious. "It's a thing, though, did you know? *Ferber? Ferberizing.* It's an actual verb."

"I'll say it was," said Clara, and then Jess started howling, punching her on the shoulder.

"Not like that," said Jess between gasps. "It's for babies."

"Good heavens." And now Clara was laughing so hard she had to wipe away tears.

Jess said, "Stop!" She was trying to get control of herself. "No, really." She wanted to explain. "A sleep method."

"A *sleep method?*"

And this was why Jess loved Clara, because Clara just understood that the idea of "sleep methods" was truly the craziest part of this absurd conversation. "The world of babies is very stupid," Jess told her. "The Ferber Method is when your baby cries and you don't pick it up."

"And they gave that a name."

"They give everything a name."

"But not necessarily *Ferber.*"

"I'm sure there's no relation." And they were howling again.

"Did you Ferber your baby?" Clara managed to ask after a while.

Jess said, "Not yet." There were tears in her eyes now too. She'd laughed so hard her throat hurt. She took a deep breath to calm down. "I didn't think you would ever come back."

Clara was quiet for a moment before admitting, "I didn't either."

"You're getting married tomorrow."

"Yup. And look at that red sky."

"Sailor's delight."

"The weather's going to be fine."

THE WEEKEND

2007

The plan was hatched on the back of an envelope about a month after the wedding when Nick and Clara were in town trying it all on for size, getting a feel for how they might make a life there. They started the day with brunch at a trendy spot near Jess and Adam's place in Corktown, a neighbourhood that Clara had never even heard of when she last lived in the city. Jess and Adam were late, even though they lived nearby, and the surly hipster waitress warned Nick and Clara they'd lose their table if their friends didn't show soon.

It was twenty more minutes before they arrived, Jess hauling the baby—so much bigger than when they'd seen her last—in the car seat, along with a variety of totes and backpacks and a list of excuses: Bella had spat up as they were heading out to the car, and then they'd forgotten her soother, and then they had to change her again, and the *traffic*. They lived just three blocks away, and Clara wondered why they had to drive.

Once they'd ordered, the waitress messed up their coffees, and then the baby refused to fall asleep. "So I have to eat fast," Jess said, shoving eggs Benedict down her throat. "Or I won't eat at all."

And this, Clara had thought, just wouldn't do. The togetherness she'd envisioned, the connection she'd come home for, was supposed to be easy, not stressful, not packed into a room so crowded you couldn't back your chair out. Adam and Jess were preoccupied with Bella, trying and failing to force all these routines instead of just letting her be. They had lost all perspective. Clara had an idea. "What if we got away for a weekend? Just the four of us?" Jess began protesting, but Clara knew she could convince her. "You both could come up to our place. Adam's sister could take the baby. You said she said she *could*." She looked at Adam, who nodded. It was possible. "A weekend together, all that time."

"But it's so far," said Jess.

"It's not." Clara fished the envelope, a letter from the bank, out of her bag. "Just outside city limits. More or less." She clicked her pen and drew the highway on the envelope, careful lines, not quite to scale, along the lake that glimmered like diamonds. The cabin belonged to the family of Clara's brother-in-law Bruce, her sister Diane's husband. It had been his grandparents', but now there were too many cousins to distribute weeks between and nobody was interested anyway—there were nicer places to go these days. Ultimately, no one wanted to spend the money to do what needed doing, and they were going to sell the property at the end of the summer, but in the meantime, Clara and Nick could live there. A summer honeymoon.

She and Nick were meant to help with the upkeep, to be a presence around the place and keep it safe from drunken teenagers and other vandals. Their job was to make the cabin home, to cut the grass, and have a car in the driveway—the driveway Clara was watching now, weeks later, as she waited for Adam and Jess to arrive.

She'd made the map as detailed as possible. "You can't miss it," she assured Jess, pushing the envelope across the table. "Just follow the directions and you'll be fine."

But now she was second-guessing herself. They hadn't called, and it was getting dark. Nick told her to relax, but she couldn't. She tried Jess's cell again, but it didn't ring through. She turned up the radio to listen to the traffic, but the route seemed okay. The highways were often jammed solid on the way to the summer homes of rich city people, bumper-to-bumper in their luxury SUVs blasting air conditioning, but none of them were on their way to a place like this, too close to the city and the lake too weedy to be fashionable. One day it would be razed for a subdivision, but that was still years away.

Adam hadn't wanted the map, insisting he could figure it out on his brand new iPhone. Clara told him, "Cellphone service can be patchy."

"How did *you* ever manage to find it?" Jess asked.

"We got lost three times," said Clara. "Drove in circles for hours." So Jess took the envelope. This was at the end of the meal, when the waitress had still not appeared to clear their plates or refill the coffees, and Bella was crying. People in line still waiting for a table were glaring at them, so they decided to pack up and go. Adam and Jess wanted to show them around their neighbourhood. Nick and Clara could never afford to live there, but this fact hadn't come up, and Clara was too embarrassed to mention it.

And what if something similar had been going on when Clara was trying to convince Jess about the weekend? What if she'd only agreed because Clara was unwilling to hear otherwise? "It's a holiday," Clara emphasized. "A getaway." She was sure she'd spied a glint in her friend's eye at the possibility of time away from the baby. "It'll be good for you. For both of you," Clara said, indicating Adam. Jess had mentioned in private that she and Adam never had sex anymore due to a complicated combination of timing and vaginal dryness. Clara lowered her voice. "Maybe a nice chance for a little romantic reconnection?" Then louder, "Come on, it's summer. What's one summer thing you've done lately?" She'd been relentless.

"They'll be here," said Nick, who was barbecuing on the deck. Clara had wanted him to wait till the others arrived to start cooking, but it was late and he was hungry, and Nick got irritable when he was hungry, so it was best to let him have his way now. They were bound to show up soon, and maybe they would arrive just as the food was on the table. Clara hoped Nick would take it easy on the barbecue, cook the meat slow and easy. She hoped the car was coming up the dirt road right now.

But then the meat was cooked, being kept warm under tin foil. Nick was waiting, but he wouldn't wait long. He'd grilled zucchini and tomatoes and halloumi, and everything was done. And still no sign of them.

There was no reason for them to be late. Clara knew they were dropping the baby off at Adam's sister's along with a cooler stocked with enough breast milk for an entire week, even though this was just a weekend trip, and there was a schedule for Bella's feedings, naps, and stimulating activities that was apparently as detailed as Clara's map.

"They'll be here," Nick kept saying, refusing to be rattled, and Clara wondered again what Jess and Adam would think of the place, a borrowed cabin on a weedy lake, once they arrived. The wood-panelled walls were kind of ironic. The whole thing suggested a domestic vintage vibe, if Clara were the kind of person who put on pearls and lipstick, ready with a drink and a light when Nick came home from work at the end of the day. Except that Nick didn't come home from work because he didn't have a job yet, and he wasn't supposed to smoke either. But Clara knew he was sneaking cigarettes down by the dock. He threw the butts in the lake. Clara thought of that song about getting married in a fever. When they first got together, Nick's chief appeal was that she loved everything about him, but the more she got to know him, the less this was true.

About half an hour later, Clara said, "I hear a car." It was so quiet out there at night aside from the sounds of nature, birds on the water and wind in the trees. The radio hummed low in the background, "Umbrella" by Rihanna—the song had been on a loop all summer. She'd heard a car, but it could have been distant thunder. A storm might be a welcome relief, a break in the heat and the atmosphere so charged with tension.

Nick kept eating.

"You hear it too?" she asked. She wanted Nick to hear it, but he wasn't listening to her, let alone to any rumbles in the distance. "Is that them, do you think?" But now she didn't need an answer because headlights swept the room, illuminating everything. Clara wondered if they'd been spotted in their tableau, if she'd been caught in her heightened expectation. She didn't want to be as visible as that.

She went to the door to greet Jess and Adam at the cabin's shabby backside with small bedroom windows and scrubby shrubs, most of the lawn given over to driveway. On the lake side things were more appealing, and maybe she could have arranged to have them arrive by boat. They were four hours late anyway, and a boat couldn't have taken any longer. "You're here, you're here, you're here!" she said, flinging the door open. "Finally."

Jess was wheeling a suitcase up the walkway as if this were an airport. Beyond her, Adam was unloading beer and a cooler from their new car, a huge SUV. "The trip was a nightmare," Jess said as they squeezed past each other, Clara on her way to help Adam.

"You had the map," said Clara. "And there wasn't traffic."

Adam said, "There was traffic."

"So much traffic," Jess called. "We thought we'd beat it if we left later, but then so did everyone. And we took a wrong turn."

"A wrong turn?"

"There was no owl," said Jess. "I was looking for an owl. Seriously, what was that map all about?"

"It would have been more straightforward in daylight."

"Owls are nocturnal," Adam said.

"Creative license," said Clara, giving a private eye-roll. She was carrying the beer and held the door open with her shoulder, ushering them both inside. "But you're here now," she said. "Nick was just starting dinner."

"Finishing," Nick corrected, pushing away his plate and standing up to greet the guests. "I got hungry."

"He skipped lunch," Clara lied.

"I did no such thing," he said. "Don't start spreading rumours. I've never skipped a meal in my life."

"But there's plenty left," said Clara. "And I'm hungry. You probably are too."

Adam said, "We stopped for a sandwich." Jess punched him in the arm. "What?" he said to her. "I'm just explaining to Clara that she doesn't have to go out of her way."

"We already did," said Clara. The spread was all over the table. "But it's casual," she said, brightening her tone. "Buffet style, help yourself."

Adam reached for some bread. "I think I will."

Clara showed Jess to the bedroom so she could stow their bags. The little room was crowded with both a double bed and bunkbeds. Then they went back to the kitchen to unpack the cooler. It was full of craft beer, fancy cheese, fresh dates, and organic strawberries—all things that Clara usually passed over in the grocery store because they were too expensive.

Jess didn't seem to have a problem with the more economical selection that Clara had laid out, however, and she and Adam both ate ravenously even after the sandwiches. Since she'd had started breastfeeding, Jess said, she could eat forever.

"I'm not going to lie, it feels good to finally be here," she told Clara and Nick, helping herself to more steak. The food was cold, but nobody seemed to mind. "To get away, I mean. I really wasn't sure if we could pull it off."

"But you did," said Clara. "I told you." She didn't understand why parents were always so resigned to everything being awful.

Jess said, "You don't understand. It literally felt impossible. That night before your wedding, I wasn't even that far away, and I got back to feed Bella before sunrise. And since then, a few times we've left her to go to the pub around the corner, just to prove we could, but we were so focussed on getting through it, getting back to her again, that we really missed the point of going out without her."

"Like you're doing right now," pointed out Adam. "Stop talking about the baby."

But then they were quiet, which was awkward, although wasn't *this* really the point, to figure out how to fill in those gaps in their friendship after all these years? To start speaking in the present tense? It was hard, but relationships were work—Clara knew this. A person had to be deliberate. You couldn't only float.

Unless you *could* float, literally, and now she was, down in the lake, and in the sky above there should have been stars, but it was cloudy. Perhaps that storm was really coming, the air was so hot that the cool water was sweet relief. Clara floated on her back staring way up into nothing. Not even a single twinkle to suggest possible benevolence in the infinite universe, but there was comfort in that too—no distractions, just Clara and Jess in that great black night, plus the other two. They'd once been a pair, but now it had turned exponential.

Clara was naked. She loved the cut of the cold water against her skin, the complete giving over to the elements, to become a part of them. Besides, darkness was its own kind of clothing—but not enough for Jess, who'd demurred at the idea of a skinny dip, though Clara imagined this was more due to Adam's discomfort than her own, because Jess never used to be a prude. Meanwhile, Nick, his white butt illuminated by the glow of patio lanterns on the deck, had bounded into the water, blazing a trail with his splash.

Floating on her back now, her breasts and belly above the water, finally almost cool now in the humid air, Clara watched Jess and Adam tiptoe in, tentatively. Jess was wearing an inconspicuous navy one-piece. She'd confessed to Clara she was uncomfortable in her postpartum body, her stomach gone slack and breasts that were alternately swollen then saggy. Jess had pumped after dinner, choosing to do it in the bedroom rather than in the open—not because of body shame, she explained, but because being hooked up to the machine made her feel like a cow. Clara had come in to hang out with Jess, and she sat on the floor watching her nipples being elongated and yanked. She found the whoosh of the breast pump almost soothing.

"It's just not very elegant," Jess said, after she'd asked Clara to look away—if she was feeling self-conscious, the milk wouldn't come. All this work was only for milk she'd end up pouring down the drain because she'd been drinking. Her freezer was already so stockpiled with extra milk that there was no room for anything else. She'd gone overboard. "I always do," she said to Clara. "But if I don't pump tonight, they'll hurt in the morning."

Clara tried to restrain her fascination and not stare at Jess in her bathing suit, trying to analyze her silhouette, which was truthfully not so different than it had been before. Skinny girls were always more neurotic about these things. She'd looked away from Jess's nipples in the pump when instructed, even though she could have spent hours watching this miracle of the body and its workings. She could have asked Jess a million questions, but she didn't, partly because she had a feeling that some of these mysteries weren't easy to articulate, partly because she didn't like her positioning, sitting here at Jess's feet. Clara ached for a baby of her own.

"Hurry up," she called to Jess and Adam, who were still taking their time getting into the water. "Once you're in, it's lovely."

"Easier said than done," said Adam. "It's freezing." He was also skinny, too skinny, Clara observed now, even though the muscles in his arms added a little bit of bulk. He worked out every day, Jess had told her. This hadn't been a big deal until Bella was born and he insisted on keeping up the habit, and now it grated on her nerves, she said, the hours he devoted to exercising. It made Jess's day alone with the baby even longer.

Adam finally dove in, and Jess disappeared under the water a moment later. They both emerged seconds later squealing and laughing.

"I told you," called Clara. "It's perfect," and she lay back again and looked up at the empty sky, her ears submerged so that she was surprised when Nick grabbed her and pulled her up into a fierce hug from behind. He reached around and tweaked her nipple, but she brushed his hand away from her breasts.

"This *is* nice," Jess was saying, swimming circles around Adam.

"Didn't I tell you?" said Clara. "Didn't I?"

Jess conceded. "You did."

Clara had envisioned staying up late and talking over wine, wrapped in towels, their laughing faces lit by firelight, although she'd nixed that idea because of the fire ban. But then Jess had gone and nixed everything. She and Adam were tired after the drive, exhausted in general, and eager to enjoy an early night with no interruptions.

And so Clara and Nick were in bed earlier than planned. Nick, inspired by their late-night swim, saw this as an opportunity to make love, but Clara was preoccupied. They had only been here alone, so it didn't matter that the cabin walls were plywood-thin and didn't quite reach the ceiling. But now she was hearing all the sounds—the buzz of cicadas outside—and listening for others: bedsprings and whispers, any indication that Jess and Adam hadn't gone directly to sleep. She could feel Nick behind her, hard, ready, and his touch had been leading her body where he wanted it to go, even if her mind was taken up with other things. Eventually her mind was won over, and the idea of other people nearby wasn't completely a deterrent.

Maybe it would be good for the others to be reminded, she considered, giving in to the pleasure of Nick's fingers at work between her legs and uttering a soft moan. Other people's sounds were so mysterious, she'd always thought, and she had ample experience of these during the time she spent in the field. Every rustle or sigh could mean innumerable things, but for the sake of propriety she said to her husband, "Shhhh." Maybe they'd make their baby tonight.

Jess and Adam emerged from their room as Clara was preparing breakfast. Jess didn't look great. "Sometimes it's like the more you sleep, the worse you feel," she said. "My circadian rhythms are a mess."

"And that's some bed," said Adam, waving his phone in the air, trying to get a signal. The mattresses were ancient and had probably been bargain-basement items back in the Dark Ages. The bed in Clara and Nick's room felt like a sack of lawn implements, but if a person was that tired, would it matter?

"Bella's probably already been up for hours," Jess commented, glancing at the clock. Adam was still trying to get his phone to work. Nick was lying on the couch, reading a newspaper that was several days old. Clara could tell that neither Adam nor Jess was going to be able to handle being so out of touch; she expected Adam at some point would climb a tree or a hill or else jump in the car and head into town to get a signal.

This was exactly what he did right after lunch, taking Nick along with him, because Nick also found the days at the cabin were long, though Clara wouldn't permit him to say so.

"So how does it feel?" Clara asked Jess once they were alone. "The getaway. Any sexual healing yet?"

"I wouldn't say so. We fell asleep as soon as we hit the bed."

"With the uncomfortable mattress."

"I didn't say it was a *good* sleep," said Jess. "But we were sleeping. And he's worried about being away from Bella, I know he is. Anxiety never brings out his best side." She paused. "I can't believe you last night, though. Running down the beach naked like that. Adam was horrified."

"I could tell," said Clara.

Jess laughed. "I knew you could."

They were lying on the deck on old chaise longues, the kind with woven vinyl that leave checkers on the backs of your thighs. "Umbrella" was on the radio again, but maybe that was okay, because there weren't enough songs about friendship.

"You're thinking about the baby," Clara said. She could tell by the way Jess was staring off at nothing with a furrowed brow.

"But I'm trying not to," said Jess. "I've just never been this far apart from her before, and I keep thinking I hear her. I can literally feel her weight in my arms." Jess wrapped her arms across her body as though she were hugging herself.

"Bella's fine," said Clara. "I promise. You've got to stop worrying. Just relax. This weekend is exactly what you need."

Clara and Nick went swimming later in the afternoon, suits on this time. They paddled out to the neighbours' raft, an ancient structure covered with peeling paint and outdoor carpeting with mildewy bits. The neighbours never came up anymore; their kids were grown. Their raft was suddenly an island, a place to escape. Nick and Clara had become so used to solitude that it was too much now, having these people in their space with all their anxious vibes.

"It's not so bad," said Nick. "And it's only till tomorrow."

"Or maybe sooner," said Clara. Adam had returned from town not feeling any more assured. His sister couldn't get Bella down for her naps. Their whole routine was shot.

Clara looked over her shoulder, considering Adam and Jess, back on shore. They looked like they were napping on the deck—or at least pretending to nap. Adam was still holding onto his phone, waiting for a miracle. "I thought I wanted to get to know him better," she said to Nick. "But now I wonder if I do."

Nick said, "He's not a bad guy." Apparently, Adam had spent the entire journey outlining his new car's safety features and the intricacies of car-seat installation. Nick was right: he wasn't a bad guy; he was steady and steadfast, and at least he tried to balance Jess's lack of chill. He'd definitely been on board about getting away for the weekend.

The sun was moving westward now, and Clara and Nick were drowsy, lying on their stomachs, heads resting on their arms. She looked away from the shore and admired her husband's tanned skin, scattered with freckles, the silver hair on his shoulders and chest. She looked back at the shore and wondered at Jess and Adam. People were funny and wanted such different things.

"But you're hard on people," Nick said, running his finger along the trim of her bathing suit, across her thigh, to where her legs came together. She rolled away from him. "What?" he asked. "You don't want to?"

She said, "They'll see."

"They're not watching," he said.

"Here?"

"Why not? There's nobody else around." They could hear the distant sound of a motorboat, but it must be around the bay. There was nothing in their sight at all.

Nick moved closer, his chest against her back, and slipped his fingers under the elastic, inside her. "You can't lie here half-naked, soaking wet, and expect me not to get ideas," he said.

"No," she admitted. Nick pulled her suit to one side and pushed his shorts down so he could slide inside her. His arms were tight around her, his body pushing against her back. She supposed from shore it looked like an innocent embrace, but she tried not to consider how it looked and instead be here and now, her eyes closed and her neck arched. The carpet beneath her hip was scratchy, but that was the only problem. She clenched her muscles so he could feel tight inside her, and he moaned in her ear.

He said, "I love you, I do," as he came and then she did. And then he started laughing. "I can't believe we did that," he said, fumbling to get his shorts back on properly. "Where anyone could have seen us."

"I thought you said nobody was looking!"

"Wasn't about to get wrapped up in details," he told her, and then he rolled off the raft and into the water. She stood up to follow him, pulling her bathing suit back down over her bum before diving in beside him. "Hello, Missus," he said to her, cheeky, wet, and handsome. His affection was so unabashed that it continually charmed her.

"Hi," she said, then started swimming, and together they returned to shore.

"You two are cute," said Jess after dinner.

"Cute?"

"I remember those days. Lifetimes ago. When you're still all swoony. It's sweet," said Jess. "Don't forget to enjoy it. I'm just saying."

"Saying what?" asked Clara, getting glasses down from the cupboard and trying hard to hold them all in her hands. Precious stems, and clinking crystal—though it probably wasn't really crystal. It was surprising they were even glass.

"That it's a good time," said Jess. "Before things get complicated." She slipped out to the porch where the guys were, with Clara behind her.

"No signal?" she asked Adam, who was waving his phone in the air again.

"I can't believe there's still a place on earth—" he was saying.

"You've been here twenty-four hours and there hasn't been a flicker," said Clara. "What are you expecting?"

They'd set up a game at the table, the sun going down before them like a show. They'd been playing old CDs on the stereo, all the female singer-songwriters who were the soundtrack to the years Jess and Clara lived together. When the sun disappeared, the sky was indigo and a triangle of stars was visible, the first of the night. They'd gone through bottle after bottle of wine while playing a popular game, cards inscribed with vulgar words and dirty ideas that incited players to be as disgusting as possible. The game was bringing Adam out of his shell. He won a round with a card labelled "Seeping Taint" and another with "Butt Guster."

"I bet you didn't know you married a total sicko," Clara said to Jess. She was delighted that Adam was loosening up.

Jess was irritated. "You don't need to make a thing of it."

"Clare thinks she knows everything about everybody," said Nick. "And what's even worse is that she's usually right."

"She has remarkable insight," Jess said drily, and then downed the wine in her glass. "But not all the time." She poured herself another drink. "She thinks she knows everything about me too."

"Don't I?" said Clara, who hadn't had this much to drink in a long time and was feeling especially defiant. "I've known you since you were a tadpole. I knew you back when you still had a tail."

"You," said Jess, sipping again, "don't have a clue."

"Oh, come on." Getting up from the table, Clara began gathering glasses and plates. "I know who you are."

But Jess wasn't finished. "No," she said. "You act like you've got it all figured out, but you're just seeing what you want to." She looked at Clara wilfully with an expression Clara had never seen on her face before. "You disappeared on me—poof! Remember that?" This was no joke, Clara realized. Jess was angry. "You were gone for four years, and you seem to think that all that time, while you were out there getting lost and getting found, I was just here waiting, right where you left me, ready to be summoned at your command. To your wedding. Your *wedding*," she emphasized. "Remember *my* wedding, Clara? Remember that?" She stared her straight in the eye, waiting; this question was clearly not rhetorical. Clara finally shook her head in the tiniest gesture. "Of course you don't. You weren't there, and you didn't even care that you weren't. You have no idea what I've been going through."

Nick and Adam were both quiet, staring off into the distance. Clara was sure that, just like she was, they were wishing they were anywhere but here.

"I cared," Clara said, leaving the plates and sitting back down again. "Of course I cared. I want to make up for all that. Isn't that the whole reason we're here?" Jess was quiet, looking away now. Clara continued, "All I'm saying is that I know you. The fundamentals don't quit."

"Well, the tadpole would probably argue with that," said Jess. "Have you ever seen a tadpole? Metamorphosis." She stumbled on the syllables.

Clara said, "I know that." Of course she did. Jess was a wife now. She'd created a *person*.

"I mean, we've all come a long way," said Jess. "Think about it—just five years ago, you were screwing Ferber." This was even worse than the game, which had opened up such twisted possibilities for things that were permissible to say. There was silence. Jess said, "Oh, come on now, guys. I am sure Nick knows that *Clare* had a sex life before him."

Adam finally came to life and stepped in. "Jess, maybe that's enough."

"I mean, Nick has *children*," said Jess. "So clearly this isn't his first rodeo either."

"I think the game is officially done," said Nick, gathering up the cards.

"You're so drunk, Jess," Clara said. This was a big mistake. It was all her fault. Adam had resumed the plate-clearing she'd started, he and Nick apparently eager to see this discussion finished.

Jess said, "So are all of you."

Nick muttered, "Not that drunk."

"And I mean, speaking of metamorphosis," said Jess, who clearly wasn't done, "you come home and you've got a different name now. Now you're *Clare*. Who even *is* that?"

"It's a nickname, *Jessica*." Clara was gathering empty bottles now. She hadn't seen any of this coming. All she'd intended was lighthearted fun, some loosening of inhibitions, but now Jess was a loose cannon. Was it the wine? What was happening? Clara wanted to stick a cork in it. This wasn't fun at all.

"I just mean," Jess insisted, "that you've changed. I get it. But so has everybody. You don't need to be all superior."

"Superior?" demanded Clara. *You two are cute* is what Jess had said, so patronizing. In June, when Clara arrived back in the country after being away for years, Jess couldn't make time for them to get together, not even just for an hour or two. She was too busy for that. "You think *I'm* superior?"

"I think you think you are," said Jess. "You think you're better than all this. Better than everything." Then she went quiet. "I'm sorry." she looked around with surprise at the world outside her mind. She looked far away now, and small. "I wish it were tomorrow."

"Are you okay?" Nick asked Clara once they were in bed.

She said, "It's nothing. But are you?" Jess had no right to bring up his past, which was none of her business, and Clara didn't care about any of it anyway. If being with someone older had taught her anything, it was that not every detail mattered. So much got lost, forgotten, or swept away, and that was even by design.

Clara wondered if her friendship with Jess could turn out to be one of those details—something packed up in a box of artifacts, like participation awards and yearbooks with earnest inscriptions by people whose names you didn't recognize.

Nick said, "So you were screwing Ferber."

"You know about Ferber. The handyman."

"The one with the biceps," Nick said. Not all of Clara's history had been packed away. She was grateful for what Ferber had taught her about the human form, but his kind of body was not her preference. The mind wants what the mind wants, Clara knew, and while she might have been drifting, she considered herself fortunate to have never been driven off-course by what society expected of women: sculpted bodies, and conventional journeys, marriage, mortgage, motherhood. She'd made her own path, however wandering, and she wondered if Jess truly wanted all the things she had or just thought she was supposed to.

Jess was right—Clara *had* disappeared. But did anyone really escape feeling superior? You make the choices you make because they're better than the other ones.

Nick said, "Shhhh."

"What?" She hadn't said anything.

"I hear them." She listened too. The sound of bedsprings and a rhythmic moan—whose, she couldn't tell.

She said, "Oh, god. This is terrible." Bounce, bounce. "We can hardly judge, though."

"I'm not judging," he said. "I only want to go to sleep."

"It won't last long," she said. "I mean, how long could it last?"

"She's so drunk," he said.

"This can't go on." They waited, but the sounds contin-ued. "This is mortifying," she said. "It's good for them though, right? Intimacy. It's healthy."

Nick said, "It's possible this is too intimate."

She nuzzled his shoulder. "Or maybe it's giving you ideas?"

He rolled away. "Eh, no," he said. And then they lay side by side listening, because what choice did they have?

"I could bang on the wall," said Nick.

"Do you think they know we're listening?"

"They'd know then," said Nick.

Clara said, "Maybe they don't even care."

"It is possible we brought this upon ourselves."

In the morning, Adam and Jess didn't get up until after nine. Jess stumbled out of their room looking like the Bride of Frankenstein, her hair gone vertical and her face green. She ran straight to the bathroom, and everybody politely ignored the sound of her throwing up, followed by another five minutes of retching.

"We were supposed to leave an hour ago," said Adam, who was loitering in the kitchen.

"Shouldn't you go check on her?" asked Clara.

"I tried," he shrugged. "She told me to go away."

So Clara went instead, knocking first, opening the door when she got no response. Jess was slumped on the floor, her chin resting on the edge of the toilet bowl. She didn't even open her eyes when Clara came in, but she admitted, "I'm pretty wrecked."

Clara said, "I can see that."

"So much for that restful, relaxing weekend you promised."

"It's been memorable."

"Sure thing," Jess said.

Clara knelt and pulled Jess's hair back, securing it with an elastic she found in her pocket.

Jess murmured, "Too late."

Clara said, "I suppose breakfast wouldn't be entirely welcome."

"Something bland," said Jess. "Toast. White-bread toast. I want that."

"I was thinking eggs and bacon," said Clara. "But toast—okay." She went back out to the kitchen to get it ready. Adam was frying bacon to speed things along, but when Jess came out of the shower looking better, she couldn't stand the smell and took her toast outside.

Adam said, "Things got a bit out of hand last night."

Clara shrugged. "It happens." She meant it. Jess and Adam owed her nothing, not after she'd made them trek all the way up here. She'd been asking more than she realized, she saw that now.

"She hasn't been having the easiest time," Adam said. "Since the baby. She didn't mean it, what she said. None of it was about you."

"No, I know," said Clara, except that it *was* about her. She'd always thought the intensity of her connection to Jess, the basis of their mutual understanding, could overwrite the need to talk about everything all the time, incessant conversation only serving to deliver you to precisely where you already were.

But sometimes you had to take the long way, and that's what Adam was doing now, fumblingly apologizing on Jess's behalf while trying not to let the bacon burn. "I'm sorry," he was saying. "She's so sorry—"

Clara flipped on the kitchen fan to prevent the smoke alarm from going off. This was friendship. "It's done," she said over the din. "I get it, totally. We're good."

HOT CARS

2 0 0 8

A few months after Bella's first birthday, with Jess returned to work, she finally read the article everybody had been sharing about children dying in hot cars. One man's motion-activated car alarm had been going off all afternoon, but he could see the vehicle from his office, so three times he deactivated the alarm with his key fob and simply went back to his job.

Jess was curled up on the sofa, scrolling on her phone and weeping. She told Adam, "You have to read this. It's going to break your heart."

There were no common denominators; the kind of person it happened to was everyone. A slight change in routine—a usual route closed to traffic, a stop to pick up dry cleaning, the other parent doing drop-off—and with that, something goes amiss, a gap in the memory as the baby sleeps in the back seat. There were scientific explanations, commentary from a psychologist. It was the sort of tragedy that, until it happened, nobody ever imagined.

Adam refused to read it; he said the article was tragedy porn. It was gross to become so caught up in a story that wasn't yours, almost voyeuristic, when at the press of a button you could have the whole thing disappear.

Except it was a kind of insurance, Jess's attention to the details and her refusal to look away—but she wouldn't tell him that. How she had to be prepared to face such disaster if ever called upon to do so. And somehow, however karmically complicated, being prepared would also mean she probably never would be.

The article was still on Jess's mind as she got Bella ready for daycare a few days later, overly conscious of her motions, still finding her way into her new life as a working mom. She fastened the baby into the car seat's five-point harness, Bella protesting until Jess popped in the soother. Once she was driving, she checked the rear-view mirror to see Bella's face reflected in the mirror that hung over the back seat.

"All right," said Jess, turning out onto the main street, ready to embark upon the latest spin on the hamster wheel that was her life now. She was still thinking about the article because she, unlike Adam and so many of the people who left comments on Facebook, could absolutely imagine how such a tragedy might happen. How a seemingly good and loving parent could have a single lapse. Jess had a newfound awareness of how easily things could slip through the cracks. Lately she'd been wondering if her life was a sieve.

She glanced back at Bella, who was looking drowsy, eyelids heavy, lulled by the car's steady hum. This wasn't part of the plan. "Hey, baby," Jess called back, as Bella's eyelids shut and stayed that way. Her nap wasn't supposed to happen until later that morning. Too bad for her that her parents' busy days didn't accord with her physical needs, just another thing to feel bad about. They had stopped breastfeeding, and Jess was troubled by Bella's ease with weaning, by what it meant that her baby had let it go so easily, that sometimes what appears to be wellbeing might be a sign of darkness lurking deeper. How do you ever know?

Of course, this was preposterous (and there you go, Bella was asleep). They were lucky to be able to afford great childcare. Bella ate better at daycare—organic food rich with variety—than she did at home. According to her teacher's report, she liked papayas, while Jess wasn't sure she'd ever tried a papaya herself. Bella's teachers were all fantastic, multilingual, with academic qualifications and electric personalities that radiated warmth. Adult-to-child ratios were above government standards. It was a very good place, but it didn't matter. No place would have assuaged Jess's anxiety at leaving her baby. Anxiety might be perceived as a manifestation of guilt, but it wasn't. The problem was the seemingly irreconcilable identities of mother and *human person*. The situation as it stood was just barely tolerable, but this didn't mean that Jess couldn't also be frustrated by her inability to be two things at once.

Her parents didn't understand this. "You don't even have to go back to work, honey," her father pointed out near the end of her leave. They'd come into the city to see Bella, the flexibility of their retirement mapping nicely onto her days with the baby. Jess had seen a lot of her parents these last few months, perhaps too much.

"But I want to go back," she told her dad. She loved her job. She'd spent years working to get where she was.

"So then you have nothing to complain about," said her mother, as though life were that simple. As though freedom to make a choice somehow took away the right to tell the complicated truth about what such choices entailed. And none of the choices were easy.

"If I didn't go back to work," Jess told her parents, "there'd be a whole lot more to complain about." She wasn't kidding. Mothering a baby had been such a primitive way of being, the world shrunk so small, and she was beyond ready to get back to reality, to substantiality.

But she hadn't anticipated this difficulty: she had returned to the real world a different person and her circumstances had changed. She hadn't realized that she'd still be expected to have boozy lunches with donors, or speak in complete sentences after missing a night's sleep because the baby was sick or teething. Just three days after Bella started daycare, Jess received her first call to come pick her up because she was running a fever, and she had been consistently sick ever since. And this was normal, all the other parents assured her. Never mind the year you'd spent coddling your baby and buoying her up with the immune-boosting powers of breast milk. Now you had to shove them out into the world to be felled by one virus after another. Immunity was a bitch.

Jess had never imagined the morning scramble: making the baby breakfast; getting her settled in her highchair and feeding her; taking time to wipe the splatters off the walls and eventually sweep up all the items that she'd hurled to the floor; getting her changed and dressed, and usually changed and dressed again; all this on top of a basic morning routine that had always tested her limits even when there wasn't a baby involved.

The commute to work was now twenty-five minutes longer, and that was when traffic was light, the weather was fine, and the baby didn't kick up a fuss at drop-off, didn't cling to Jess while pitching a gigantic fit, didn't hold on so tightly that one of the teachers would have to pry Bella's tiny fingers, furious fists, and solid grip off her.

Even once the baby was installed at daycare, she occupied a huge percentage of Jess's too-limited attention as she
anticipated the phone buzzing with news that Bella was sick
again, or imagined that no call meant something even
worse—a gas leak? Carbon monoxide poisoning? Jess would
then flip the coin to envision catastrophe befalling *her*
instead, her poor baby left motherless, an orphan. At some
point she and Adam should get around to making wills.

Jess was lucky that her job provided her with some lee-
way, a door that shut, lots of flexibility and work-from-home
options, but she had to be careful. As the only parent on
staff, she had to make sure no one thought she was letting
the team down, particularly now as she was looking to
advance. So in the meantime she kept on, like a woman
whose physical and mental capacities were not stretched to
their limits. It was clearly an act, but she had no choice.

Though she was not above complaining. She vented to
everybody: supermarket cashiers, janitorial staff, streetcar
drivers. The morning of the day it had all gone wrong, she
sent a text to Clara explaining the situation: there was an
outbreak of *scabies* at daycare, so she would understand if
Clara preferred to cancel their plans for the evening. But the
text was really just another excuse to share her disbelief at
the absurdity of it all.

"It's understandable, though," Clara told her at the end
of the day, once they were finally face to face. (Face to face,
and *on a weeknight*! They'd been able to take such casual
closeness for granted once, but Jess would never do so again.)
"I mean, actual scabies. I'd be complaining too." Clara had
come over anyway after Jess stressed that Bella didn't actually
have scabies; the outbreak was in another building, and the
chances of Clara being affected were remote, but still.

"Five kids are down with a rash," said Jess, "and they've had to call in Public Health. But now there's all this trouble on the listserv because half the parents are blaming it on the school's policy of non-toxic cleaning supplies, which is apparently a violation of public health rules. And the other half are furious, terrified of toxins, and replying in all caps that they'd RATHER HAVE TO DEAL WITH SCABIES THAN AUTISM. Which, understandably, has rubbed the parents of children with autism the wrong way. To be honest, I've never even stopped to worry about whether Bella might have scabies—which means she probably does. The worst thing about having children is that the list of terrible possibilities is endless."

So daycare drop-off that morning would have been drama enough, but Jess was still hung up on the article about hot cars—even though the day wasn't really that hot, and she was certain she had not left Bella in her car seat today, because her hands were still raw from the vigorous hand-scrubbing routine required upon arrival at daycare and she had a lingering paranoid itch. But still she kept second-guessing, glancing back at the car seat as she drove away from the centre—definitely empty. She could be sure.

But everybody was always sure, and they weren't always right. Wasn't that the problem?

When she arrived at the library she parked her car in the lot, gathered her bags from the passenger seat, and checked the empty car seat twice. She imagined what it would be like to return to the car at the end of the day and see a little body there. To be that mother. But she wouldn't be, not today at least. Jess breathed deeply and clicked her key fob. Her daughter was at daycare, perhaps right now contracting scabies—but at least scabies was treatable. And now Jess was barely late for work, with very clean hands to boot. Silver linings, good vibes only. Her baby was fine. And outside the exhaustion of the everyday, Jess had something good to look forward to: scabies notwithstanding, she'd be seeing Clara in just a matter of hours.

Clara was coming into the city for an interview—another one, this time for an impressive-sounding position with the municipal government creating a master plan for the city's archeological resources. After many delays, things were moving forward for her and Nick. He'd received his permanent residency permit and could start looking for work too. For the last year, they'd been living at Clara's brother-in-law's cabin, helping with renovations and winterizing the place, but it was about to go up for sale and they had to come back to reality. Clara no longer talked about trying to get pregnant, which Jess knew didn't mean the longing was gone, just that nothing had happened yet. It would have been easier if Clara had been able to share what she was going through, instead of leaving Jess to tiptoe around guessing, but that was Clara, always keeping what was most tender to herself. The more present she was in Jess's life, as she was these days, the clearer this was.

The itching, Jess prayed, was psychosomatic, but it continued as the day progressed, on the back of her neck and under her arms, behind her knees. She kept glancing out her tiny porthole window to the parking lot, not that she could even see her car, or that it would mean anything if she could, because Bella was at daycare. The proof was in the itching. Jess did a presentation for a school group and felt wooden in her performance, a year out of practice, but she wasn't sure the students even noticed, which was almost worse, underlining her niggling sense of the pointlessness of all of this, the exhausting rally of her day, a relay with a single runner, holding onto that baton for dear life.

She spent that afternoon shut away in her office trying to finish up grant applications there was never enough time for, emerging only to check out the "Sleeping Beauty" exhibit she'd helped to curate, hundreds of different versions of the story and similar versions from Italy and Egypt and from *One Thousand and One Nights*. There was a recent graphic-novel version narrated by a hamster, pop-up books and miniature books, full-colour spreads and books that were so old their pages were brittle enough to crumble. All of this under glass, of course, climate-controlled. You could look but not touch, but there was so much to see.

"Sleeping Beauty" wasn't a story meant to render readers weak with desire, but Jess had a different feel for it now, at the end of a long day on a trail of sleepless nights. Wouldn't she like to prick her finger and fall into a century of rest and have vines grow thick around the palace walls. Impenetrable. No need for the hero, the prince on his steed. Turn back, good sir, and let me sleep. Why did everyone think the curse was such a bad thing? Benevolent witch, that fairy was. Maybe everyone had gotten the story wrong. Jess was so tired.

The exhibit was good, though. She hadn't altogether lost her groove and she was part of a great team, even though they had their challenges. Nancy and Imelda had been having a feud since the replacement of the carpet. When Nancy lost the battle to get the pattern she wanted, she decided the one that was installed triggered her migraines. She'd been on sick leave half the time ever since, which left Imelda to carry both workloads. When Nancy made it in, the two of them were always squabbling, and Jess sighed now as she saw them emerging from their cubicle. She wasn't in the mood for diplomacy.

There was concern about the new girl on reception, they explained, who had offended everyone by dying her hair blue and wasn't keeping the pencils in the reading room properly sharpened. "There have been complaints from *scholars*," Imelda disclosed.

"Could you just sharpen the pencils yourself?" said Jess. A reckless suggestion.

"It's not part of my job description," Imelda reminded her.

"The sharpener's noise aggravates my headaches," Nancy added.

Jess tried not to snap as she told them, "I'll take care of it." She wondered what they would think if she showed them the article about babies dying in hot cars, if it could possibly provide them with an iota of perspective. *Do you ever look out the window?* she wanted to ask Nancy and Imelda. Could they fathom how microscopically she cared about the pencils, the carpet, about somebody's blue hair?

On Wednesdays Jess finished work early and picked up Bella before all the other parents arrived. Now that Bella had settled into daycare, she cried when it was time to go home, and this felt like a punch in the gut. Lately Jess was driving more and more slowly to pick-up, because there seemed no sense in rushing to inevitable torture. She took the tears personally, even though the teachers told her that it happened all the time and was part of a necessary period of adjustment. But to Jess it was another indication of her failure at all things.

This day in particular, after being wracked by anxiety with scary images strobing through her brain again, she had been looking forward to taking her squishy, miraculous, perfect girl in her arms and burying her face in her neck, inhaling her sweet-sour scent. But Bella was having none of it. The teacher doing pick-ups was the cold one who had no truck with Jess's feelings.

Perhaps no one batted an eye as Jess carried out her screaming child, but she didn't look around to see. The point was to get out, because Bella would calm down eventually, even if she was still screaming and wriggling as Jess fought to get her fastened into her car seat.

"Transitions are difficult for everyone," Bella's other teacher, the nice one, had reminded her the other day, and as Jess put her key into the ignition she thought what an understatement that was.

The irony was not lost on her that the car seat was an instrument of safety in the event of impact. Before the invention of airbags, babies rarely died from being left in hot cars. Back then, car seats were fastened to the front seat beside the driver, where it would be difficult to forget who was along for the ride, even if the baby had fallen asleep.

Out of sight, out of mind—although listening to Bella's screaming, Jess wasn't sure how this was possible. A better mother would count her blessings: a baby as furious as Bella could never be forgotten. Such a baby could almost make you want to forget her on purpose . . . but no, Jess was joking. It wasn't funny. It was important not to think of things, because if you did they might come true.

But surely the universe wasn't so methodical. No one was up there keeping a tally of Jess's darkest thoughts. Bella's rage began to subside, or perhaps it was just that her voice had gone hoarse. Jess turned on the stereo, and the CD launched into "You Are My Sunshine," the darkest brightest song that Jess had ever heard. She didn't even like it, but Bella did, and she finally calmed down. Jess checked her out in the mirror, red-eyed and teary-faced, runny-nosed. Jess wanted her to stay calm, so she started singing along with the track. The verse about waking up from a dream to discover her sunshine gone, all empty arms and crying—it was the kind of despair she'd been imagining all day.

She pulled into the driveway, and there was Clara, delivered like a wish come true, waiting on the front steps beside the pretty planter whose flowers had been dead for weeks. Jess felt a rare surge of energy as she jumped out of the car to rush over to her friend, her lodestar.

"You're like a vision," Jess told her, clicking her key fob, the car locking behind her with a beep. "I've been out of my mind, and Bella screamed and screamed all the way home. My ears are still ringing."

Clara had come down the steps to greet them. "She's asleep," she said.

"What?" Jess said, looking toward the car, where Bella was still strapped into her car seat, her furious, snotty face now angelic in slumber. Jess had left her in the car. Not for long, it was true, and she hadn't gone far, but it had happened just like the article said. They can disappear from your mind, fall between the cracks. She'd forgotten about Bella and had just now turned around to find her there, the same thing they'd all seen, those poor parents—the very image, the sleeping baby, an illusion. As though they could reach out and brush the soft curve of that cheek and the baby would stir.

"Jess?" Clara was calling from far away. Jess's heart was pumping in her ears, sounding like traffic, even though there wasn't another car in sight. She couldn't stop staring at the baby. She was frozen. She couldn't even breathe, she realized, struggling to do so now. Clara was holding her, and Jess could hear a voice saying, "The baby, the baby," and she recognized the voice vaguely as her own.

"Jess?" called Clara. "The baby's fine, Jess. The baby's fine." She held Jess by the shoulders and tried to get her to look her in the eye, but Jess was looking through her. She couldn't focus. "Where are your keys, Jess? Bella's fine, Jess. We've just got to get her out of the car."

"I don't even know," Jess said once they were inside and Bella had been changed and her grubby face wiped. They were sitting in the kitchen with a bottle of wine. Bella was in her highchair eating little defrosted cubes of pea risotto. "Nothing like that's ever happened to me before."

"A panic attack," said Clara, as though it were simple, as though it were nothing. She topped up their glasses as Jess tried to explain the article about the poor babies and their poor parents. "You have to realize that's the kind of thing that happens to hardly anybody," Clara reassured her. "Those stories are outliers."

"Tell that to the people it happened to."

"But think about all the people it *didn't* happen to," said Clara reasonably. "Child mortality rates used to be brutal. Parents today have less to worry about than at any other time in history."

"The risks are real, though," Jess insisted. "I mean, last week Bella choked on a grape. A *grape*. You're supposed to cut them in half, but this one should have been quartered."

"And Bella was fine."

"She coughed it up."

"Things happen," said Clara.

"There is not enough room in my day right now for things to happen," said Jess. She refilled her glass. It was easier to be calm now. Twilight was cozy, and Clara was there. "I feel like you literally saved my life today."

"But if it hadn't been for me, nothing would have happened at all," Clara said. "You would have gotten her out of the car right away." They looked at Bella. She was banging on her tray with a plastic spoon, smiling her not-quite-toothless smile, green peas smeared around her mouth, unaware of the emotional havoc in her midst; the catnap in the car had rendered her cheerful. She adored Clara, who was such a baby charmer. Clara had carried Bella into the house, not missing a beat as the baby transitioned from sleep to chatty wakefulness.

The house was a mess. Breakfast dishes were piled beside the sink, two baskets of clean laundry were stacked in the hall, and a bag of dirty diapers was tied up by the door, still waiting, after three days, to be taken out to the garbage. They paid premium for bags that masked odour, so the bags didn't smell, but maybe they did and Jess was just immune to it. It was possible that the whole house reeked, so Jess apologized for everything being such a disaster. She should have tidied up.

"Hey, I invited myself over," said Clara. "You don't need to be sorry." She was happy to report that her interview had gone well, and she wanted to talk about it. Jess considered, as she filled Bella's sippy cup and tried to listen, that maybe Clara hadn't come over tonight to go through an itemized list of Jess's struggles, to hear about the panic, the mess, and how the house had started to feel like Jess's days: confining, claustrophobic. The walls were closing in and there wasn't enough light.

When they bought the place, Jess recalled, it offered so much space they couldn't even imagine how to fill it. There had been a spare bedroom and a linen closet; now they didn't have either, because the spare room was the nursery, and the linen closet was stuffed with small appliances in need of repair, outgrown baby clothes, and a decapitated wooden rocking horse. At the start of her maternity leave, Jess had entertained all kinds of notions—she would learn about carpentry, she'd fix up the horse!—but then the year was up and the horse still had no head.

"It's too small," she complained, the house. They'd been trying to put down roots, but instead of roots, it was baby stuff that had spread everywhere, all that gear that had to be stored somewhere, and that somewhere was everywhere, and it sometimes occurred to Jess that nearly every surface in their home was made of plastic and played a stupid song.

"We need a house with a basement," said Jess. Not a condo, but somewhere planted firmly in the ground. A place to store boxes of photos and her grandmothers' china, camping equipment and fishing rods.

"But real estate's a nightmare," Clara said. "I mean, there are basements, but they're all tiny apartments with five-foot ceilings that smell like backed-up toilets. I should know— I've been looking." She sighed. "I never thought it would be this difficult to find work. It doesn't matter how long my CV is. If all the experience is international, it's like starting from nothing. It's dispiriting."

"But it will come together," Jess assured her. She knew it would. Clara and Nick would find their own way, and it would be thoroughly unconventional. They had no desire for a home like Jess and Adam's anyway. Nick thought modern buildings had no soul, a proclamation Jess had tried not to take too personally.

The water on the stove was boiling and Clara got up to help, adding the gnocchi from a package. With the jar of pesto from the fridge, this would be instant dinner. Some things, at least, were mercifully uncomplicated.

"It's a lot right now, your life," said Clara once they'd finished eating. "It must feel like it's sucking you under."

She wasn't wrong, but Jess didn't want to admit it, because then what? Bella was using the sign for "more" now; they had taught her that at daycare. Signs certainly beat unintelligible screeching. Jess refilled the sippy cup. "It's just the stress of work, and that article," said Jess. She sat back down again.

"When's Adam coming home?"

"Seven or eight. I don't know. It depends." She saw where this was leading. "But this isn't about him."

"Except that you're carrying all this on your own," said Clara. She got up and started loading the dishwasher. "A full-time job on top of another full-time job. Is it any wonder you're stressed?"

"You don't have to do that," said Jess, meaning the dishwasher. But Clara paid her no mind, "And Adam does a lot," she reminded her. "When he can. He takes Bella to her swimming lessons. Most of the time. He has to work." She had to defend him.

"You work too."

"But my job is more flexible. And his job *is* paying the mortgage. Adam carries more than his share. He's supporting us."

"But you're supporting him too. You were the one who made that risotto. You bought the pesto, I'm sure. Taking the baby to daycare and bringing her home again after work, day after day. Invisible labour, but I see it."

"It's just really hard," Jess emphasized. "And not because I'm doing it wrong. It's easy to prescribe solutions. I know, I used to do it. But when you're in the middle of the mess, there's no way out. You really just can't fight it."

"But that sounds hopeless."

Jess wiped Bella's face, then poured Cheerios in her tray for dessert. "It's not as bad as that," she said. "But some days are tough. And now it's like my mind is conspiring to make it even harder. I'm not getting enough sleep. It's exhausting being back at work."

Clara refilled their glasses. "Things will get easier," she said. "I mean, they must. If everybody goes through it."

Jess took Bella out of the highchair to stop her from hurling the rest of the Cheerios to the floor. She held her close. "There are consolations," she admitted. "And sometimes when Adam's home, he does her bath, and I get fifteen minutes, sometimes twenty. And so I sit down and read, I take time for that. For me."

"Twenty minutes," said Clara softly, horrified.

"I know how it sounds," said Jess. "But it's the greatest. I fell asleep getting my teeth cleaned the other week—sitting back in the dentist's chair was like being at a spa."

"Jess, that's *sad*."

"You'll see," said Jess. "You think you won't, but you will."

Clara said, "I'm not pregnant."

Jess said, "You will be." She sniffed Bella's diaper. "I can't believe I haven't put you off the whole baby thing with all this."

Clara said, "But I want that too. The good, the bad. I want everything."

"It's going to happen." It had to. And then came a splendiferous squelching sound as Bella had her postprandial shit. Jess said with emphasis, "I promise."

Jess and Adam's new house had a backyard with an actual lawn, and a deck big enough to accommodate a patio table. The tumbledown garage beyond would be torn down one day, but in the meantime they marvelled at having an out-building, and so much space besides: walk-in closets and an ensuite, a fully finished basement with a home theatre. The renovated kitchen, perfect for entertaining, had been the thing that really sold them. They'd already taken Nick and Clara on the tour.

"Everything is so gorgeous," said Clara, perched on a stool at the counter with a drink—non-alcoholic—in hand.

Jess had just drained the pasta in the ceramic sink. "Since the first time I saw this room, I've been picturing you sitting right there," she said, gesturing at Clara with a wooden spoon. "I just can't believe it took this long to get you to come across town." They'd moved in three months ago. Bella, beneath Clara's feet, was stacking Tupperware towers.

The Tupperware had come from a party, but not *that* kind of Tupperware party. They didn't live so far from down-town that irony was dead, Jess explained. No, it was a *vintage*

Tupperware party, with Pyrex mixing bowls and casserole dishes, stuff her neighbour Nahlah plucked from garage sales and sold on eBay. Nahlah held the party a few times a year, and it was a chance for the neighbourhood wives to get together. Which was ironic too, because Nahlah was a wife who also had a wife, Nads. Nads and Nahlah, the next door neighbours. They'd be stopping by later for a drink after their kids were in bed, because the houses were close enough to be in range of the video monitor. "We do it all the time," Jess said.

It was strange for Clara to see Jess living next door to somebody else, a worn path between their back doors. Perhaps she and Nick should have come across town a little sooner, but it had seemed like such a long journey on the transit map, and they didn't have a car anymore. It had also been difficult for Clara to conjure the requisite enthusiasm for Jess and Adam's next step up the property ladder just as it was becoming clearer that she and Nick might never be able to purchase a home anywhere. The housing market had gone bananas.

In the backyard, Adam was showing Nick the mess that was the garage, the spot where the raccoons were getting in through a hole in the roof. They'd paid over half a million dollars for all this. Clara watched them from the window as they sipped their beer, two men paired off without any say in the matter, almost nothing in common except that their wives had found themselves in the same room on a curious night more than a decade ago.

Jess followed Clara's gaze. "So Nick hasn't found anything yet?"

Clara tried not to prickle; the question had been innocent. "Oh, you know," she answered, even though Jess didn't.

"But at least you're working," said Jess, stirring the sauce for the pasta. Clara now had a six-month contract running educational programs at the museum across the road from the university residence where she and Jess were living when they first met. Clara had had to scramble to get this job because she wasn't a teacher, but her affiliations were impressive and her references good. She had done more fieldwork than many of her colleagues, even if she lacked that essential graduate degree. But she'd been hoping for something permanent. And the pay wasn't much; it just barely covered the bills in the condo they were subletting, a place with bland beige walls and a balcony you couldn't sit on without inhaling exhaust fumes. None of it was really ideal.

"It's just a contract," said Clara.

"But it's all you need," said Jess. "Until the baby comes." She turned back to the sink, where she was dealing with the pasta, so she couldn't see how it made Clara uncomfortable, this naming of the situation. *The baby.* As though Jess were talking about the season, the weather, the inevitability of heavy traffic in late afternoon. Other than Nick, Jess—and presumably, Adam—was the only one who knew. Clara hadn't even told her family yet. It was all very early, still not fit for ordinary conversation.

Jess turned around again. "I have to tell you now, while they're still outside." Nick and Adam, she meant. Her tone was urgent, confidential. "I'm pregnant," she said. "I mean, I'm pregnant too."

Clara felt as though the wind had been knocked out of her. She said, "How?"

"Just. Adam doesn't even know yet. I mean, he won't be surprised. We've been trying. I found out this morning, and I knew you were coming. I wasn't sure if I was going to tell you, to tell you first, but I had to. We'll be pregnant together. We'll be on mat leave together." Jess was practically dancing, waving the wooden spoon.

"I don't get a mat leave," said Clara. Six-month contracts didn't come with a mat leave. She shifted on her stool and sent a Tupperware tower toppling, which made Bella shriek. Clara got down on the floor to make things right. To hide.

Jess called over the counter, "But you know what I mean." She sounded disappointed. And all Clara could think of was that Jess had gone and jinxed everything. She tried to stack the tower again, but Bella kept taking the pieces and hurling them across the room. "Clara?"

Clara reluctantly returned to her feet. Jess was waiting, waiting for her to say something, anything, except what she was really thinking. That the symmetry was too tidy, as if they were tempting fate. That Jess should have known better—but then really, how could she? Jess didn't know what it was like for pregnancy to be so fraught, literally unspeakable. She didn't know that if Clara dared to say the words, to truly acknowledge her situation, then all of this could be taken from her, and while this might be illogical, wasn't all of it? To be standing here staking everything she had on a microscopic embryo. All of it was perilous—how did anybody ever manage to be born?

Jess looked concerned now, so what Clara said was, "This is incredible." And it really was beyond belief, to be here together after all these years, in the same place at the same time, finally, and now to both be pregnant. She could feel this, on top of everything else she was feeling, which was a lot.

Clara had abandoned the Tupperware so Bella was yelling, and Jess came around the counter, got on the floor, and gathered her daughter while organizing the plastic containers—all at once, in a feat of dexterity. "But you can't say anything. I don't want Adam to know I told you first. But how could I not tell you when you're right here?"

"You have to tell him." Clara couldn't imagine keeping such a thing from Nick.

"Oh, I will," Jess said. "But he would have made me wait. It's early, he's cautious. But I needed to tell you first." She stood up with Bella hanging off her body.

"I won't say anything," Clara reassured her. "What would I say?"

"Oh, no!" Jess said. Behind her on the stove the sauce was boiling, splattering. She popped Bella back down and rushed to turn off the burner, knocking the wooden spoon off the counter. She picked it up off the floor and tossed it into the sink, selected another from the jar on the counter and stirred the pot. Then she wiped the splatters off the counter, the wall, and the floor. "Never, ever get white tiles," she called, disappearing as she got down on her knees, then popping up again. "They're a disaster." She wiped her brow and looked around. "There was a method to my madness," she said, "but I seem to have lost it."

"I know what that's like," Clara was saying just as Nick and Adam came inside.

"We're never buying a house," Nick said. "They've got raccoons in the roof."

"The garage roof," Jess clarified. "It's not like it's our roof."

"You gave the raccoons their own roof," said Clara.

"That's how it works out here in the suburbs," said Adam. He didn't know, Clara was thinking. His wife was pregnant and he didn't know, but Clara did. He scooped up Bella from the ruins of her Tupperware city. "Raccoons are actually the least of our concerns with this wild animal on the prowl." He lifted her in the air and blew a raspberry onto her belly, making her squeal.

"We used duct tape," said Clara. "Back when Jess and I lived together. We had squirrels then—remember?"

"And that actually *was* our roof," said Jess, finally putting the lid on the pot. She pushed a cutting board across the counter with a serrated knife and a fresh baguette. "Could you?" she asked Clara, who was happy to start slicing, to focus on something other than Jess's news, now the elephant in the room, in her brain. "Clara and I used to literally live in a hovel. Haven't we come a long, long way?"

"Speak for yourself," said Nick, pouring another drink for himself and Adam. "Who knows where we're going to end up?"

"You could let us live in your garage," Clara proposed to Adam and Jess. "With the raccoons."

"Might be hard to climb up to the roof in your condition," said Adam.

"Couldn't I use the door?" Clara asked.

Nick put his arm around her. "I never knew you were so fancy."

Bella was toddling around the room and arrived at Clara's feet, wrapping her arms around her knees. Clara picked her up, inhaling her scent. "Did you know," she said, "that baby powder is a carcinogenic? I had no idea. My sisters used it on their kids all the time. I don't know how else you're supposed to make a baby smell like a baby, but apparently you shouldn't use it at all."

Adam shrugged. "We don't."

"Oh, you're getting steeped in the mom facts already, Clara!" said Jess, who was putting plates in the oven to warm. "This is all so exciting."

"Make sure you get it written down now while you still know it all," said Adam, getting Bella to high-five him. "When this baby comes, you won't remember your own name."

They sat down to eat, and Jess told them about a display she was creating at work about giants and fairies. "I spent yesterday morning cutting out diaphanous wings. Not an easy task, actually. Who knew cutting and pasting could be a thing you do for a living?"

"What a dream job!" marvelled Clara. Then she turned to Adam, who worked for a consulting firm specializing in finance and executive compensation. "Still busy linking pay to performance?"

Adam said, "There are worse links."

Nick was feeling feisty. "Capitalism is a scourge. Why should everything be about the money?"

"Except everything already is about the money," said Jess. "The point is to tie that money to something tangible."

"Shareholder value," said Nick. "The rich just get richer."

"Not if business is bad," said Adam.

"But it's your job to fudge the numbers, right? The dollar took a nosedive last year, but I bet everybody still took home a fat paycheque."

"Relatively speaking, yes," admitted Adam.

"It's manufactured," said Nick. "The whole thing's a scam."

"The economy?" asked Adam.

"This is getting heated," said Jess, holding Bella on her lap. "Clara, why don't you just give us more parenting advice? Much less controversial," she joked. Bella was meant to be eating spaghetti noodles but was mainly hurling them to the floor. There was a piece in Jess's hair, and Bella picked it out and ate it.

Jess eventually put her to bed. Soon after, Nads and Nahlah knocked on the sliding door with video monitors in hand and two bottles of wine. They shook off their shoes and got glasses from the cupboard because they already knew where everything was. When Clara held out her hand, Nahlah hugged her instead. "The BFF. I've heard all about you." Everyone toasted to the house, to friends new and old.

And then they were back to talking about money. Nads was a banking renegade, having left the industry to co-found a credit union, so she was able to bolster Nick's anti-capitalist arguments, leading Adam to throw up his hands in mock-frustration, or at least Clara thought it was mock. She didn't mind that her husband hadn't been proven a fool.

And then they all sat down to watch the baby monitors, which apparently was a normal thing to do. Nads and Nahlah's children were sleeping, one not so soundly, and Bella was still awake but quiet, pulling her blanket over her face and then hurriedly pulling it off again.

"They're yuppies!" Clara exclaimed when she and Nick were on the subway going home. "I thought the yuppies had all gone extinct." For a long time, they'd been observing parents, promising each other they'd do it all in a different way. But this was the first time since parenthood had become so imminent. "We're never going to be like that."

Nick said, "Never."

"But we're going to be good at this, right?" They'd been waiting so long. Clara was cuddled up against Nick's shoulder. It had to be kind of okay, having babies. Especially if people were having one and even another one after that.

"The truth?" he asked.

She looked up at him. "What do you mean?"

He said, "I'm terrified."

"Okay, I get that," she said. She was scared too. She took his hand and squeezed it.

He said, "I'm happy, but I am so bloody scared that I'm going to mess this one up too."

She squeezed his hand again, "It's different this time."

He sighed. "I always think it's different this time." Their train pulled into the station, and from there they'd catch the bus.

They walked down the platform and rode up two escalators in silence, and when they were outside, she said to him, "So?" She had no idea what kind of ground she was standing on.

He said, "So what?"

She said, "So you're just going to leave that here? You're supposed to reassure me. You're the one who brought me to this moment. You're the one who brought me halfway around the world—"

"I brought you *home*," he said.

"I thought you did." She took a breath and looked up into his eyes. "I'm scared too." She wanted him to reach out and touch her, to hold her, but he didn't.

"It's complicated," he said. Sometimes she hated the way he always had to be so honest. If Nick lied, she might not be fooled, but maybe it would feel better than this.

She said, "I thought this was what you wanted."

"It is," he said, with no hesitation. That had to mean something. "I don't know if you know what it's like, to go over there and see your friend and her house and her life, and I really don't know if I can do that. Be the kind of person who owns a set of those fancy orange pots. Everything is so shiny. I don't know if we can be the kind of people who get together and watch their babies on TV."

So that's what this was all about. Clara said, "I don't want you to be anything but you." But not *this*, she was thinking. Please let this moment be an aberration, because right now you are failing me. "I just want to know that we're building something real here. That's what I want. Not pots." She paused. "Of course, we need some pots. Useful for boiling water."

"But what's a kettle for?" he asked. "I mean, I've got nothing against pots in general. But did you see that thing? It's like a big orange cauldron. And everything matches in their kitchen."

"It all cost a fortune," said Clara. "And they hardly ever cook." She wasn't going to tell Nick that Jess was pregnant, not yet. He took her hand now and squeezed it. She said, "I think it's normal to be scared about having a baby."

"It's just upped all the stakes."

"But isn't that what we signed up for?"

Nick put his arm around her, held her close. "Isn't getting what you wanted sometimes the scariest thing?"

"We're going to be fine," she said. She needed him to promise that they were going to be fine.

He said, "I'm going to show you," as their bus pulled in. He whispered in her ear, "I promise, I won't let you down."

Clara was at work when it started. She was directing the kids in sketching replicas of Roman water jugs and deciphering narratives from the images etched into their sides. These were the kinds of actual artifacts she'd once helped to unearth, working long days in the hot sun, the neck kerchief a necessary accessory to soak up all the sweat. She was so far away from that life now, and as she moved through her first trimester she was grateful for things such as flush toilets, air conditioning, and medical care in her first language.

"I'm getting soft," she complained to Nick more than once, and he'd only agree, grabbing her bum, her swollen breasts. Her body was no longer her own, and Nick said he liked it, but Nick's desires weren't the problem; it was the disorientation of no longer recognizing herself or who she was becoming.

She'd come so far—twelve weeks, which was nearly home free. "There is absolutely no reason you can't bring a healthy baby to term," the midwife had told her, and by twelve weeks Clara even believed her.

She was in the room with the jugs and little kids were sprawled on the floor. Here there was none of the formality required by the quiet and austere UK museums. This museum was a fantasyland of unpeopled dioramas, woolly mammoth skeletons, Regency furniture and a terrarium of cockroaches. It was an extension of these children's playrooms, a place for today as well as ancient times, which was the way things should be. This is what Clara was thinking when she first felt the rush.

Springing to her feet, she alerted a colleague and headed to the bathroom, hustling into a stall to reveal what she'd expected: blood. But it was dark brown, which was a good sign, at least according to all the pregnancy books. Spotting was normal, and brown blood was old blood, which was better, though Clara couldn't remember why. She looked in the toilet. There was blood there too, but not so much. And she'd been having cramps, she realized, now that she was paying attention. She folded toilet paper into a makeshift pad, a temporary measure, and for the rest of the day she could only focus on twinges and pangs. By the end of her shift, the cramps were worse, her makeshift pad soaked through. She paged her midwife, Rachel, who called back as Clara was walking out of the museum and into the street.

"Did you bleed through a pad?" Rachel asked her.

"I don't even have a pad," said Clara. "It's a wad of toilet paper."

"We don't worry until you've bled through a pad in an hour."

Clara said, "That's a lot of blood."

"Go home," said Rachel. "Lie down for a while and try to relax. Give me a call if things get worse."

When she got home, Nick wasn't there. She saw with irritation that his phone was on the counter. Clara set her shopping bag on the table—a pack of super-pads she hoped she wouldn't have to crack open. She made a pot of ginger tea (she'd quit caffeine months ago) and sat down to watch TV. She didn't like TV and would never have brought one into her home intentionally, but she was grateful for the distraction now. There was a reality show on, this one about real estate. She sent a text to Nick, only to feel immediately angry when she heard his phone vibrating on the table. By the time he walked in the door, she'd watched three episodes of the real estate show.

"What are you doing there?" he asked, taking her in, all curled up in a blanket in front of the TV. "Are you sick? You look terrible."

She told him about the bleeding but tried to play the whole thing down. "Rachel said it was probably fine." Except the cramps were worse, and her head was fuzzy.

And then in the middle of the night she woke up to find their bedsheets wet. She flicked on the light and saw all the blood, and Nick freaked out, which was good, because it meant she didn't have to. He was ready to call an ambulance, but she wouldn't let him. It was important for things not to be crazier than they already were, so she doubled up on the enormous pads and they headed to the hospital in a cab.

"I think I'm losing it," is what she told him on the way there, and she didn't mean the baby until she realized what she'd said and what was happening.

At the hospital, they were only one of many couples who were miscarrying, a situation that was established after an ultrasound. There were a few hopeful seconds in which the technician searched for a heartbeat and Clara held her breath, daring to hope. But there was nothing. The baby was gone. Nick and Clara stared at the monitor as they had done on previous visits, but there was no magic left to see.

They sent her home without pain pills. "Over-the-counter will be fine." There would be days of bleeding, so the pads would come in handy after all. Clara would be okay, and although she knew this—feeling despondent and at the same time entirely numb at the enormity of what she and Nick had lost—more than anything else she was shattered by the thought of the pain and the blood that she'd have to go through for nothing. She felt like such a body, a bag of flesh, and a useless one at that. It was all so familiar, this feeling. She was bloated with self-pity.

"But sometimes there really is no one to blame," said Nick as he handed her a tub of ice cream and a spoon.

Clara said, "That feels like a cop-out."

"I can't believe how shitty I feel."

"How shitty *you* feel?"

"Not worse than you," he said. "I'm not saying that. It's not the same, but I'm just so sad. And I wasn't expecting that.

It barely seemed real to me, the baby, so it seems strange to be mourning."

"I know," she said. She put the ice cream down on the side table.

Nick climbed onto their bed and put his arms around her, and his tenderness made her cry. "I just love you so much," she said. "And I loved our baby too." It was the first time she had ever articulated this, because she'd been so afraid of what she stood to lose. A creature with a physical body, even one insubstantial enough to disappear with the flush of a toilet—there had been so much blood, but most of it was hers. "I didn't want this to happen."

"I know," Nick said, turning her face his way and holding her chin. "This is not your fault." And then, "We're going to have a baby," he said, pulling her against his chest, his sweater. It had been washed a million times, but she could still smell the smoke, the smell of him, embedded deep in its fibres. That sweater was older than all of time. "I promise."

The shore was a distant blur, an outline, a suggestion. Clara had thought she was adrift before, but she had no idea. Her baby had been a lifeline, and once she let it go there was nothing to hold her. Even Nick's arms didn't count, because he was drifting too. With his age, and her history—there was significant scarring in her uterus, the doctor said, that made her vulnerable—the odds might be working against them. She would never be able to get pregnant naturally, according to the doctor, and Clara hadn't known how badly she wanted this until they told her it couldn't be had.

There was one good thing: her contract at the museum was renewed. And Nick agreed that he'd have to quit walking around the city imagining he was John Lennon in New York in the 1970s. He'd have to buckle down, get an actual job. Clara had found a fertility clinic with five-star reviews. "This is going to be expensive," she warned him.

He found a position coordinating banquets at a hotel downtown, something she knew was a compromise, but it came with health benefits and better hours than a bar. She was so grateful and surprised that they'd hired an older guy with very little related experience, but he told her they were struck by his erudition. To the interviewers, who didn't know any better, Nick sounded like someone who had gone to Oxford or Cambridge, and he acknowledged that there were some advantages to emigrating after all.

And so a shore—albeit different from the one they first envisioned—was just perceptible on a faraway horizon.

But Jess was out of reach. The break between them finally arrived after nearly six months of distance—they'd both been so busy, schedules misaligned, they could easily manage to avoid each other in perpetuity. Clara didn't want to see Jess—it felt too much like pressing on a bruise, and she knew that Jess was avoiding her too. Especially after she'd signed them both up for weekly email updates about fetal development. These started arriving about three weeks after Clara's miscarriage ("Your baby is the size of a navel orange!"), and it wasn't until the baby in the email was the size of a large mango that Clara finally told Jess she'd lost the pregnancy. Jess felt terrible, but she was just as upset that Clara had waited ten weeks to tell her the truth. Clara had no explanation for this, words failing her, which had been the problem all along: she'd started writing texts and emails but ended up deleting every one, and she was unable to just pick up the phone and call, because what could she have said that would make any sense?

They met up one last time in the new year, because Jess insisted on taking Clara out for her birthday. Clara wouldn't have gone, except Nick urged her to, reminding her, "She's your very best friend," even though Clara couldn't summon the sentiment that invested the phrase with any meaning. And this seemed like just one more thing that she was failing at—Clara felt as numb to her friendship as she did to everything, except for the grief and intermittent rage she'd been walking around in for the last five months like a fug.

It wasn't Jess's fault, not really, and it was likely that no matter what she did, everything still would have been wrong. Even if Jess hadn't been pregnant, Clara would likely have pushed her away, because Clara was pushing everyone away.

The restaurant was called Tabala, way out in the east end. Its decor was spare and minimalist, and it was so expensive that the mains didn't come with sides and Clara could only recognize every other word on the menu. Jess was already seated in a booth when Clara arrived. She was just eight weeks away from her due date, her pregnancy so conspicuous, but it was one more thing they didn't know how to talk about, along with Clara's miscarriage, Bella, and those email updates Jess would have continued to receive, which Clara knew all about because she'd never unsubscribed. This week her baby would have been the size of a cantaloupe.

I should never have come, Clara thought, as Jess prattled on about landscaping, cleaning women, and idle gossip about people Clara barely knew. She stared at Jess across the table, barely recognizing her, trying to channel steel so that she wouldn't crumble. She'd suffered so much lately that it seemed absurd to have to endure this as well—the affront of a relationship that seemed to have been drained of all meaning. She could just walk away. Away from Jess, who managed to get pregnant with ease. Whose body was burgeoning and blossoming and doing all the things that women's bodies are supposed to do, and who was really here only because she was waiting for Clara to assure her that all this was fair and fine.

"You're so quiet," said Jess at last, as close as she could get to acknowledging the situation, possibly finally running out of words to string together. "But listen," she said, as though Clara had been doing anything else. "I've got a proposition." And Clara just knew, the thing that could make this worse.

"Would you be willing," asked Jess, "to be this baby's godmother?" As though such an offer could tip the scales towards balance.

Clara said, "We don't believe in God."

"Well, we don't have to call it that," said Jess, still looking hopeful, excited. "We could call it anything."

"A consolation prize?" Clara asked. Jess's face fell, she looked wounded, which wasn't fair—*she* was the one who had steered this so wrong. And Clara thought of the evil fairy godmother in "Sleeping Beauty," the one who laid the curse, and she wondered whether that godmother had simply been pushed so close to the edge she couldn't bear it anymore.

"I have to go," Clara said, getting up from the table, pulling her coat around her shoulders. She headed for the door, leaving Jess scrambling in her wake, no doubt struggling to get unstuck from the booth, pay the bill, all the while calling after Clara to wait.

But Clara didn't wait. She imagined that this was the end of it, of them, finally. It felt good, like ripping off a bandage. Clara was free now, wholly unencumbered, lighter than she'd felt in forever . . . until she heard Jess calling her name just in front of the subway entrance, waving her arms, Clara's bag in her hand. Clara had left her bag, with her wallet, her keys, and everything else, at the table. Jess's entire body heaved as she struggled to recover her breath, falling against a brick wall for support, a disturbing sight for passersby. She was just barely able to form the words, "This is all so hard, I know."

Jess gave Clara her bag and placed a hand on her shoulder, creating the slightest window of possibility that things were salvageable. "What you're going through—" she started. And then three words that would hurt more than anything else did: "*I can't imagine.*"

And maybe if Jess hadn't articulated the horrible truth of it, her own failure of imagination, of empathy, the distance between them might not have widened so impassably. Perhaps Clara could somehow have found a way to be generous, reaching for Jess's hand, pulling it even closer. Somewhere there was an alternate universe in which Clara could find enough room in her heart to answer, "You have nothing to feel bad about. All this, you deserve to have it. I want it for you." But it wouldn't be this universe. Because she couldn't. She didn't. Jess would have to live without this one thing.

A SPELL FALLS OVER THE CASTLE

2010–2014

Once upon a time, there were two women who were both with child, and then the first woman's baby died, and the second one's baby didn't, and the second woman had no choice but to carry on, leaving her oldest friend broken and grieving behind her, without even a trail of breadcrumbs or shiny pebbles allowing the possibility that they could come together again.

Jess wished she could take it back. That fateful dinner in the tiny booth, whatever the words were that had sent Clara spinning, and everything she'd done before that, which she'd imagined was benevolence, sealing their collective fates. Getting pregnant just because she could, which turned out to be reckless, a disaster. Jess had convinced herself that everything would work out, because for her it tended to, and therefore that it would *have to* work out if she and Clara were pregnant together, because surely no destiny could be so cruel . . .

She'd gone about it so clumsily, awkward and desperate, because the stakes seemed so high, and they really were, as the circumstances of their rift would attest to, dramatic and devastating. Clara had whirled around on that street corner, charging out of her life forever, and even if Jess had been

willing to humiliate herself in such a fashion, she couldn't
have kept running after her. She had finally reached her limit.
Stranded on that corner, so enormously pregnant, struggling
to catch her breath, creating a spectacle, people stopping to
ask if she needed help, which meant she must have really
looked like she was in trouble, because this was a city where
people didn't talk to strangers.

A man had helped her call a taxi, because her hands were
shaking so much that she couldn't work her phone, and
someone else had offered an energy bar, which she accepted,
because she realized she was ravenous—she'd been too nervous at dinner to eat anything, and maybe something was off
with her blood sugar, or her iron.

No one wrote self-help guides to processing the grief of
losing your best friend. Jess considered this a few days later
as she stood in the bookstore on her lunch break, perusing
an entire shelf of titles about toilet training. Life goes on.
The next aisle over were books about marriage, widowhood,
divorce, raising teen girls, and postpartum depression, which
Adam thought she should also pick up, even though the
baby wasn't born yet.

"You seem so sad," he said.

"Of course I'm sad," said Jess, but he didn't understand,
not really.

"You've still got me," he said, kissing her hair, holding
her as she cried, and she cried a lot, her emotions all turbo-
charged. *Hormonal.* And Jess hated that, how easy it was to
explain away, and therefore dismiss, the weight of her loss,
of her grief. Losing Clara was not as immediately conse-
quential as losing her partner, it was true, but this was an
essential, albeit invisible, wound, distorting Jess's sense of
herself, of who she was in the world.

She was powerless to stop the grief. Clara had gone, disappeared. She'd scrubbed her social media (not that she'd ever had much of a presence there). Jess's texts remained unread, and when Jess called, she didn't answer.

"Send an email?" Adam suggested. "You could write her a letter and buy an actual stamp?" He really thought the whole thing would blow over.

But then Miles was born, two weeks early, and he had a heart murmur, which would turn out to be fine, but for a while things were scary, and not long after, Jess was diagnosed with postpartum anxiety, which she realized she'd been living with ever since Bella was born, a very long time. The drugs brought relief, finally, and by the time her brain was sorted out, the matter with Clara had simply been added to a never-ending list of things to do, right after finally putting away all the laundry, which was never going to happen. Filed away under the subheading That Very Bad Time.

Months went by, a blur with two kids under two, and then the months turned into four whole years. Sometimes Jess felt as though she was barely holding on as the children grew. And there were days and weeks when she didn't think of Clara at all because her life was so incredibly full, if often overwhelming. Perhaps it was only natural, Jess considered, on the occasions when Clara came to mind, that they'd drifted apart. Perhaps the mistake had been trying to hold on for so long.

Eventually, as she started to emerge from the storm that had taken hold of her, once she'd processed the grief, once she had found a therapist who managed to unlock so many of the mysteries of her mind, Jess was able to take responsibility for her part in what had happened, to understand how insensitive she'd been. One day while cleaning out the children's bookshelves, she came across the copy of *Outside Over There* that Clara had given Bella for her first birthday. Such a weird and creepy story, the kind of gift that no one but Clara would have given. Jess reread the loving inscription, "To Arabella, for the rest of your life . . . ," and she remembered how much Clara had loved Bella (*Oh my god, Jess. Look what you made*), realizing for the first time how hurt she must have been to cast that love away. So absorbed in her own life, her own storm, Jess had been oblivious to everything Clara was going through, how far apart their stories were, how fraught their common ground.

And then one day a package arrived on her doorstep.

AVOCADO STONES

Nick and Clara moved out of their sublet into an apartment of their own, the ground floor of a Victorian that had a backyard with an apple tree and big patio doors through which the sun poured in. In the doorway of the second bedroom was a line marked in increments with pencil, representing a child's growth, inching halfway up the frame. Clara, who wouldn't let Nick paint over it, would sit on the floor staring at the marks, imagining the force that must have driven that kind of growth. Somehow the child whose height had been measured in the doorway became her ghost child, the baby she'd miscarried, but she could see far into his future now. He was a boy with freckles, a bowl haircut, and gaps in his teeth. (The previous March, Jess—whose approach to Facebook privacy settings was pretty slapdash—had given birth to a son.)

Clara started making bread, preserving pickles and drying herbs for tea, all the things she hadn't felt comfortable doing in the condo, that cold and sterile space that was never really theirs. When the weather was warm, she'd go into the backyard and lie in the sun, her skin absorbing the heat from the concrete patio slabs, a hat over her face because the sun hurt her eyes, and she didn't care for sunscreen. She wanted goodness and she wanted light, vitamin D. She imagined the sun was an elixir. She started eating avocados by the crateful, having read that they had magic properties for fertility, perhaps suggested by their egg shape. Every time she cut into one and removed the stone, she'd clutch it in her hand and make a wish: "I want to have a baby." As if magic was all it would take.

But there was also science, which was another kind of magic—magic that ended up costing all their savings, the money they'd been sitting on when they came across the sea. "It will all be worth it," they kept telling themselves as the bills mounted. As one cycle failed and then another, the seasons passing until, finally, they had to wonder when they'd stop.

Every morning before work, Clara travelled to a fertility clinic downtown (the streetcar passed right by the library where Jess worked) to be examined by a nurse named Donna, whose perkiness seemed at first insufferable but then a promise, and soon Clara was in love with her and had placed her heart in Donna's hands. At the clinic, Donna and her colleagues would take Clara's temperature, examine her cervix, perform ultrasounds, and help track her weird menstrual cycle. When Clara's eggs were ripe, they were injected with Nick's sperm, which he'd be summoned via text to deliver. Nick and Clara didn't talk about any of this at home. If they tried to, he'd end up confessing his fears that she was unhealthily obsessed with becoming pregnant, which would only make her angry. So she did her thing and left him alone to do his, both of them working toward the same imagined outcome.

They felt oddly estranged through all this, though they were often together, usually holding hands, but biology

emphasized their separation. And while it might have helped
to make love, to provide some kind of connection, even ceremony, to the whole endeavour, Nick had been restricted
from ejaculating outside of a schedule. He didn't complain
about this, as his remarkable sexual appetite had dissipated
somewhat when he clued in that the only reason Clara was
interested in having sex at all was for the purpose of procre-
ation. And when she said she didn't understand what difference it made, Nick protested that it made a big difference.
They were both aware that this was a messed-up dynamic,
but they crossed their fingers and hoped it was something
they could work through once Clara finally became pregnant. Getting pregnant, Clara was sure, would be the answer
to everything.

Before, she and Nick used to imagine what their child
would be like. Boy or girl, his dark hair or her blond?
Definitely crooked teeth, short-sighted. Clara thought a scat-
tering of freckles. Their baby would be chubby, with fat rolls
on its thighs, a pokey belly. She'd seen baby pictures of Nick's
son once upon a time and wondered if they were a clue.
Gummy grins. Dimpled wrists. But now she didn't care what
the baby looked like. It didn't matter.

The baby, to Clara, was mostly abstract now, an idea.
Sometimes at the clinic, she forgot that a baby was even a
possible outcome, that she was undergoing all these curious
procedures and rituals as a means to an end. All the waiting
and wishing and hoping had simply become the framework
of her existence. Without all this longing, she wondered
sometimes—by then it had been going on so long that she
wore it like an itchy sweater—who would she even be?

"A baby isn't everything," Nick would sometimes dare
to remind her. At one point they had decided to forgo the

trying, to take a break, for a whole year. It was a relief, but it also made her despairing. Clara had felt so lost.

"Don't you think we could have a good life regardless?" Nick asked, but Clara refused to give in, as though it were a matter of will. He'd promised her they'd have a baby and she believed in that promise, even if Nick was willing to let it go because he feared it might destroy her. She really was obsessed. Even during the months when Clara wasn't frequenting the clinic, she clutched her avocado stones. She ordered a necklace online that represented Heqet, the frog-headed goddess of fertility and childbirth. "Did you know," she said to Nick, "that thousands of years ago Egyptian women wore amulets just like this?" And if it was good enough for them, she would take it.

It was unsurprising that it wasn't only the Grimms who had the frog fetish. Frogs were archetypal. (At times like this, Clara could hear Jess's voice in her head. Infertility in "Sleeping Beauty," that poor woman in the bathtub. Clara was realizing that everything she ever needed to know had been right there in front of her all along, but she just wasn't paying attention.) Maybe it was obvious: the connection between sperm and tadpoles? Or was it the symbolism of any animal who could have as many babies as that?

Though having even one baby, thought Clara, seemed extravagant. She considered what it must be like to have two children, as many babies—or more—as one had arms to hold them. Such juggling would be required. A kind of a dance, she imagined it, requiring fluency, balance. (When she thought of Jess, Clara had visions of spinning plates in the air. And also of bathtubs and frogs.)

At home alone, Clara took up her place in the doorway, watching the marks on the wall, although they began to seem like less of a promise as seasons went by and no baby came.

For the first time, Clara envied her sisters, how easily their babies had arrived, and this became just another reason to keep her distance from her family, from everyone. She knew her sisters would try to talk sense into her, broaching fostering and adoption, listing all the reasons why fertility treatments were against God's will. No thank you, she didn't need to be around her sisters, especially because being around her nieces and nephews only made her heart ache. She got enough of that at work with the children she taught, their lisps, pigtails, knobby knees, and tiny noses, and their certainty about their futures: they were all going to be paleontologists and archeologists, celebrity zoologists and butterfly scientists. When she told them that butterfly scientists were called lepidopterists, they looked at her as though she were stupid. Of course they already knew that. They stood for everything Clara had ever wanted and had become so far out of reach.

When it happened, after so long—years—she thought they were kidding, that there had been a mix-up. She made the nurse—not Donna, she'd retired—double-check, triple-check. But there it was on the ultrasound screen, in her womb—her *womb*! Three weeks along—most people wouldn't know this early, but the fortune they'd forked over came with benefits. It was all still early, the nurse said, but the baby was just fine.

Those early weeks crept by slowly, and Clara tried not to hope, steeled herself, because she'd been here before. As the first trimester progressed, she made excuses at work for her pallor, her regular exits to throw up in the bathroom, the days she couldn't come in because she couldn't get out of bed. She was so sick.

"This is a good sign," Nick told her, parroting something she'd told him after reading it in a book—that morning sickness was a sign of a healthy pregnancy. Clara hadn't been ill at all with the baby she miscarried. But hearing her words in his mouth only made her realize how desperate she was for any assurance, how flimsy the foundation of any hope was.

It was September but still so hot outside, and she'd come home from work to collapse into the chaise longue in their backyard, desperate for some semblance of a breeze. Since she'd been pregnant, she couldn't stand thinking about food, so she hadn't been cooking, although she would eat whatever Nick delivered—barbecued meats and vegetables, corn on the cob, asparagus slathered with butter.

She was counting the days, the hours, every square on the wall calendar with an X through it, another day she'd made it through, although she wouldn't allow herself to feel relief until morning because things could go wrong in the night, Clara knew that now. At twelve weeks, she passed the day that had been furiously circled in red in her mind, the day she'd miscarried during her previous pregnancy. She said nothing to Nick because she didn't want to curse it, because she was still waiting for something terrible to arrive.

That night Clara had enough energy to sit upright at the table in the backyard and she was actually hungry for dinner, burgers and grilled tomatoes. It would be the last night before the heat broke. The apples on the tree looked ripe and almost ready to eat, and it was as though fall was waiting, just like she was. The giant pitcher of ice water on the table was drenched in condensation. Clara drew a heart with her index finger, then wiped the moisture on her face, which felt cooling for about a quarter of a second.

Nick commented on how different she seemed, how there was colour in her cheeks again.

"It's because I'm sitting in a chair," she said. "It's an optical illusion." She told him this rare burst of energy was probably due to the nap she'd taken at her desk that afternoon.

He said, "You won't be sitting at that desk too much longer—" but she made him stop. Let's not tempt fate. Let's not mention this date, or the future, or all her crazy superstitions, the frog head around her neck or the avocado stones. It had to remain unspoken, how much she wanted this baby.

And then one day around thirteen weeks, Clara woke up in the morning and felt like getting out of bed, as though seven hours of sleep had been sufficient. She sat up and stretched, and her head didn't feel fuzzy. She headed to the kitchen to make breakfast, poached eggs and kale with buttered toast, her appetite remarkable in its specificity.

But her euphoria was cut short by the thought that she might not be pregnant anymore. It was still too early to feel her baby moving, and her belly was only soft, not round. There were no outward signs of what was happening to her, except for the sickness and fatigue, and now that they had dissipated, she was left with nothing.

Hysterical enough on the phone to be alarming, she got in to see the doctor that afternoon—not the crunchy midwife she'd embarked with last time, but now a specialist in high-risk pregnancies. His nurse had taken her blood pressure and apparently it was through the roof, and he came into the room, full of concern. "What brings you here?" he asked her.

And she told him. How she'd woken up that morning feeling totally fine, and the logical conclusion was that the baby was dead.

He pulled out an instrument she hadn't seen before, a heart monitor. "At thirteen weeks," he told her, "the baby's heartbeat is generally audible."

She lay on the table. He instructed her to lift her shirt and coated her belly in gel, seemingly blasé about the procedure. But then:

So much noise. It was like cruising an FM dial, static and feedback. Like holding a shell up to your ear and listening to the sea. That's what it sounded like, the same rush of blood.

"Don't panic," he said. "I'm getting this." And indeed, there it was, a steady beat at the centre of all that noise. Like the thunderous gallop of a team of horses that went on and on and on. "Healthy baby with a heartbeat," said the doctor. And Clara just knew then that the baby would be okay.

She tried to articulate her certainty to Nick later that night as they dug into a cake she'd picked up from the frozen foods aisle at the grocery store. It felt good to give in to a craving, to listen to what her body was telling her, which was mainly, *deep and delicious*. Her mouth was full, but she was still talking, trying to get to the point, which seemed elusive. Or maybe it was that every time she nearly got there, she realized how flaky she sounded.

"It's an intuition," she said. "Even though everything I intuited before turned out to be wrong." Once she had been sure she'd felt the embryo implant. A kind of pinch. She could have sworn it. But it was all in her head.

"I thought I'd been certain," she said, "but now I know what certain is. That heartbeat, the way it just kept going and going, and I've never heard anything else like it. It was something to believe in, constant and unceasing, and maybe what I figured out is that all this is so much more than me, like it's up to a higher power and I should just sit back and let it happen."

"So you've turned religious after all," said Nick.

"No, it's a different kind of faith." She'd recorded the heartbeat on her phone and she played it for him, and he admitted that it touched him, but it was too devoid of context. He hadn't been converted yet. "It's really going to happen. I can feel it." Just think of it: to want and to receive. A simple thing, as perfect as a heartbeat. Such extraordinary design.

Now that the world had been returned to her, Clara suddenly felt what she'd been missing like a phantom limb: Jess. The ache of it had been lost for years in the pain of everything else she couldn't have, and now she craved it the same way she was craving orange juice and cartons of sweet-and-sour chicken. She was powerless to resist these urges, especially when they didn't make sense. She wanted Jess to know this baby, to be part of her life.

But how do you do it, send a message to a friend when you were the one who blew up the bridge between you? How do you begin to rebuild? How do you know you have the right to? Clara didn't think she had the right, not really. When things had fallen apart five years ago, she was so heartbroken and furious at the injustice of her situation that the opportunity to make Jess feel as terrible as she did was frankly satisfying—when Jess said "I can't even imagine," Clara decided, "I'll show you." But only for a moment. Afterwards she was immediately delivered back to her darkness, a place so essentially lonely that the loss of Jess barely registered.

But she was feeling it now, the loss, just like she was feeling so much else that had been lying dormant with her life on hold. She'd actually picked up a book again when she was off work for the holidays, a novel, the first one she'd tried in such a long time because all those hours she used to spend sitting in doorways and clutching stones had to be filled now. It was *My Brilliant Friend*, by Elena Ferrante, a copy that had been passed around the lunchroom at work. After failing to get through more than a quarter of it after weeks of trying, Clara finally knew what to do.

With a pencil she composed a note on the inside cover: *Jess, I hate this book. Everyone promised I'd devour it, but they lied. And I can't figure out if it hits too close to home or if it doesn't hit at all. It's melodramatic, not fun, and way too long. I feel like maybe you'll understand?*

My Brilliant Friend would cost a small fortune to mail across town, but it would be worth it if Jess got the message. This mission was a worthwhile distraction from her pregnancy, which continued apace, but it felt good to have something else to hope for.

When Clara opened the door two weeks later and saw the package had been returned, still wrapped in its plain brown paper, her heart didn't even fall. By now she had become skilled in the art of resignation. And what kind of olive branch was a book in the mail anyway? And not even a book she'd been able to enjoy.

But maybe . . . She picked it up—no small feat at thirty-two weeks pregnant, bending around her belly, trying not to put too much pressure on her knees—and turned it over, and there it was, Jess's familiar handwriting, Clara's name neatly penned. Not "Return to sender" but something different, which was why Clara had printed her return address so carefully. She wanted Jess to know how to reach her.

Jess had mailed back the book with a piece of paper tucked inside it. The paper was worn so thin it was soft, and there were remnants of tape stuck around its tattered edges, the whole thing so delicate that Clara had to unfold it with care, and it took her too long to realize that what she was holding had been created by her hand. The map was from a time she could barely remember, but she remembered drawing it, remembered the impulse to hold the world in its entirety. Clara had once been so confident that all of it was hers to have and that nothing beyond its margins really mattered. Here they were, the two of them, Jess and Clara, the centre of the universe.

Inside the book, Jess had added to Clara's message: *I thought I was the only one. I tried and I tried but I just couldn't love it. I just don't think anything has to be this bleak. Surely there's a possibility for a different kind of ending?* She'd written her phone number, her email, both the same as ever. She'd been waiting all this time.

Clara sat down with her laptop to write a message to Jess. Jess, who was now a seasoned mother of two kids, seven and five, who'd already travelled the road Clara was on now. Jess, who'd known Clara longer and better than anyone. Even though Jess had known her last when she was a different kind of person, someone who hadn't lost so hard and bet all of it anyway, Clara wasn't sure she'd be able to do this without her.

She wrote, "*So here's a shocker: I am having a baby. It's a girl and she's the size of a napa cabbage, whatever that means. Apparently normal in every single way, and with little else in common with vegetables. This is happening even though I'd started to think that any offspring of mine would be more like that tiny bit of woolly mammoth DNA scientists found preserved in amber— do you remember that? The smallest fraction of possibility, science fiction instead of probable. But it's actually true, the opposition of extinction. PS: Did you ever hear about Heqet?*"

Jess responded within the hour: "*Oh my frog-headed goddess.*"

Then Clara: *I'm just so sorry.*

Jess: *Me too.*

They made plans to meet, and then those plans came true. Clara had been waiting, she answered the door before Jess even knocked. There was a split second of awkwardness when the door flew open and neither of them knew how to be.

Jess broke the spell. "You just won me a hundred bucks."

"What?"

"It was a feeling I had. Not since always, but in the last little while, that you were going to come back. I was ready. I couldn't chase you, I had to wait. And Adam said maybe it was just because waiting felt easier than accepting, and I guess it was. But here you are."

"What about the money?"

"We made a bet. Adam lost. I don't think Adam's ever lost a bet before, but you're sort of a wild card. And I was betting on that."

"Adam!" said Clara.

"Don't take it personally," said Jess. Clara led her inside. "He didn't know you as well as I do." Jess was still talking as she followed Clara down the hall. "I don't even know where to start, how to say how sorry I am."

Clara stopped abruptly. "How about we just don't," she said. "Start, I mean. We've wasted so much time already."

"You disappeared," said Jess. "And I just *let you.*" They arrived in the kitchen, and Clara poured two glasses of iced tea. "I had no idea at the time what you must have been going through. Everything was just so intense, so exhausting. Maybe by now you understand." She gestured towards Clara's body. "You're blooming," she said, which Clara figured was code for *Where in god's name have your cheekbones gone?*

"I look fat," said Clara. No use skirting the issue.

"You look pregnant," said Jess.

"I," said Clara, "have never ever felt so good." Not for her the list of complaints from women in their third trimester. Sure, she'd lost her second-trimester bounce, but for the most part, especially while in repose, she felt buoyed by a sea of wellness, not even minding the weight she'd gained, her thickening legs and arms and the hugeness of her belly and her breasts. Or her chins. She didn't care about her chins, because she'd fallen in love with herself. She could celebrate. And eat brioches when the urge struck her, because her body was telling her something and she would listen to her body, and for the first time in a long time it was a body she trusted, and everything was unfolding as it should.

"But I'm sorry too," Clara said as she led the way outside, carrying her glass and a plate of cookies. "I've been desperately sorry ever since. It was shameful." She interrupted Jess's protest. "It was. I know it. I always knew. I was lost in my own head, and maybe we can get on with it now?"

They took their seats in the shade. The patio doors were open wide so that the living room, stuffed with books, rugs, blankets and throw pillows blended seamlessly into the outdoors. "Oh, I know this aesthetic," Jess said, looking around. "You've still got your steamer trunk." With the Cunard Line stickers, and Nick's turntable and a stack of vinyl records were piled on top of it.

Jess looked good, Clara realized, once she'd examined her more closely. A bit thin, and wan. Tired, of course, but only as tired as anyone with small children who had almost made it to the end of the day. Her hair was coloured nearly blond now. She was wearing one of those beige sack dresses, surely made from organic cotton, that only looked good on two percent of women. Jess and Adam must have a lot of money. "This is delicious," she was saying, holding up her drink.

"The key is sugar," said Clara, who'd already downed hers. A look of distaste crossed Jess's face. "What?" Clara said. "Sugar's good for you. It comes from the earth." She picked up a cookie as if to prove it.

Jess nibbled one reluctantly. "Nick's not here?"

"He's at work." Clara explained that he was working overtime, which they were grateful for. She had a few more weeks left at the museum, and then they'd have to learn to live without her income. She'd qualify for unemployment, though it wouldn't be much.

"But you're going back eventually?" There were lines around Jess's mouth, new ones, and they came out when she was frowning.

"Who knows, who knows," said Clara.

But Jess would not be deterred. "You must have some idea."

"I have none at all," said Clara. "This, a baby, was the end point, and we never thought past it." The last few years had taught her plenty about taking things as they come.

"But won't you miss it?" asked Jess, and Clara hardly knew what she was talking about. "Your job," Jess clarified. "You've always loved your work. You knew what you wanted to do before anybody else we knew did."

"But that was such a long time ago," Clara said. "And I don't even do that anymore."

"You're going to be bored," said Jess.

"I guess we'll see."

"*I* was bored. I couldn't wait to get back to work."

"How's it going, anyway?" asked Clara. "Work."

So Jess told her about her promotion, and how they'd been granted five years of extra funding, which would provide latitude for new creative projects. "I'm home by five thirty, and I can set the nanny free," Jess said.

"And Miles," said Clara. "I've never even met Miles." She paused. "These last couple of years . . ."

"Seriously," Jess said. "I barely made it out alive. Two kids, and Adam's working all the time. One day I went out wearing socks on my hands. I thought they were mittens. It was August. I don't even know." She took a breath. "I wish I'd been a better friend, but it was just so hard. I could barely keep my own life together, but I want to do better now. I want to be here for you."

"Okay," said Clara. She'd been waiting for an entry point. "So how about this: I want you to be here when the baby's born."

"What? *Here?*"

"At home. We want to have the baby at home."

"That's insane," said Jess.

"It's not," said Clara. "Especially not if you're going to be here. Because you know how to do this. You've done it—twice."

"I've never had a baby at home." Jess seemed horrified. Maybe this was a bad idea.

"You've had a baby, though," Clara said. "I want that matrilineal tie."

"I'm not your mother."

"But you're *a* mother. You're the closest thing I've

got—well, except for my actual mother, but if she were here while I was having a baby it wouldn't end well."

"But what if it doesn't end well for us, either?" asked Jess, sounding desperate. "I mean, our track record hasn't been great lately."

"Maybe the idea is too weird," Clara admitted. "It's been such a long time."

"*That's* not why it's weird," said Jess.

Clara said, "I just want to do everything right. You don't know how hard it's been, how much it cost, and I don't just mean money. It almost cost me you."

"But it didn't."

"I need my people around me now," said Clara. "I want to bring our baby into the world surrounded by so much love and strength, and you're the only person I trust enough. Except Nick, but it can't all be on him. This whole thing's so scary, just like—" She tried to think of a way to explain it. "It feels like jumping off a cliff."

Jess said, "Oh."

"What?"

"No, it is." Jess was silent for a moment. "Clara, this is a big deal. A huge thing. I'm worried you don't really know what you're asking." She was warming to the idea. Clara knew she could persuade her.

"But I do know," said Clara. "Will you consider it? Entertain the possibility?"

"I don't think I'd be very useful," Jess said.

Clara said, "I don't even need you to be useful. I just need you to be you."

THE WATER BIRTH

2015

"She did it," Jess announced from Clara's front porch. "She really did. I was there. I saw it." She was on the phone to Adam just thirty-five minutes later. She had exited the scene along with the midwives, leaving Clara and Nick and the baby, the new family, alone. "I can't believe it," she kept saying to Adam, exhilarated by what she'd witnessed but also tired and stunned. She'd been convinced that having the baby at home was a terrible idea, that anything and everything would go wrong, especially given her friend's track record. She couldn't understand why Clara would be willing to risk everything, why she'd replace her high-risk OB-GYN with a midwife, playing fast and loose with life and death . . . but everything had gone according to plan.

Although there hadn't actually been a plan—this had been the most exasperating point. "We'll just take things as they come," Clara had pronounced as Jess pressed her for details, wanting to know what she'd be expected to do. Clara said she didn't want her to do anything, she just wanted her there, but this made Jess uneasy; when her kids were born, during the worst of it, she'd hated every person in sight for their powerlessness to take away her pain.

"And I had an epidural," she underlined during their back-and-forths weeks before the birth, giving Clara another reason to reconsider her cockamamie idea. (According to the midwife, it wasn't a plan but a *vision*: "You have to be able to see something in your mind to make it so.")

But Clara was undeterred by Jess's doubts and protests. "You've got wisdom and experience," she said. "I need you to share that with me."

"Well, can I share it now?" Jess responded. "Because I remember what labour was like, when it felt like my pelvis was being shattered, and my vagina was on fire. Is that enough? Do you want more details?" But Clara shook her head, raising her hand to make her stop. Clara was doing hypno-birthing meditations. Everything else was just noise.

So Jess went along with it. She was squeamish about the details, but she was going to be there because Clara needed her.

Nick called her after dinner one night in the middle of May to say it was finally happening, could she come, so she kissed Adam and the kids goodbye and headed downtown, taking transit because she didn't want to worry about parking, and who knew how long it was going to take? She felt she was setting off into the unknown, which was something she rarely felt these days. Adam had assured her that they'd do just fine without her, crossing his fingers that it wouldn't take days and days.

Clara was standing in the kitchen stirring batter for a cake, wearing nothing but a T-shirt that wasn't long enough, her thighs mottled with cellulite, the hair between her legs and down her thighs thick and impossible not to stare at, but

Clara wasn't attentive to such details. She didn't seem to care about anything except stirring the batter and taking deep breaths, most of the time with her eyes shut. She acknowledged Jess's arrival with a nod and stopped stirring. Then she placed a hand on her belly and breathed deeply again. "Born Slippy" by Underworld was playing on the stereo. Nick and Clara still had CDs.

The kitchen opened onto the living room, where the pool was already set up and lined with garbage bags and being filled with a hose connected to the sink. Nick was watching TV with the sound off. He got up to greet Jess and whispered, "It's happening." He was nervous, she could see it. Normally he was a consummate host, in strong possession of himself and his home, but he didn't know how to behave right now. "She's doing okay," he told her. "She wants her space."

Clara was stirring again, swaying. The midwives were in the garden and Nick had turned the music down, Clara's moaning loud against it, like the lowing of a cow. She was bent over the counter, her hands braced against the edge.

"Darlin'?" Nick called, but Clara waved him away. "She's going to bake that cake," he muttered to Jess. "I told her we didn't need to have a cake, but she insists. She read about it in a book. And she's never going to get it done because she keeps putting down the spoon and leaning over and moaning."

"Shut up, Nick," called Clara from the kitchen, through clenched teeth.

"Are you sure it's all right that I'm here?" Jess asked him, now in even lower tones. They ducked into the hallway.

"If it wasn't, you'd know it," he reassured her. "Get ready though, she's going to turn on the cooker. As if it wasn't hot enough already." The temperature outside already felt like summer.

The song ended in an explosion of drums and noise, and then immediately started playing again.

"She's got it on repeat," said Nick. "Don't even mention it."

"She's doing okay?" Jess asked as they watched Clara, who was upright again and stirring the batter to the rhythm of the song, as though she were under a spell.

He said, shaking his head, "She's amazing."

Jess remembered her own early labour lasting two days, contractions coming on strong in the evening and fading away during the day. Eventually she went to the hospital to be induced. She'd been ready for a similar lack of progress with Clara, but everything was unfolding at an even rate, one thing leading to another. Jess's main job was not to forget the cake in the oven; the baking smell was meant to fill the air while Clara laboured.

When the midwives declared Clara's contractions sufficiently strong and close, they permitted her to finally get in the pool. Her relief was immediate. Her eyes were open again and she was smiling, riding her pain, going with it. It was incredible to witness the way she was present yet not present, the way she went so deep inside her brain that the pain of her contractions was a distant thing, something to roll with rather than fight.

Jess had even thought it might be boring, watching and waiting, but there was momentum even when it seemed like nothing was happening. Clara's lumbering body was efficient, and Jess thought back to the advice she'd been given when she was in labour—*Your body knows exactly what to do*—words that hadn't been even vaguely true. Watching Clara now, however, she could see how it worked. Jess understood the physiology—the contractions that open the cervix to let the baby pass through, and the stronger ones that get the baby moving—and now, before her eyes, it all was unfolding, fascinating, and oddly outside of time.

Eventually one of the midwives got in the pool with Clara, and then Nick too in his shorts, and they were all so focussed that Jess didn't even feel weird at the sight of her friend's husband's baggy chest and the grey hair that covered his shoulders. Clara wanted people around her now, and so Nick sat behind her and held her, whispering encouragement in her ear, kissing her hair. And Jess sat just outside the tub, Clara squeezing her hand, the force of her grip the only thing revealing the intensity at the heart of her calm. She was here. This was happening. Jess had never felt so much a part of anything so far outside herself.

The cake was ready shortly before Clara started to push. Jess pried her fingers free and got up to remove it from the oven, surprised to see that she was dripping with sweat. She couldn't find oven mitts, so she used a dish towel to pull the pan from the oven, burning her thumb in the process. "Ouch," she said to herself, and put her thumb in her mouth. She picked up a knife from the dish rack to test the cake— the knife came out clean. Done. It smelled like cloves, apples, and molasses. She turned the oven off.

She went back to the pool. There were puddles on the tarps on the floor and a slight breeze blew in from the yard. It was dark by now, and she could see bats swooping outside. She remembered the night she and Clara slept outside on the balcony, the line between outside and in as blurry as it was right now. Moths were clustered around the lights and there were animal sounds all around her, Clara's moans and growls and the hums and murmurs that encouraged her. It smelled like sweat, like bodies, and Jess didn't know if it was hers or everybody else's, but such distinctions didn't matter now. She noticed the raised moles dotting Nick's arms and shoulders which now wrapped around his wife in the water, holding her steady. One of the midwives announced the time was getting closer. She said to Clara, "You are doing so great. Not much longer."

When the time came, everything changed. The lights got brighter and the world outside drifted away as they all came together in this moment, which was centred on what was happening to Clara's body now. None of this was remotely similar to Jess's births. She'd stopped analogizing. This was a different experience altogether, and she didn't know what she could offer here besides not letting the cake burn, and she'd done that.

And now the world was gone and it was only Clara and the midwife in the water, who had her hands all up inside Clara's body, split open, and the baby was coming, she was coming, Clara delivering the most guttural growl, a noise that might have been the sound of the world being born. And then here was the baby, born in water like a fish. A frog. Amphibious. Blue, then purple, then bright pink, greeting life with a squall. A shock of black hair wet with water and vernix, a wide-open mouth. Everybody waiting for confirmation, the hearing that is believing. This tiny creature, a new life, opening her little mouth and unleashing a sound that birthed the world. A shock of breath and light and air, and then they brought her to her mother, her father. A bundle of baby, limbs so furled that they could hold her to themselves like a package they'd received. All those years of waiting and loss, so much longing, and now they were here, and she was too.

Everyone drifted away from Nick and Clara and their baby girl, leaving them alone in their little universe. Jess went out to the porch to report to Adam on the night as the sun rose orange and rich in the east. She had never seen the sky this way. Day was breaking, an expression she finally understood now that she saw it: the sun shattering the night and all the darkness that had gone before.

"I don't know how she did it—it was like she was possessed," she told Adam. But not by anything evil, or alien, something fighting its way into the world; instead it was something more essential, ethereal. "And everything is okay," she said. "Everything is fine." Jess choked on her words, recalling all her fears, which she'd completely forgotten about while everything was happening. "The baby's here, and she's perfect." Clara had delivered the placenta, but Jess hadn't stuck around to watch that. "No name yet." In fact, since the baby had taken her very first breath, neither of her parents had said a word.

Jess's own family had got through the night just fine, Adam reported. Bella had joined him in bed. Althea, the nanny, would be arriving on schedule at eight o'clock, and everything would proceed from that point; the universe evidently had not received the memo that the whole world had changed. Jess stared at the extraordinary morning sky and wondered how anything could ever be the same again. While the arrival of her own children had been world-changing, certainly, shattering everything she thought she knew or had been expecting, watching the birth of Clara's baby was the complete opposite, an exercise in the connectedness of all things. Now there was this tiny, furious life where there had been nothing before. Jess watched the sunlight spread across the world, trying to decipher the meaning in it all.

She'd been up all night, but her body was still so charged with adrenaline that it hadn't yet occurred to her that she was tired. She went back inside and surveyed the room and its chaos. Clara was wrapped in a blanket sitting outside under the apple tree with her daughter (her daughter!), trying to get her to latch onto her breast. Nick was collapsed on another chair facing them, a cold beer in his hand, nearly naked, but past noticing.

So Jess started assisting with the cleanup, mopping up puddles with old towels, stuffing tarps into garbage bags, returning the room to its natural disorder. She cut the cake into slices and offered it around but there were no takers, and in this, at least, she was gratified. She knew that nobody would want any cake, but there were certain things, Jess was figuring out, you had to let people learn on their own.

The outside scene was a remarkable tableau—the bright blue sky, the tree a brilliant green, the newborn baby at Clara's breast. It was the kind of image that would drive an artist to pick up a paintbrush. Jess snapped a photo instead, Nick and Clara oblivious. They'd forgotten about the world, and it was all right. This part Jess remembered well, although the setting had been different—a sterile hospital room under painful fluorescent lights, bells ringing, alarms sounding, and the rumble of trollies and stretchers going by. But she and Adam had scarcely noticed, because their baby had arrived. Maybe it didn't matter where you were at the moment the world was made entirely new.

The baby was suckling, and Clara looked content, serene. Jess continued to reflect, remembering her own experience. It would be three days before the milk came in, three days in which the baby might just sleep and Clara rest, and they'd think they had a handle on it, they'd start thinking it was easy.

But then on Day Four, the milk would arrive. If being pregnant was like jumping off a cliff, Day Four was crashing down to earth, made even more complicated by hormones. On Day Four, Jess had cried because she finally understood what they meant when they said having a child was like going out into the world with your heart outside your body. How that external heart felt just like a gaping wound, and Jess had also cried because she actually *had* a gaping wound, her vagina held together with crude stitches. Crying, too, because never had she done something so irrevocable, and she knew now that it was all a trap. But she also cried because love had bowled her over, the miracle of this person, this being whom she'd created out of nothing. What had she known about anything until she held her daughter, suddenly privy to the universe's deepest secrets? What had ever mattered before?

It was all so complicated and fraught, the highest mountain she would ever climb, but Jess would not say a word to Clara. She would let her enjoy the high while it lasted, and this would be her gift.

THE TOMB

2016

They had made a date to go on a family outing to the museum, where, in another lifetime, Clara used to teach. It was across the street from where Jess and Clara had first lived together, several lives before that. This was hallowed ground, an area steeped in resonance, with ghosts around every corner and the past nipping at their heels, eager to trip somebody up. All of it was a little bit dangerous.

Adam and Jess were museum patrons, a distinction that meant their names were displayed on the Donor Wall, they received regular invitations to swanky galas in the atrium, and Clara and Nick could get free admission on their pass. Clara hadn't been to the museum since she left her job, even though it would be an ideal place to wander while the baby slept in her carrier—more intellectually fulfilling than the mall, she meant, but then again, the mall was free. She had once worked at the museum, but now she couldn't afford admission.

Nick and Clara had arrived early, seven-month-old Lucinda strapped to Clara's chest, fast asleep. They waited outside for Jess and Adam in the falling snow, and they didn't realize how wet it was until their friends were in front of them, exclaiming, "You're drenched!" Jess hauled Clara in through the sliding doors, her children trailing behind her holding hands, like toy ducks on a string.

There was a scramble at the coat check; Clara wanted to keep her jacket as a layer of protection between Lucinda and the world, but Jess insisted. She had become so command-ing these last few years, as managerial as her job required. Of course, wearing a wet coat around the museum was a stupid idea, Clara admitted, but it was two dollars for each coat, Jess scoffing as though dollars were pennies. She handed over everyone's coats, giving the attendant a twenty.

They headed for the dinosaurs, naturally. The thing most people didn't realize was that only a fraction of these skele-tons were actual dinosaur bones. Most of them were plaster-cast, something that Clara wasn't about to tell Miles and Bella, who could recite paleontological facts forever. Although Miles' recitations were a challenge for him—he had a speech delay—he showed off his knowledge in other ways too, and had used a felt marker to carefully label the dinosaur species printed all over his backpack. Bella had been in paleontology summer camp at this very museum, where she learned shortcuts between the different wings and exhibits. The children essentially guided their tour that morning—final destination: the cafeteria. Bella confided to Clara that the chocolate tarts were delicious.

"I know," said Clara. "I used to work here, remember?"

And Bella looked suitably impressed, which perhaps meant more to Clara than it should have.

When Clara and Jess finally got a moment alone, linger-ing at the back of the crowd before the stegosaurus, Jess asked her, "So, how *are* you?" There was something in her emphasis.

Clara said, "What do you mean?"

Jess's eyes were too wide. "Just asking." She took a step back to stand directly under the wing of a pterosaur, an enormous terrifying bird that could have picked her up with a swoop. She ducked around to escape Clara's scrutiny, but Clara wouldn't let her go.

"I'm good," Clara said carefully, following her. "What's up?" It was more of a demand than a question. Jess had never been very hard to crack. She was already flushed. "You *know*," Clara said. "But *how* do you know?" She followed Jess's glance across the room toward Nick. "He told you."

Jess shrugged and gave an embarrassed smile, making corkscrew gestures with her arms and shoulders, as though if she twisted enough she might disappear, shimmy into a different realm. But she didn't.

"What did Nick tell you?" Clara asked, turning back to look for her husband. Adam was struggling to keep track of the children in the crowd, and Nick was behind all of them, examining the carapace of a prehistoric sea turtle. "When were you talking to Nick?"

"He called me," said Jess. She was anxious now. "Don't tell him I told you. I wasn't supposed to say anything."

"Nick called *you*?" Clara couldn't imagine what could possess him to pick up the phone and dial Jess's number, not even under duress.

"I thought it was weird too," said Jess. They'd made their way to the edge of the room, out of range of the dino enthusiasts and to the fossilized fern display. Nobody ever got excited about fern fossils. "I thought there was something wrong. Like, life-and-death wrong. He was worried. And maybe he wanted someone to talk to? He wanted me to touch base and make sure you were okay."

"So here we are," said Clara.

"Don't be mad," said Jess. "And seriously, I can't believe it. When were you going to tell me? Are you really okay?"

"It's not a death sentence," said Clara.

"Well, what are you going to do?" Jess asked.

"What do you think I'm going to do?" Clara peered under the blanket to check on Lucinda.

Jess said, "But how, Clara?"

Clara stared back at her in disbelief. What kind of a question was that?

Nick, Adam, and the children came over to join them. They'd exhausted these dinosaurs and wanted to move on.

Clara looked at Nick. "You told her."

Jess said, "I didn't mean to—"

Clara said, "No. Stop now. The two of you with your collaborating. You're both supposed to be on my side." She could see by their expressions that she was scaring them.

"But of course we are," said Jess, sounding desperate. "He was only trying to help."

Clara turned to Nick. "This was you *helping*?"

He looked sheepish, an expression Clara hated. It was the look he wore when he had given up responsibility for something he'd done. "You weren't supposed to know," he said.

"You think that makes a difference?" Adam was leading Bella and Miles away from the tension, and Clara wanted to get away too.

"I didn't know what else to do," Nick confessed.

"You could have asked me," said Clara.

"I did," he told her. "Really. In all kinds of ways. I've been trying, you haven't been answering." He said it again. "I didn't know what else to do." Jess was beside him, looking concerned.

"Well, how about I leave you to figure something out," she said, walking away so Nick and Jess could continue their speculations as to her mental health and capacity for good choices, because she didn't want to hear it. They'd get to feel wise and superior, and she wouldn't have to stutter so stupidly as she struggled to defend herself. Did they realize how hard it was to articulate anything on so little sleep? She couldn't win this one. No matter what she said, they'd put it down to her condition. And now they were holding that against her too.

She disappeared into the old wing of the museum, which had been the way to her office back when she'd had one, although she shared it with seven other people. The baby was on her chest, and she realized that Nick had the backpack with the diapers, blankets, change of clothes. To be caught so unprepared with a baby was a kind of emergency, but Clara tried not to think about that. As long as she kept walking, Lucinda would sleep. Clara contemplated making her way down the old staircase with its century of grooves, all the way to the exit, but Jess had her coat-check tag. She had put herself in a precarious situation, as dependent as a child. She didn't even carry a purse anymore; her wallet and keys were kept in the backpack that functioned as diaper bag. She had two free hands, for the moment, but nothing to hold.

So she went up to the third floor instead, away from the crowds, the dinosaurs, the families cruising for animal skulls and wolverine dioramas, brushing away sand to reveal dinosaur thigh bones. She crossed over to the Greek, Roman, and Egyptian rooms, where she taught back before she really knew how much she stood to lose. It was another life she could barely remember, supplanted by years of struggle and then Lucinda and motherhood, a whole new civilization to discover.

In the Egyptian room, people were staring at the preserved body of a boy who'd died thousands of years ago as though they were waiting for something. There were mummified cats too, and birds, and other objects discovered in tombs. A small girl in a yellow dress was staring at the display, looking confused. She asked the adult holding her hand, "Whose mommy is that?" and Clara thought of the picture book by P. D. Eastman.

There was a tomb, a replica made of stone with symbols etched upon the walls. Clara ducked to get through the doorframe. She used to have children do crayon rubbings in here, all of them crowded inside, trying to carve out their bit of space and wall. The effect had been claustrophobic, but now the tomb was empty except for her and Lucinda. The stone walls filtered out the sounds of the museum and everything was quiet.

Was anybody—Nick, Jess—coming after her? And did she even want them to?

Clara knew that her behaviour wasn't rational, that escaping to an Egyptian tomb would do nothing to lend credence to her insistence that she was of sound mind, but she had to get away, and she was tired after climbing the stairs and standing around for so long with the baby on her chest. Sinking down onto the cool stone floor, she leaned back and relaxed. This made the baby start fussing, but this was the idea; she wanted Lucinda unfurled, awake. The baby was hungry, and Clara could give her what she needed, and life could really be so simple.

———

Four months ago, when Clara began to understand what was happening, she ignored it, hoping the problem would just go away, which was not entirely delusional. The number of times the problem (even when it wasn't a problem) had gone away made this a statistical likelihood. The situation felt surreal, but it would have anyway, because Lucinda was four months old and Clara was delirious from lack of sleep.

She was having trouble processing. She had fainted, and she was anemic, which didn't make sense. Then the doctor called her back for an appointment. Was there a possibility she was pregnant? She said no way. She was breastfeeding, and Lucinda was just four months old. Not to mention that she had spent years completely barren and the odds of her conceiving on her own were next to nil.

But she *was* pregnant. And when the doctor told her this, she started to cry, and he presumed she was upset, because what woman with a four-month-old baby wants to be pregnant?

"I realize this is unexpected," the doctor said, "And not necessarily welcome news."

"But I'm that woman," said Clara.

"What?"

Clara was perched on the edge of the examination table and she moved softly back and forth to keep Lucinda asleep in the carrier on her chest. She said, "I used to visualize. There were books that said if you saw it happen, it could come true, and I did it. I imagined being here, and you telling me I was pregnant. By accident. We have been through this so many times in my mind, you and me, although you probably didn't know."

The doctor handed her a tissue, and Clara wiped her eyes. The tears weren't exactly heartfelt, but since Lucinda was born, she tended to run like a tap.

The doctor wanted to refer her for an ultrasound, but Clara said not to bother.

"I've been here before too," she said. "My pregnancies don't keep." She left with the referral and promised to make the call, which was a lie. What she was going to do was take the iron supplements, because she didn't want to faint again, particularly not while holding Lucinda.

She said nothing to Nick. It didn't seem dishonest because they'd been occupying separate spheres since the baby was born, since even before that, if Clara was honest. He was busy at work, booked with seasonal parties and late nights all the time. She hardly saw him. Lucinda was her planet and she was in her orbit, and Nick and the rest of the world were far away.

Clara kept waiting for something to happen. She was well versed in miscarriages, but there was no sign. She was tired and slept when her baby slept, but she would have been doing that anyway, particularly as Lucinda didn't sleep at night. So the weeks crept along and Clara was only vaguely keeping track of time, finally booking the appointment because it had been long enough now. She wasn't so far gone to be that irresponsible.

So she went for the scan and of course, something was wrong. She knew it by the blank expression on the technician's face, the way it fell over her like a mask, and when Clara saw it, she realized she'd been fooling herself. It turned out she was not hardened enough for this to be old hat, to not be devastated by what was about to happen to her body.

To think that she could be here alone, suffering without a hand to hold, without Nick to put his arms around her while she cried. But even if she'd been honest and he knew the real reason for her appointment, he couldn't have come. He was at home with the baby they already had.

"This is your first ultrasound?" the technician asked, moving her wand across Clara's stomach, back and forth, squinting at the image on the screen.

"Well, for this pregnancy," said Clara. "But I mean, this isn't my first time. It's happened before." She wanted to ask the technician to just wipe the gel off her belly and let her get dressed again, let her go home to lose her pregnancy in private and with her dignity intact, before she fell to pieces about a baby she never even knew she wanted.

"Twins?" the technician asked.

"What?" Clara said. "Oh, shit." And then she started to cry, this time the emotions so far beyond her comprehension that she couldn't have said what she was feeling. There was a whole other spectrum for moments like this.

So instead she started babbling through her tears. Never in a million years had she imagined twins, she told the technician. Stupid really, because they'd done IVF with Lucinda and that increased the likelihood, but Clara had been so stuck on the miracle of just one baby that she hadn't allowed herself to consider any more. This time, however, it made no sense: she'd conceived these babies naturally. How on earth had she conceived these babies naturally?

"Bodies can do surprising things," the technician told Clara, still exploring the wonders of her womb. "Nobody really understands." She kept searching. "There," she said, holding the wand still, pointing to the screen, at an incomprehensible blob. "Baby A, and Baby B." She tried to find a better angle. "Two healthy babies," she said. "Fourteen weeks, more or less. But don't tell anyone I said that. Don't tell anyone I said anything. You'll need your doctor to go over your results."

Clara's head was swimming. She was thinking of this baby that was supposed to have disappeared, and how it had turned into two. And if she held on longer, would there be another one? Was that how these things worked?

"You really didn't know?" the technician asked. "Because most of the time with twins, you feel terrible. So tired you can't see straight."

Clara said, "I have a five-month-old at home."

"Jesus Christ." The technician recovered. "Well, then," she said, only now conscious of her slip, never mind that she had been breaching protocol throughout the appointment. "I mean, it's a blessing, it is." Clara wished she would stop talking.

What was she going to tell Nick? What were they going to do? Three babies. What a disaster—but not completely. This *was* a blessing. Clara knew the technician wasn't wrong.

She felt like a pinball, bouncing from one side to another, bells ringing, lights flashing. The child she had imagined as an only, now with siblings. A pregnancy that had happened just like anybody else's. An "oops baby." Two oops babies. This was not a terrible thing.

But it was terrifying. And these were the thoughts she entertained once she left the clinic, on the streetcar ride back across town, where her husband waited, unaware. He'd just spent a morning with their baby daughter, and he'd be feeling good about holding up his end of the load because he'd changed a diaper. He didn't have a clue.

How had she been so stupid that she hadn't realized what was happening? It was a question that didn't need answering.

She'd been lost in newborn moo-baa-lalala-land. Lucinda was like a drug, and Clara couldn't get enough of her scent, and her sounds, and the feel of her skin against her body. Since Lucinda was born, there had been nothing else. Clara had shut out the world. And what else had been going on without her noticing? She thought of frogs raining down from the heavens, a kind of prophecy. Was that from a fairy tale, the Bible, or just that Tom Cruise film? She was about to open her front door right now, and what would she find inside? A plague of locusts? So many possibilities because everything was on the table.

But she got home, and it was ordinary, the way she'd left it. Piles of books and newspapers, flyers and magazines, and the usual things scattered everywhere. Everything Clara needed was usually within arm's length, and she only had to dig to find it.

Nick was asleep, lying spread-out on the couch, Lucinda sleeping on his chest. Oh, this poor man, Clara thought as she watched him. What if she'd left him there in his pub in Derbyshire with that tiny little flat upstairs? His life had been far from perfect, he would tell you, and Clara hadn't had to drag him here kicking and screaming. But he didn't like his job here, organizing hotel parties. None of this was what he had planned for.

Recently he'd proposed moving into a caravan, and she liked the idea of wheels rumbling beneath the floor. A rumble would put one baby, Lucinda, to sleep, but then she wondered if it could put three babies to sleep. Where did you put three babies in a caravan? Where did you put three babies at all? Clara imagined telling her sisters the news. They'd give each other that look. *This was going to happen to you all along*, they'd say. *You're going to turn into everybody else.*

There's a house for sale, they'd tell her, *just down the concession.*

She watched Nick and Lucinda sleeping, listening to their quiet parallel breathing.

So much was about bodies. How she fed and bathed Lucinda, changed her diapers, and the way that she and Nick found solace and pleasure in acts just as intimate. The way she knew the smell of his sweat, his piss, the way he held his head when he was tired. It was all bodies, the way they came to each other, what they took from each other. Clara thought of Lucinda at her breast—she wondered how Nick had got her down to sleep without it. The way her daughter overwhelmed her senses, the smell of digested milk on her bedsheets, and how she inhaled it, slightly rank and wholly sweet, thinking that if there was such a thing as an essence, this was it. Watching her family sleep, conscious of the life growing inside her, Clara considered, What if this was the universe, and who was she to find fault with that?

Nick's eyes opened as if he'd heard something.

"Well, I'm about to blow your mind," Clara said.

"What?" He was struggling to lift his head, but he couldn't move or he'd wake Lucinda.

"How was she?" Clara asked, handing him a pillow so he'd be more comfortable.

"She was fine. Went down easy." He said, "Blow my mind?"

"About my appointment," Clara said.

His eyes widened. "What's wrong?"

"Nothing's wrong." And then she began backtracking because that wasn't true. "I mean, nobody's going to die," she said.

"What is it?" She knew that look—Nick was steeling himself. It was the way he used to flare when toughs got rough at his pub, how he'd just look harder. Except now he was supine with a beautiful baby snoring on his chest.

"I'm pregnant," she said.

"Clare," he said, like a warning.

"With twins."

"Are you fucking kidding me?" He had to whisper. And what would he have done if he had been able to get up, she wondered, if he wasn't immobilized by Lucinda? Would he have sprung to his feet and punched a wall?

He said, "How?"

She said, "I don't even know. The usual way, I suspect."

"But I thought—"

"Me too," she said. "The universe is messing with us."

"With twins," Nick said. "Like, two."

"For real. And I'm fourteen weeks now. And they're growing well, the technician said. Off the record, I mean, but I could see. I honestly never thought I'd get this far."

"You knew?" he demanded, sitting up quickly, waking the baby up.

"I kind of knew," she admitted. "But I didn't think anything was going to happen. The doctor recommended iron supplements. I've been taking them."

"You saw a doctor?" Nick was furious. "All these weeks and you've never said a word?"

"I didn't think it was going to matter," she said. "I was sure we were going to lose this one too."

"So you said nothing?"

"I've had a lot on my mind." Lucinda was warming up from confused snuffling into a full-blown wail. Nick tried to hand her over, but Clara waved him away. "*You* woke her up," she said.

"She's hungry," he said. The default, but Clara didn't move. "Clare, what honestly is this?"

"What is what?" Lucinda had started to scream.

"Seriously, just take her. I've had her on my own all day."

"So what?" said Clara, unmovable. "I have her on my own every day."

"And now you're bloody having twins?" said Nick. "That's a fantastic plan." He was shouting over the baby's screams. "Just take her," he said, and she did. She unbuttoned her shirt, unsnapped her bra, and the baby found her way. Now it was easy, natural, a relief.

She said, "It wasn't exactly a plan. I mean, it happened. I'm pregnant. I'm as stunned as you are."

"I just don't know what you want me to do with this."

"You don't have to do anything," she said. "It's not going to make any difference. The thing is the thing."

"But the thing is twins?" said Nick. "Who has twins? Fucking twins!"

"My mother had twins," said Clara, and what this meant exactly suddenly dawned on her for the first time. Family history meant that twins were genetically more likely, and Clara also couldn't help but consider what the news must have meant to her mother, and her father too. By the time Clara was born, her twin sisters were an established fact, a unique quirk of their family, but eventually it had ceased to matter much because the girls didn't look alike, even less so as they grew into women. Had this news, all those years ago, also blown her parents' minds?

"It's not going to happen," Nick said. "It's just not possible."

"I'm not sure we get much say regardless."

"You mean me," he said. "*I* don't get much say, do I?" When she said nothing in response, he continued. "Clare, I don't think we can do this. I mean, I don't think I can. And you—" He shook his hand at her, as though she were already a lost cause. "I mean, it's not just the twins. It's the money. Kids cost money."

"Not necessarily," she said, realizing that he was going to make her fight for this. She was going to talk herself into it, and then she'd have to bring him along with her. She hoped she could, because the other possibility was that he would walk away from her forever. So she told him, "You could leave. Rather than us having it out like this. Rather than you holding it over my head. I'd even understand." She wasn't bluffing. She didn't want Nick bound to her because he thought he had to be. The last thing she wanted was that.

"But I can't," he said.

"You could," she told him.

"Don't you know me at all?"

The baby was still suckling, and Clara tried to relax. She couldn't carry all this tension with her. What if stress was a chemical that got passed on in mother's milk? She knew there was some truth to this. She closed her eyes, just like the baby.

But Nick was suddenly there in front of her, flapping his arms. "No, no, no!" he was shouting. "You can't do this now. You can't deliver news like that and then just disappear. We've got to deal with it."

She said, "I'm here." Eyes open.

"You're not at all," he said. "Clare, what's happening to you?"

She said, "I'm having twins."

He said, "What, like a side effect?"

"I don't know what you're talking about." Sometimes Clara felt as though language had become incomprehensible, as well as human behaviour. It was probably a natural conse-quence of never leaving the house, but she wasn't sure this was a bad thing. Ever read a newspaper? Why would anyone ever leave the house if they didn't have to?

"I feel like we've been here before," she said, closing her eyes again. She was so tired. "So are you in or are you in?"

"What kind of a person do you think I am?" Nick didn't sound angry anymore, even when he said, "I notice that you didn't give me any other option."

She pulled herself awake. Lucinda was slowing down, nearly done. "It's not like this is a tragedy," she told him. "Like an earthquake, or a genocide. An airplane disappearing from the sky. Or an erupting volcano, with ash that sweeps an entire city away. Those are the sorts of things we should spend our shock on. The rest of it, it's just life. This news, twins, is a *gift*, if you look at it."

"I'm looking," he said. Lucinda shat her diaper, and they both tried to pretend it hadn't happened. He said, "How are we going to make it work?"

"With some planning," she said. "The rest we could play by ear. I don't know. People manage. It's what people do. The trouble with now is that everybody thinks too much."

"But what about the money?" said Nick. She knew she was trampling on his dreams. He hadn't given up on the idea of opening his own business, a bar or a bistro. The work he was doing now was soulless, and the only people he spoke to were brides' parents looking for deals, and the people who cleaned those gaudy floral carpets. Stacks of chairs being wheeled in, set up, then stacked and wheeled out again. Once a mother-of-the-bride had slapped him because of a foul-up with the head table's floral arrangements. Other people his age were close to retirement, but for him it got further away every year.

"I don't know about the money," she said. "But we can make it work. Kids don't need competitive gymnastics and chess lessons. I mean, does anyone?" She thought about Jess and Adam, their whole life so carefully structured. Absolutely nothing grew wild. "We could live on love." She knew she sounded stupid.

"You can't eat love," said Nick.

"Then we'd live on lentils." He smiled, and she smiled back. "It doesn't make sense, I know, any of it—the pregnancy, twins, that I didn't tell you. But even *this* doesn't make sense." She nodded her head towards Lucinda. "That she's here. That she's real. Do you see why I'm confused?" Nick nodded. "For so long, I wanted this. All of this. And wanting became my reason, the whole point. But to want and then to get—it's mind-bending. What do you do when you don't have to want anymore? And then to get and get. It's like praying for rain, but then the creeks burst."

"But this is not a tragedy," said Nick.

Clara said, "I really don't think it is. I mean, it's shocking. And it's going to be hard. But imagine if two years ago someone had told us I'd be pregnant and we'd be waffling. Nick, I was crazy. You remember. And now, it's just that I'm a bit stunned. How are we going to make it work? I don't know. But we'll do something."

She added, "I'm sorry, though. You didn't know what you were in for. *I* didn't know what you were in for."

Nick said, "I *like* not knowing what I'm in for, actually. Most of the time. Life turns out to be a grand surprise."

Clara got up and sat beside her husband on the couch, the baby in her arms, wide-eyed and calm. She felt as if the couch was a raft, the weather was good, and everything they needed was here. There would be no land in sight for days, but who cared? "I like being a family with you."

He said, "Me too." He leaned over and sniffed her hair, which she'd washed that morning on the occasion of going out into the world. He kissed her neck, her ear. She batted him away.

"This is the kind of thing that got us in trouble in the first place."

"Trouble's not all bad, then."

"The baby needs changing."

"I did it last time," Nick said. This was usually Clara's line. But if they waited any longer, Lucinda would do it again, and shit would come seeping out of her onesie, down her legs and up her back. "Just go," said Nick.

She went to their bedroom. The room had been crowded before the baby. Now, piles of laundry towered on every surface, and racks hung with drying diapers covered the floor. She changed Lucinda on the bed, which was made, at least, because Nick had been home this morning. It was the one clear space in all the mess. Nick stood in the doorway and watched as she took off Lucinda's clothes, cleaned her up, replaced the dirty diaper with a clean one from yet another pile of stuff.

"I think we're going to run out of room here," Nick said, and he was only kind of kidding.

"There's room," Clara assured him. And there was. There was another bedroom in the front that was going to be Lucinda's room when she got bigger, and there was the basement too, a dingy space, but they could make it work. "Part of it, too," she said, "is a question of getting organized. Actually putting some of this stuff away." She gestured towards the dirty laundry and realized that this was all on her. Everything was. She could do it.

"Hey, I need you to help me, though," Nick said. Clara could tell that he didn't want to have to say this. She could see it in the way he held his head, the tension in his shoulders, how he hesitated. "You need to keep me in the loop," he said. "You can't go away like you did."

"I was here," she protested.

"But you weren't," he said. "Maybe I lost you in the piles of laundry, I don't know. But I feel like it's been ages since I saw you, and then you came home and told me we're having twins. I need you to be *here*, with me."

"I'm here," she said, standing before him and handing him the baby dressed in a fresh sleeper.

He said, "I want to take care of you. To give you what you need. But you have to tell me things. We have to stay connected."

"We'll have date nights?" she offered.

He gave her a pointed look. "I mean more than that. It's you I love, Clare," he said. "It's you. The point of origin, of everything."

"I love you too," she said. "I love you too." She repeated it like a mantra.

They were going to be all right.

In the tomb, Lucinda squawked, attracting the attention of a passing security guard with a walkie-talkie. Stooping over to see inside, he backstepped when he realized it was a woman unbuttoning her shirt and averted his eyes. Clara tried to ignore him.

He said, "There's a nursing mothers' centre on the second floor."

"Yep," said Clara, securing Lucinda's latch, "But I'm good here."

"You might be more comfortable," said the guard.

She said, "I'm comfortable." She knew her rights: she could breastfeed anywhere. Even in an Egyptian tomb, or at least a replica. They might have a case against an actual historical artifact, but she'd be willing to argue it. With her background in lactating and archeology, she'd be uniquely qualified for such a position. It might be the one thing in the world Clara was really meant to do. Apart from this, of course: feeding her baby now, feeling grateful for the wall that kept her posture straight. She needed some structure, it was true. She was all slump these days. She had this vision of herself as a worn-out sofa, barely held together, mostly stuffing but comfortable. She was comfortable, and what was wrong with that?

The security guard had left her to her business and Clara closed her eyes and listened to Lucinda's snuffling. They were going to be all right, she'd convinced herself—but then Nick had called Jess. It was a sign of desperation. Had things gotten that bad?

There was a gauge in Clara's mind these days that flicked between excitement and terror. She was supposed to have been content with one baby because she had nearly not had any, but she always knew it wouldn't be enough; she knew that, for the rest of her life, she'd feel the dull ache of longing for another, and that there would be a hole in their family. She would've had to live with that, and so too would she find a way to live with what fate was delivering now, which was more than she or anybody needed, but she would find space in her arms to hold it all.

And here the dial moved. She was already so stretched— what was going to happen to Lucinda? What would Clara lose in nurturing a pair of newborn siblings just as Lucinda was beginning to discover the world? Clara thought about attachment parenting, and all the ideals she'd inhaled, things that were so instinctive—co-sleeping and babywearing and breastfeeding and responding to a child's needs. How did you do that with two, with three? Could she be the kind of parent she wanted to be?

But somewhere between the two extremes there was a middle ground, a place where Clara could breathe, and think, *Yes, this is how life happens.* This was her good fortune, her extravagant blessing, and she would take each moment as it came, and she would be challenged, exasperated, exuberant, and exhausted, but it would be okay. One step at a time was the way forward, and she could do that. But only if she knew for certain that Nick was walking alongside her.

Lucinda burped and Clara looked down at her, tucked against her. Right here with the baby on her chest, the other two growing inside her, was as close together as they would ever be. It was possible that Clara's arms would never be so free again, able to hold all her children at once, so she wrapped those arms around them now, around her baby, and her belly, and herself. Her self.

A child peeked in, confused to find a woman with a baby, unsure what parts of the scene, the diorama before him, were part of the display. Clara smiled. She didn't want to make him feel uncomfortable, but she didn't want to move either because Lucinda was back on the boob, suckling now for comfort. "You can come in if you want to," she said. "We're just sitting."

She kept forgetting that she didn't want to be left alone after all. No, she wanted company, but perhaps she wanted it too much. The boy sensed her longing and backed out slowly, and she heard the scramble of his footsteps as he hurried over to a parent, a responsible adult who came to look inside and find out what the boy was talking about, the half-dressed woman and the baby in the tomb.

Clara ignored the curious adult and instead stared down at Lucinda, who was gazing back up at her, coming off the breast to smile, this incredible baby that Clara had grown all by herself once science had given her a jump-start.

And then Jess was there. "Hey you," Clara said, easy. Jess would always be the one to find her.

"They have a nursing station downstairs."

Clara looked at her, incredulous. Her too?

"Nick went to look in the minerals gallery," Jess said, "because Lucinda likes shiny things, but I knew I'd find you up here." When Clara didn't respond, Jess said, "Clara, I can't keep chasing you. I don't have the energy. It's too hard right now. It's all too much."

"I know." It was a relief that Jess was here, so much easier than it had been to wait for her. "But sometimes there's just this pressure, like a weight, like the whole world's about to come crashing down. It's excruciating. I just had to get away. It's hard to explain."

"But you don't have to," said Jess, settling in beside her. "I know exactly what that's like." Jess had fallen apart after Miles was born, though it was all over and done with by the time she reappeared in Clara's life, the whole experience neatly tied up with a bow. "And maybe Nick called me because he knew I'd understand. He's such a rock, Clara, he really is. He thought it was postpartum depression, and he was scared. He thought something was wrong."

"But nothing's wrong," said Clara. "For the first time, maybe ever, it feels like nothing's wrong."

"These last few months have been a lot," said Jess. "I think they are for any new mom. And now *twins*. I almost didn't believe him."

"I almost don't believe it either."

"And I'm not really sure that you're actually okay," Jess said carefully, looking around the tomb.

"I just couldn't handle it, you and him," Clara said. "Talking about me like I'm a child." Lucinda was looking around now, eyes wide. A tomb was a funny place to be.

"Nobody thinks you're a child," said Jess. "Nick's just worried. And we should probably go and find him." She pulled her phone out of her bag, then put it back. "Why does nobody in your family have a cellphone?"

Clara shrugged. "We have one, we just keep losing it. Anyway, it's hard to get a signal in a tomb." Lucinda latched on to her breast again.

"You aren't always in a tomb, though," said Jess.

Clara said, "Maybe I'm thinking of staying here."

Jess said, "Come on."

Clara said, "I need you to trust me."

"Of course I do."

"You don't," said Clara. She closed her eyes as the baby fed, feeling the ease of her milk's flow. "You and Nick both think I'm crazy. Which will probably be a foregone conclusion if I have these babies, and you two aren't there for me. I need you."

"But we need you too," said Jess. "Can't you see that? How every time you run away or disappear, it doesn't get easier. It hurts, Clara. And I just can't keep doing it over and over. I can't."

Clara kept her eyes closed and focussed on the steady rhythm of Lucinda drinking her milk, the pull she felt deep inside her body. Jess's voice was far away, on the periphery of her life now. Things had shifted, things were always shifting, nothing ever stayed the same.

"You're lucky," Jess continued, off in the distance. "I don't know that I've been clear enough about that. I know it hasn't been easy, but you've got Nick, and this baby, and the other ones you're going to have."

"I'm spoiled for babies." Lucinda came off the nipple. Clara opened her eyes.

"We need to get back," Jess said. "He's going to know you're not in Minerals, and he's going to think you left. And the kids are getting hungry."

"I want lunch too," said Clara, refastening the straps on the baby carrier.

"How are you feeling?" asked Jess, hauling her up to her feet. "Really?"

"Good," said Clara. "Really. Nobody believes me." Not Nick, the doctors, or her midwives. Every time she said she was feeling good, they saw it as proof that she was delusional. "Hungry, though." Jess could grasp that. "I'm eating for three. Actually, four," because she was Lucinda's food supply too. "I've got energy though, and my moods are stable." The hormones she was taking during her fertility treatments had been much more difficult to endure than her pregnancies. She looked at Jess. "I was going to tell you."

"Well, I guess so," said Jess, "because at a certain point you'd have to."

"No, I meant, I *wanted* to tell you," said Clara. They were walking through Egypt, Greece, and sub-Saharan Africa now. "But I think I was trying to figure it all out for myself first. I'm *still* trying to do that. And there's never really an optimum time to spring that kind of news."

"Because you knew I was going to freak out," said Jess.
"Yeah."

"And I did freak out, when Nick told me," said Jess. "Of course I did. Because it's always so much. Sometimes it just seems like motherhood has taken you over completely." They were making their way down the stairs, where totem poles rose up to the glass ceiling. Ideas about the top of the totem pole were a cultural misunderstanding, Clara had learned somewhere along the line. It was the figures near the bottom that had a kind of supremacy, the necessary strength for a foundation. You could climb to the top of a totem pole, and where would you be? That much closer to the sky. But then what?

"Maybe it has," Clara dared to admit, once they reached the main floor. "Taken me over, I mean. But is that such a bad thing? Because it's really like I finally know what the point is, of my life, of everything. Nothing else I've ever done has seemed as meaningful as being this baby's mother." She wrapped her arms to hold Lucinda close. She was being provocative, but it was the truth. Even though so many women had worked so hard so that there could be other choices, Clara was choosing this one.

"Life is long," said Jess. "Remember that? You're the one who told me. A baby can't be everything, not forever."

"I never said anything about forever," said Clara. "I'm thinking about right now, these few months ahead. For the first time in my life, I think I know what it means to be present. I'm here. I'm really here."

"But see, that's what we weren't sure of," said Jess as they arrived at the atrium, where the others were waiting.

Bella and Miles were squirming and wriggling, impatient, Adam on his phone again, and Nick all out of place. She'd left him all alone, Clara realized, and she wondered how she would feel if their roles were reversed. It had been a very long time since Nick hadn't been where she needed him to be. She said to Jess, "I swear," as everyone scrambled to their feet at the sight of them. She said to the rest of the group, "I'm sorry. I just had to get away from the dinosaurs." Grabbing Nick's hand, she squeezed it and repeated, "I'm sorry." He squeezed it back. Thank goodness he squeezed it back. She might run away, and even if he couldn't find her he'd wait for her forever. She'd never been so sure of anything, and that was why they worked.

Jess said, "I suspect lunch will probably cure all."

Bella slipped in between Clara and Nick and nudged her. "Remember? The tarts?"

"I remember," Clara said. She smiled at this funny little girl who had her mother's face, reminding Clara of all the stories about her friend that she knew but would never tell.

HERE AND NOW

MONDAY, MAY 14, 2016

The Charlotte Nordstrom Institute for Folk and Fairy Tales' Board of Directors was threatening a coup. Jess knew this sounded over-the-top, too much like her colleagues Nancy and Imelda, who had imagined the carpet was a conspiracy, but it was true. The Board of the institute where Jess had worked for nearly her entire career, where she had been expecting to succeed the executive director, Edith Morningside, when she retired in June, had decided to shift in a new direction. They wanted to hire somebody's nephew, a young hotshot, Elliott Lubbock III, a man just barely out of school. But he had done a co-op program in information studies, spent a few seasons dabbling in fintech, and now he was looking for a new pursuit. The general feeling was that he had connections that could bring in a lot of money. The Board chair had paraded him through the office the week before, where he shook hands and was affable, as if it were an election. And maybe it was.

"Plus, he's a man," Barbara "Babs" Corningware, another Board member, pointed out. "Might be nice to add some diversity." Everybody who worked for the Institute was a woman, except for Todd in IT.

And because of the composition of the Board—seven men and three women, every one of them white—nobody seemed to find Babs's perspective unreasonable; or if anybody did, they kept their mouth shut. As did Jess, because she served on the Board as a non-voting member, and if she spoke up, it would be seen as speaking on her own behalf, instead of in the Institute's best interest.

But it was both. Jess had been instrumental in growing the Institute, in modernizing its practices and raising its profile, making it relevant, creating vital community connections. And it was a fact that Jess could have been making more money someplace else, but the value of the work she was doing and its extraordinary nature had always seemed entirely worth the difference.

This made it particularly galling now that the years she'd invested in the Institute, along with her value and experience, were being wholly dismissed.

"It's infuriating," said Miranda, a librarian who'd been working there almost as long as Jess. "He wouldn't know the difference between a folk tale and a Little Golden Book." They were having their standing Monday lunch date at the restaurant down the street, a place specializing in healthy salads and vegan rice bowls. "It's sexism, it's nepotism. It's all the isms."

"He's such a worm," said Nahlah, who was fervently on Jess's side. Nahlah, Jess's neighbour, had joined the Institute part-time three years ago when Jess hired her to work in fundraising. She had worked in philanthropy before her kids were born, and she wanted to get back into it now that they were in school. This was not nepotism necessarily, because Nahlah's work was excellent, though Jess supposed it depended on your perspective.

They talked about what was now her impossible quandary. In order to fight for the job she wanted, Jess would have to backtrack on so many of the gains she'd made—she'd need to work late, give up her Wednesday half-days, and the one day a week she worked from home. The Board would be expecting a skills upgrade. Edith herself, who was actually on Jess's side, had tried to pitch the situation as not a big deal—"You've just got to prove yourself," she said, shrugging. Like Elliott Lubbock III, Edith was unmarried and had no children, and so she too had had less to balance in the whole work/life conundrum. Unlike Elliott Lubbock III, however, Edith did not claim that sleep was unnecessary and wasn't forever rhapsodizing about "24/7 pingability." Elliott Lubbock III loved a buzzword.

"I really do want to hear about the party, though," said Nahlah. The celebration for Lucinda's first birthday had been on Saturday. Nahlah and Miranda both knew Jess had advised Clara that a big party wasn't necessary. Clara didn't need the extra stress, and Lucinda was too young to understand any of it. First-birthday parties were really for the parents, even though a better celebration might have been to put the kid to bed early and indulge in a bottle of wine. But Clara wasn't drinking, and nobody ever put Lucinda to bed. Any time they tried, she spent the whole night screaming.

"We love having her with us," Clara insisted when Jess would suggest that a firm bedtime might help establish a routine, and Jess might have called bullshit if she'd heard that from any other mother. With Clara, however, she believed it. There was something in her delivery, her ease in the moment as she held her child in her arms. So languid, cool, and certain—sometimes Jess could see traces of the long-gone Clara in the woman her friend had become, that radiant girl who'd saved her one night a thousand years ago.

Jess's advice to Clara about first-birthday parties was also self-serving. The last thing Jess wanted to do on a Saturday afternoon was attend a small child's birthday party. Her own children would only be bored and stir up trouble when there was no one their age to play with. But because accepting advice was against Clara's religion, the party would proceed.

Adam buttoned up the clean shirt he'd just ironed. "You don't need to get all fancy," Jess had told him. A T-shirt would suffice at Nick and Clara's, and Clara would likely be wearing no clothes at all—she'd spent most of the last year feeding Lucinda, flashing her giant breasts unabashedly, magnificent and horrifying at once.

But Adam dressed up anyway, because he wasn't great with advice either, and pleats were in his programming. He'd taken Miles to hockey that morning while Jess and Bella did the gymnastics run, one of Jess's favourite parts of the week because she got to spend fifty minutes in a nearby café with a giant mug of coffee reading the new Lauren Groff, which was sprawling and resplendent.

Jess couldn't recall if Clara had attended Bella's first birthday, which they'd held at a restaurant since their old place was too small for the occasion. It had been so long ago. And even if she could remember, it didn't matter, because missing Lucinda's party was not an option. The party was a big deal; they'd sent invitations in the mail.

Nick greeted them at the door, urging them inside, reminding them to keep their shoes on because everyone was out back. Everything was just getting started.

The place was crowded, but it always was, because the

apartment was so small. There were no other children, except Lucinda, who had learned to stand, was even taking tentative steps, hanging onto the edges of furniture. Clara didn't have mom friends, not the way most women did, not the way Jess had. She might have acquired some, but she'd been put off by the mothers she met who heard her story and said things like, "I wouldn't wish that on my worst enemy." And then everything started going wrong, and her pregnancy became so complicated and all-consuming that there wasn't a chance for diversions like music class, indoor play-spaces, and the library storytimes that had helped save Jess's life when she'd been home with her own kids.

So it was a different crowd, a strange vibe for a child's party, but Nick had the hospitality right—it was his profession. He put a drink in Jess's hand, Pimm's with berries and mint. He'd even remembered juice for the kids, and there were bowls of chips on all the tables, so Bella and Miles were happy enough, wholly absorbed by the tablets they'd brought. Jess went outside, greeting Clara's sisters briefly on her way to Clara, who was sitting in the corner under the apple tree. Not the guest of honour exactly, but she might have been, looking queenly, in the Victorian sense, laid out on her chaise in a blue caftan over yoga pants. She was the centre of a small group wrapped up in conversation, but when Jess caught her attention, Clara's eyes lit up. "You!" she exclaimed.

"Don't get up," said Jess.

"Don't worry, I can't," said Clara, shifting to sit up higher, her physical discomfort evident in her movements and the expression on her face. She held her arms out for a hug. "My best friend," she told the others—Pam, who lived upstairs, and Emily, one of Nick's co-workers.

"Happy birth-day to you," said Jess. "To both of us, really."

And Clara explained how Jess had been there a year earlier when Lucinda came into the world. "She cleaned out the pool," she said. "It was disgusting, apparently. The nicest thing that anybody's ever done for me." She smiled. It had been so important for her to have Jess there when Lucinda was born, but this time everything was different. If Clara had a birth vision, she wasn't sharing it, and her health had been so unstable. Jess had offered to be there again, or else to take Lucinda when the time came, but Clara was being vague about her plans, refusing to commit to anything.

The others got up and gave Jess space. "Adam and the kids are inside," said Jess, finding room to perch on the end of the chaise beside Clara's swollen ankles. "How are you?" She could infer by how pale and tired Clara looked, but she wanted to hear what her answer would be.

Clara shrugged. "We're hanging in there." For so long, she'd felt excellent, then one day her iron levels plummeted and she fainted at the bus stop. Her breast milk dried up and she was devastated, even though Jess tried to convince her that weaning wasn't really a big deal. Lucinda was growing well and had already started eating solids, but Clara would not be reassured.

Clara never worried about the things that really mattered. She felt terrible, she'd confess on her worst days, and she looked awful too. Her body was swollen, the circles under her eyes heavy and dark, and her hair was falling out. She ached when she moved and she ached when she lay still, her body spread all around her, but on her face Jess could still, unmistakably, read contentment.

"I was feeling strange last night," Clara was saying. "I

started worrying today would be the day and that this party might not even happen. After Nick had done all that planning!" She gestured all around, at Jess's drink. "It's going to be such a relief when the babies come, so nice to no longer be living on hold like this."

Clara didn't know, Jess thought. Lucinda wasn't even a toddler yet—she had no inkling of the chaos down the line. The way Jess understood it, Clara's life was going to be on hold indefinitely, way off into the horizon.

"But the feeling turned out to be nothing," Clara continued. "Truthfully, I feel strange all the time. Maybe it was wishful thinking to suppose the babies might come today. It's still too soon, but I just want everybody to be here." She meant her little family, finally complete.

"But you need to take care of yourself in the meantime," Jess reminded her, knowing how futile her advice was. Clara was unmovable, in every sense of the word.

She wasn't even listening, sunk back in her chair, smiling dimly. She raised her glass and took a sip of her drink, which was pink with berries floating in it. She said, "Good, good. I'm feeling good." The most annoying kind of delirium. As though Jess has asked her the question. As though the answer might even be true.

"And your blood pressure? It's okay?" The midwives had been monitoring it, Jess knew.

Clara shook her head, "Stop fussing. Last time I checked, you weren't my nurse." She put her hand on her belly but looked Jess right in the eye. "And I really want to know: how are *you*?" Sometimes she'd do this, briefly surfacing from the spell, as though she and Jess actually still inhabited the same universe. As though she had the bandwidth to follow her line of inquiry beyond a superficial response. But right now she seemed to be waiting for Jess to answer. Maybe she wasn't so far gone yet.

So Jess told her, "Things are fine. Busy, but fine." Should she leave it at that? She waited to see if Clara's attention had already drifted elsewhere. But then everyone was busy. Busy was boring. "Work has its . . . challenges," she continued. She was up for her promotion, she reminded Clara, but the politics were getting complicated, plus the day-to-day workplace matters that were now her jurisdiction. It wasn't all bad: she was putting together an exhibition on the role of luminescence in stories, how images of light, sparkle, and shine—ordinary flax spun into gold, golden plates at Sleeping Beauty's christening—informed a tale.

Clara said, "What the frog foretold came true."

Jess was surprised. "You remembered!" Sometimes she wondered if she occupied any part of her friend's crowded consciousness.

"How could I forget?" asked Clara. "I mean, just look at me."

Jess said, "I don't know that any frog foretold that." Fairy tales were full of stories of barrenness, but rarely of fecundity. Maybe twelve brothers or twelve princesses lined up in a row, but you never heard how it was for their mother, all that laundry. *Once upon a time there was a couple who longed for a baby, and then they got what they wanted, and then some.*

"The old woman who lived in a shoe," said Clara.

"But that's a nursery rhyme," Jess said. There was a distinction. "I always had sympathy for that poor woman, her children shamelessly multiplying, ducking in and out of eyeholes."

"I've been reading it," said Clara. "It's good to be prepared." She smiled. "And how's Miles?" This question was a hook on which a lot of freight hung. Jess knew she should be glad that Clara was thoughtful enough to ask at all, that the inquiry did not come with the pointed insensitivity she'd come to expect from the people who relished vicarious misfortune. Or the pitiers—Jess hated the pity, although the people who couldn't even muster pity were worse. The smug people, who figured she and Adam were making a big deal out of nothing, indulging their son. People who thought the problem was "too much time on the tablet," which was a sensitive point because it was true, there really was too much time on the tablet.

"He's doing okay," said Jess. Most people wouldn't even notice, not at first. Miles had friends at school, got along with them at recess. He played hockey, rode his bike, and in the Instagram photos she posted, he looked like any other kid. He had the same wide smile as his sister, but he didn't have Bella's words. Bella, who talked all the time—she always had, so most people never realized what her brother was lacking. Bella covered for him the way they all did. Miles was smart, but he struggled with the connections between thinking words and actually saying them. Childhood apraxia of speech was the official diagnosis, and Jess tried to be grateful they'd received it early, even though at the time it felt like an infinite corridor of doors had slammed shut. It was a valuable lesson too, with both of her children, to observe that something that came so easily to one person could prove incredibly difficult for another.

"He's doing well," she told Clara. "There's been progress. Little steps." Most people wanted a narrative with forward motion, instead of stasis and disappointment. Most people eventually stopped asking altogether. "Speaking of little steps, I saw Lucinda standing," she said. "Nearly walking." Mundane milestones never ceased to be remarkable, and Jess knew this now better than she ever had.

Clara said, "We're in for it now."

"But this is where it gets good," said Jess. "Once the kids are big enough to be actual people, it gets harder, but it gets better." She said this forgetting that Clara and Nick were still in the eye of the storm. "I mean, it's going to be good," she corrected herself.

"I know," said Clara with a smile. Sometimes it was as though her brain had gone as loose as her skin. Where were her edges? Jess could have sworn she used to have them. "I feel like the luckiest mama in the world," she went on, completely sincere, even though she couldn't move, was swollen to the size of a mountain, and Jess wondered if her friend had really lost her mind.

Adam came outside and greeted Clara with a hug, Nick behind him with the baby in his arms. When he put Lucinda down, she pounced on her mother, who strained to pull her up, to make a space beside her body. But her body itself was what Lucinda wanted, palpable pleasure on her face as she breathed Clara in, her features transformed, her ringlets bouncing. Lucinda looked like a child one might order from a catalogue.

But then she was distracted by Bella, who wandered out alongside her brother. Indoors, Bella had been delighting Lucinda with cartoons on her tablet, Nick explained, and now Lucinda was partial to her, raising her arms for Bella to pluck her up. So Bella did, setting her down on her little feet and holding her hands to help her walk. Miles took her other hand and Lucinda beamed.

"Look, Mom," Bella called, looking as proud as Lucinda. Here were all their children, like something she and Clara might have imagined on those nights when they sat out among the rooftops planning happily-ever-afters, the sun filtering through the sprawling apple tree, the air still redolent with blossoms though they'd scattered weeks ago.

Nahlah said, "I bet it feels like you've only just got her back, and now you're losing her all over again." She scraped the last morsels of rice from her bowl. Nahlah knew. She'd been there for Jess when Miles was a baby, during all those years after Clara disappeared. Without Nahlah (in addition to therapy and pharmaceuticals), Jess wasn't sure she would have still been standing when Clara decided to find her again.

"I have to let her go," Jess replied. "It's the only way. And it turned out to be a good little party after all. There was cake and everybody sang, and the baby smeared icing all over her face, so they got that part right."

Miranda said, "She's going to need you."

"She's pretty insistent that she doesn't need anybody this time."

"A fast blow to the head is what she's going to need," said Miranda, who was quite certain, and possibly not wrong, that anyone who embarked upon parenthood was playing recklessly with life itself—or at least with life*style*. She'd spent her career as a children's librarian, thus satisfying whatever maternal yearnings she had. She saw no real difference between what Jess, Nahlah, and Clara were all going through. They were all women indulging in inappropriate levels of self-sacrifice, and she was having none of it. "Put her out of her misery."

"Harsh," said Nahlah.

Jess said, "I hope it doesn't come to that."

If Jess were in charge—this is what she told Adam, Miranda, Nahlah, and everybody else—she would have locked Clara in a tall tower for safekeeping, because Jess had so much else to worry about. She just didn't have the capacity for one more impossible thing because her entire life was already an impossible puzzle, something that no one else seemed to properly appreciate. There was a calendar on the wall before her now, a wipe-board whose patterns would flummox even the most brilliant mathematician. A schedule, as though to suggest there could be a scaffold to hold all this: hockey, choir, and gymnastics during the week, plus computer-coding classes on Saturday mornings, which started conflicting with math club, so they had to quit.

There were not enough hours, not enough days. What was one supposed to do with the doctor's appointments, trips to the dentist, allergy shots, speech therapy, and then more speech therapy? Jess had counted herself lucky that the Institute was generous and flexible with her hours, but she wasn't sure how much longer that would last. None of it was remotely possible either without Althea, their long-time nanny, who was as capable as Jess at coordinating the madness, the juggling. Maybe in a few years Clara too would have a calendar as maddening as this one, a calendar where Jess had just noticed out of the corner of her eye a conspicuous blank space for the forthcoming Saturday. A blip, or an error? But no, Bella had karate. Jess had forgotten to write it down. She got up from the couch, where she had been sitting with Adam, so she could add it with the dry-erase marker. This oversight made her nervous—what else was she missing? So much could go wrong. It was a whirlwind, this life. Terrible and dizzy-making, though exhilarating at the best of times. All too much—but this meant Jess had a better idea of what Clara was going through than Clara knew. Jess imagined herself as a cautionary tale about the dangers of saying YES to everything, but all she had ever wanted was to open up her children's horizons. And with Miles's struggles, it seemed even more important to push his limits. To leap them. Hurdle after hurdle, she hoped.

"But this isn't about Miles," Adam replied. "Miles's problems aren't Clara's. Clara's problems aren't even yours."

"But they are," said Jess, slinking back down beside him. Everything was connected, one thing leading to another. So why would anybody tempt fate? Clara never thought things through. For example, she was planning to name her babies Paulina and Shadow. "Who does that?" Jess exclaimed. "Who names a set of twins 'Something and Shadow'? Who gets to be the shadow? It's cruel and inhumane, that's what it is."

"And you told her that," said Adam.

"I did," said Jess. "And she laughed, like I'd said something foolish. As though the implications of a name like Shadow were something to be scoffed at. Can you imagine that? Growing up as a twin and being called Shadow?"

"What about Paulina?" asked Adam. "Where did that come from?"

"Nick's grandmother—the one who wasn't called Lucinda. And now that they've run out of grandmothers, Clara finally gets to name one of her children, and she comes up with Shadow. I never thought I'd be wishing that Nick had more grandmothers."

"So you don't like it that Nick named the kids," said Adam. He picked up her hand and started kissing her fingers. "And you don't like it when Clara does either. Could the root of the problem be that you don't get to name the kids? They aren't your kids. You know that, right?"

What she also knew was that Nick and Clara would soon have a house full of girls, and they didn't even have plans to buy a house or move to a bigger apartment. Clara just kept shrugging and saying that babies were small. She had been even more strange and evasive than usual at the party on Saturday. There was something she wasn't telling her, Jess was sure.

Adam was nuzzling her neck now. The children were solidly asleep, and it had been forty-five minutes since they'd heard a peep. Jess understood that he was seizing the moment, and even admired his initiative, but her mind was elsewhere. She pulled away from him. "What?" he said.

"I don't understand how you do it. Just flick on the switch and start thinking of sex."

Adam said, "I don't have to flick. It's always on."

"But what about all the other things?" she asked him. "Here I am thinking about scheduling karate, and how I can get back from Miles's appointment in time for my meeting tomorrow. If we had sex right now, I'd just be visualizing the calendar the whole way through."

"The calendar?"

"The whiteboard. I close my eyes and see it on the back of my eyelids. Seared on my brain."

"That's what turns you on?"

She hit him with a throw pillow. "No," she said.

He knocked the pillow to the floor and came at her again, kissing her behind her left ear. "You've got to relax," he said, which was normally the kind of instruction that would annoy her, but Adam was right. She'd spent the whole evening wound up like a top, and if she tried to fall asleep with her mind like this, her dreams would be awful and her sleep would be wrecked.

"Adam, it's Monday," she murmured. "Monday's not a sex night." He didn't back away, though. "And I haven't made the kids' lunches yet."

"I'll do them in the morning," he said. He had his hands up her shirt. "I like Mondays." The effectiveness of his touch was decreasing her interest in talking him out of it. "Are you still thinking about whiteboards?"

"Whiteboards?" She was thinking of Clara now. Her body. Her life. Jess had sounded the alarms, but Clara refused to listen. Could she let this go? Somebody and Shadow. She was still thinking this as her husband pulled her top over her head, it catching on her earring. "Ow!" she said, and she was brought right into now, and there he was, Adam, so intent upon her body. She pulled away but only to tug off his shirt too, and to unfasten her bra and climb onto his lap. To put Clara out of her mind.

He said, "We're going to do this here?"

And yes, they were going to. Because when you're a woman with a whiteboard on the back of her eyelids who finds herself lucky enough to be in the moment, you just go, and that woman's husband should know enough not to ask questions.

She tried to stay here, concentrating on Adam's body, feeling what she was feeling with her fingertips—his soft skin, the hair on his chest, the compelling firmness of his stomach muscles, and down inside his pants, where he was always ready. He was right about the switch.

"I'm not thinking about the calendar," she said, and it felt wondrous not to be thinking about the calendar. She tugged off Adam's jeans, and the rest of her clothes, and climbed back onto his lap where he was sitting on the couch, more than ready, and she took him inside her.

And now she was here in this moment, but Adam had gone somewhere beyond it, his eyes closed and his mouth moving silently, slowly, as she moved up and down on top of him. He pulled her close, her breasts to his face, where he kissed and sucked them, and she reached down to touch herself, so they could come together, her other arm braced against the back of the couch, and when she turned her head she could see their reflection in the window. They hadn't closed the curtains. They had a view straight through the backyard and across the laneway since they'd torn the garage down the summer before. If not for the reflection of them in the window right now—adding to her arousal; they looked pretty hot—she'd be able to see right into her neighbours' kitchen, the same way they were able to see right through to hers. But no, she stopped this line of thinking. Although when she turned her head the other way, she only saw the whiteboard, so she stared straight ahead at the wall. The closest she'd ever get to Zen.

But that was weird, and she was glad when Adam looked up, his eyes on hers, and she could feel the pleasure building even though her hand was cramping, but she kept going, and he did too. She could tell by his breathing, the pressure of his grip on her shoulders, the pulsing muscles in his arms, that he was getting close. So she stopped holding back and let it happen, the orgasm moving through her and lasting as long as she could hold her breath and make it so, feeling him coming too.

Adam pulled her close, sweaty and shaking. "Not bad for a Monday," he said, his voice still unsteady.

But she had already moved on to the next thing. "Bella's slip for the field trip. You remembered to sign it, right?"

CONCURRENTLY

Clara had become comfortable living on the edge—which was, in some ways, a joke. Their life was so risk-free that all their household cleaners were edible, and she hadn't had a drink in years. She was up all night most nights, but not for reasons that would make anyone's hard-rock memoir. Lucinda's sleep was still patchy, and the pressure of nearly full-term twins on Clara's bladder meant a lot of getting up to pee, and then afterwards she'd lie in bed and wait for them to move, or for Lucinda to rouse again, and perhaps the sun would already be rising, making its way down the alley outside to arrive at their bedroom window.

They'd reorganized everything so Clara's whole life could be conducted from her bed, snacks and diaper changes, games and puzzles. An entire life within arm's reach, so she'd be okay with Lucinda while Nick was at work. He didn't want to go, didn't like to leave them, but he was taking six weeks off when the babies came and working overtime in the interim to help fill the gap. And while they'd considered having somebody come to help—Clara's mother? One of her sisters?—Clara was sure it would be more trouble than it was worth, because the whole point of bedrest was to avoid stress and upset, so why would they go and invite these into their home?

No, it was easier to be on her own, making do, passing the time with games and stories, naps and cuddles, but still, the edge was close, along with the warnings from her OB-GYN about the risks of her pregnancy: she was geriatric now, all the trouble she'd been through already with miscarriages, and now twins, barely a year since her last birth. She had high blood pressure, the doctor had told her, but he was the reason why, Clara knew, which was why she'd quit going to him.

"He's doing me no good," she said, and it was true, she didn't like him at all. Lucinda had been born in a dream of a birth, and there was no reason her twins should have to enter the world in different circumstances, fall into the hands of a man with a pointy chin-beard who didn't even know that he should hide his eye-rolls when she talked to him. "I am not having it," she said, and Nick didn't argue.

Except then, her previous midwives wouldn't take her on. "High-risk," they kept saying. There were strict protocols, and their relationship with the hospital depended on taking those protocols seriously. "And this isn't just red-tape bureaucracy," explained Rachel, who'd been the one to catch Lucinda. "Sometimes the hospital really is the best place." Clara felt as though she was being backed into a corner.

But there was another way, Clara learned as she scrolled on her ancient laptop, reading about the unassisted birth movement, the most empowering rabbit hole imaginable for a woman confined to her bed. She came at Nick when he got home with stats and anecdotes about the patriarchal conspiracy of medicalized birth, unleashing her inner goddess. "It's doesn't have to be like this," she insisted to her husband.

"No pregnant woman should have to submit to a man who rolls his eyes."

To which Nick rolled his eyes, and she threw a stuffed cat at him, but he'd also just brought her dinner—fried chicken and coleslaw—so there was only so much she could do. He had drawn the line: she was not going to give birth to twins alone. "Unless you really want to be alone," he said, "because I'm not sticking around for that."

So they made a compromise. Searching online forums, she found a local group of renegade midwives who took on complex cases, women who listened when Clara told her story and whose eyes showed nothing but understanding. Women who made her aware of the risks, but also told her that these risks didn't have to define her experience. Women who recognized that she was more than a pile of statistics. Finally, for the first time since her pregnancy became so complicated, Clara started to feel safe.

Though others were less assured. Rachel was no longer speaking to her, hadn't even shown up to Lucinda's party. Jess didn't know the half of it and still disapproved, projecting all her own anxieties onto Clara. It was not helpful to hear everybody else's fears and concerns, especially since it was only going to be Clara in the moment anyway. She'd learned the first time around that the only person she could really count on was herself. Even Nick, ever faithful, loving, and patient, would not be able to reach her in the eye of that storm. Nick, who was the one person who trusted her enough to give her the freedom to walk her own path, to listen to her heart.

But then it started to slip sometimes, Clara's confidence, her certainty. Was it too much to ask that anything be so sure? When Lucinda was playing down on the floor and Clara felt

256   KERRY CLARE

a twinge in her belly—what if it all went wrong and she couldn't get to the phone? What if Lucinda was hurt and Clara couldn't reach her? What if she had gambled their safety away, betting on too much, as delusional and stubborn as everybody told her she was? Could everybody be right?

Clara couldn't share these fears with anyone. Not with Nick, who she'd had to persuade to join her here in the first place. She had to be unwavering. And certainly not with Jess, who'd predicted all along that she'd start feeling this way, that she'd change her mind.

Clara knew what the stakes were. She'd been shown the statistics, warned of the dangers. Rachel said she was being selfish. "They could lose you," she wrote in the last text she ever sent. "Maybe you're doing all this for the babies, but what are they going to do without you? Everything would fall apart."

But it hadn't. Not yet. The way the world keeps on turning was one thing Clara knew for a fact. The sun arrived at her window every morning, something to believe in, and so she would.

HERE AND NOW

TUESDAY, MAY 10, 2016

Adam had remembered to sign the permission slip for Bella's trip, but he dropped the ball on the kids' lunches, something Jess didn't realize until she'd delivered Miles to school after speech therapy and discovered his backpack was empty. So she had to drive to the store to pick up cheese buns, apples, and a box of granola bars, splitting it all into two plastic bags, which she dropped off at school, finally arriving at work forty minutes later than the two hours late she already informed them she'd be. The Board meeting was in progress because they'd already waited as long as they could. All the seats around the table were occupied, including one taken by Elliott Lubbock, who didn't even work there (at least not yet), and so Jess had to settle for a vacant chair by the door, which at least meant she could slip in less conspicuously.

Her phone buzzed. She'd sent an irate text to Adam and was waiting for his response, but this message wasn't from him, instead from an unknown number: "*Clara rushed to hospital early this morning. Massive hemorrhaging. No word yet. Her mom's coming into the city to be with Lu. Will send details when I've got them. —Pam.*" Clara's neighbour. And while the message should have sent Jess into a panic, instead it seemed impossibly abstract, almost absurd and just left her confused. How could this be real? And what was Jess supposed to do now? Surely not stay here listening to the men talk incoherently about blockchain and NFTs.

She texted back, *"How can I help?"* She could leave this useless meeting and be there in a heartbeat. *Massive hemorrhaging.* She could have called it after seeing Clara at the party: something was not right. But being right felt wrong now. Jess would have given anything not to have known this was going to happen, and she hoped she still didn't know what was going to happen next. She tried to keep her mind open to all possibilities: They were at the hospital. Clara was in excellent hands. And nobody died in childbirth anymore, she told herself. She kept telling herself.

Her phone buzzed again at a moment when the room had gone quiet, so the sound was like a siren. Everyone turned to look at her.

"Anything to offer, Jess?" asked Edith Morningside, looking disappointed with her protegé for not knowing anything about blockchain and the part it would play in the financial future of the Institute.

"Um, I—" said Jess. Pam had written, *"Just stay put. Nick is there. Lu is with us right now. All we can do is wait and hope."* Jess held up her phone. "I've sort of got a personal emergency going on here." She knew what they were thinking: her kids. That they'd made her late already. She said, "It's my friend." Elliott Lubbock had turned around to look at her, as smug as any mediocre man who had just stolen a job from a woman who'd worked ten years for it. She'd like to hear just what he had to say on the topic of luminescence and golden flax.

Another text arrived from Pam: "*Her sisters are praying.*"
Of course they were praying, they were always praying, but
now Jess was grateful. She could pray too, for her best friend,
and for those babies, and she just couldn't spend another
moment in that suffocating room with those people who
were plotting her downfall, who were staring at her now
waiting for her to crack.

So she left. She'd scarcely arrived, so it wasn't hard to go.
She threw the strap of her bag back over her shoulder and
walked out of the room, not even turning around to note the
questions or hubbub she was leaving behind her. She called
the elevator and went downstairs, then outside—not to her
car, but to the street, where everywhere was empty. She'd forgotten it could be like this on a weekday morning, when the
only people out were old men who still wore hats and shuffled
down the sidewalks with their canes, nannies pushing strollers
with sleeping kids inside. She walked north, the wind whip-
ping through her light coat, making litter dance in sweeping
circles up and down the sidewalk.

Her coat was so light she didn't have to check it, and she
slung it over her arm instead. She didn't even have to wait in
line for admission because the museum was as empty as the
sidewalks, quiet and echoing. Where had everybody gone?
Jess showed her membership card to get a ticket for the special exhibit, the reason she'd made the trip, and took the
elevator down to the basement.

Downstairs it was dark, and there wasn't any weather.
The walls of the exhibit were painted black, and the bright
spotlights focussed on cases displaying jewelry still shiny after
centuries buried in ash. There was another case with a dog
rendered in plaster, its legs awkwardly contorted. Jess was
glad to be without her children. They wouldn't have liked

this. Or maybe she wouldn't have liked having to explain it to them. They'd be asking if it was a real dog, and she would tell them it wasn't, which was a lie. Or not exactly. Which was no real consolation for the enormity of what had been lost.

Jess saw a face, a child's face, round cheeks and plump lips, the kind of face you might see on a vintage Christmas card, the face of an angel, a face from a statue, all its details preserved. It was rendered in plaster as well, but in a different fashion, no accident. Its eyes were watching Jess. The rest of the statue was fragments now.

So much had been preserved in ash: an actual loaf of bread, a tile with an etched image of a bakery. Busts with broken noses, the identity of their subjects now lost to history. Kitchen utensils and weigh scales from the market. All these things had been buried, although the irony was that with their unearthing came inevitable breakdown. Submerged under centuries of ash, pieces of ancient, ordinary life could be preserved forever, but when they were unearthed, they began to decompose. What a paradox. Was there a folly in searching, in wanting to know?

Pompeii. There had been rumblings. None of it had been wholly unexpected. What kind of person builds their house in the shadow of a volcano? It's asking for trouble. *Vesuvius.* Like the name of a comic-book villain. Etymology unknown, apparently. When Vesuvius erupted in AD 79, it sent black clouds up into the sky for miles.

Walking around, Jess learned about ordinary life in Pompeii, about plumbing and housing and aqueducts. She wasn't alone; there were a few other visitors down here too. The exhibit was new, a big deal for a museum that was struggling with its bottom line. A museum was such a permanent fixture, you would think, culturally speaking, preserving all of time . . . and yet this museum was just a hundred years old. A chronological blip in a grand scheme, the newest wing replacing another that had been built two decades ago. That nothing is permanent is something Jess hadn't realized years ago when she and Clara had made their home across the street, the museum an imposing shadow that blocked out the late-afternoon sun.

Jess remembered when Clara worked at the museum on six-month contracts, how they never hired her permanently, all the precarity. How difficult it had been during those years after she returned from abroad and all her experience counted for nothing. Clara had never known how to play the game, and she claimed she didn't even want to know. Sometimes she was so reckless.

But now Clara could die. This is what Jess was thinking as she turned a corner and saw an image of the exploding volcano projected on the wall, audio rumblings enhancing the experience. Miranda's partner was a doctor—a psychiatrist, but still, he'd gone to medical school—and he told Jess that a home birth with twins in the condition Clara was in was the craziest thing he'd ever heard.

On another wall, a chart depicted the height of the ash as it fell, a suffocating storm that buried everything. It had been four stories, higher than a house. You couldn't expect to crawl out of that. You could imagine yourself, furiously digging, trying to rise through the debris, to keep your head above the deluge. Was it still called a deluge if the force wasn't water? What was the word for a deluge of ash?

Jess imagined herself to be the exception. Surely everybody did that. She would be the one to survive, to persist, in keeping with the rules of narrative. Though it was impossible to imagine how she could make her way through the torrent of suffocating ash and have her hands free. There would be no way to survive and also bring her children, and without them, what would survival be?

Around the next corner were plaster casts of human bodies made of cavities left when the bodies eventually decomposed, the bodies of the people of Pompeii, people who'd built their homes, and their bakeries, and their aqueducts in the shadow of a volcano. It was terrible to see, a violation of their humanity. An invasion. It seemed wrong to be a witness to such a horrible private moment, such startling vulnerability, parents with their arms wrapped around their children, using their entire bodies as protection, a futile measure. Because the ash came down and buried them all, and there was not a single thing that anyone could do.

Those poor people, thought Jess. They were no different than her, or anyone else strolling through the exhibit this morning. They were people who got up on an ordinary day and were going about the motions of their daily lives, never anticipating what was going to happen. And how do you ever know when or where it's going to come from, what is going to rain down from black clouds over your head, subsuming your world and your life?

At the end of the exhibit was a gift shop, though Jess didn't linger there. She made her way out, and up in the elevator to the lobby, and outside to the light, and the fact that the world was still there was surprising.

EVER AFTER

But Clara survived. She lived. She *lives*. She feels this point can't be emphasized enough, even though the people who loved her were all too keen to dismiss it, almost as though the actual outcome was beside the point.

And how do you measure that, the line between everything that could have happened and what actually did? A hair's breadth. The skin of your teeth. Lately Clara was preoccupied by idioms—what exactly *was* the straw that broke the camel's back? Clara pictured drinking straws, the bendy kind for milkshakes. Her children chewed on those, their tiny tooth marks along their lengths. Tricks of language kept tripping Clara up, and teeth were part of the trouble, erupting from the softness of her children's gums in a seemingly endless process, keeping everybody up at night.

Clara just couldn't visualize it—the breadth of a hair. As though it were nothing, when such a space contained infinity: the distance between life and death, huge and intractable. But maybe the problem was her. These days, Clara had trouble visualizing most things, trouble seeing anything except for the scene in front of her eyes, which was usually a mess, spilled juice and a carpet of toys, a leaning tower of laundry that was sometimes clean but never folded—because who had time for folding? Who had time, when there were children to catch, and grab and cuddle and feed and comfort and rock and sway and love and devour?

Two years ago, for weeks after the twins were born, Clara had been confined to her bed while her incision healed, and there were bedpans and gross bloody gauze, and it was terrible, but she just fed her babies and they grew, and Lu climbed on top of her and lay down as though her mother were a sofa, and it was here that Clara gave in, submitted to, and just became a sofa. *I am plush and for comfort*, she affirmed to herself, and just rolled with it. At night Nick came to bed and curled up against her, and they were all of them there—the little babies on one side and Nick on the other, and Lu curled up at the foot of the bed because she liked to sleep splayed out like a star. There they were, floating, and the bed was their world, and never mind that her wound wasn't healing, that it couldn't air properly, tucked as it was inside her rolls of flesh. This was why babies weren't supposed to be born that way, on a surgical ward, and the only thing that really caught Clara up in those wondrous early days was the injustice of it all and the indignity of her experience of birth. She was furious at having been reduced to an object, a body that bled and bled.

But she had recovered, impossibly, and her body was doing its thing again, after it had all gone so wrong, after the night she still couldn't think about, even though Nick had never stopped. The one thing about having it happen to her was that at least she didn't have to see it, but Nick couldn't get the picture out of his head, he said. Even when he closed his eyes it was there, the way the blood came and how life had appeared to drain right out of her—"I'd never seen anyone go that colour." And how the midwife, the one they'd never liked anyway, had panicked. She freaked out, and Nick thought he'd have to call an ambulance for both of them, though it had almost been a welcome distraction from the sight of his wife dying before his eyes.

"I wasn't dying," Clara reminded him.

"But I didn't know that," said Nick. "It really could have gone either way." The midwife finally gathered her senses before the paramedics arrived and turned on the overhead lights, the whole scene transformed into something glaring and pounding. All the adrenaline, and the flashing lights of the ambulance out on the street illuminating the neighbourhood with alarm.

How does a person get over that? Clara didn't know, but you can, and you do. There had been the infection, but her wound healed eventually, and one day she could get up, go to the bathroom, even take a walk beyond the end of the street. It was the kind of experience that makes mere newborn twins seem almost easy. "After that," Clara said, "everything else is a picnic."

Things were good now. But part of being good meant understanding that this life had limits, and you couldn't push too hard. Clara kept her expectations low. All she needed to be was a sofa, and if she could manage that then the day was a success, and so they stayed curled up all afternoon. Lu was watching Elmo on TV and the twins were eating—still breastfeeding, and Clara hadn't even had to supplement after their second week. She was amazing. She was a superhero. She'd never been so pleased with herself, and nobody could tear her down.

And as the babies grew, she didn't get any more ambitious. There would be time for ambition, and right now it was autumn in all its glory, and then winter when there was no point in going outside, and spring again—they watched it all unfolding out the window, those seasonal scenes, and nothing ever stayed the same. So it would actually be unfair to accuse Clara of lacking in vision, because she was paying attention, even with everything she'd lived through—the blood and the recovery, the building of two more humans into toddling, terrifying bundles of motion that never stopped.

"They're bouncing off the walls," said Jess, "all cooped up in here."

Clara ignored her. Jess thought her wisdom was applicable to everybody. She and Adam now owned a sprawling summer place beside a lake, and she was insisting that Clara and the kids come up and stay for a week or two.

"Honestly, can you imagine?" Clara reported to Nick.

But he looked confused. "Why not?"

Clara was aghast. "Because of all the reasons I already told Jess that we couldn't." She shouldn't have to explain it to him too. Because the kids would be a handful. Because taking care of all of them in a space that was somebody else's would hardly be a holiday at all. Most of all, that it was exhausting, all that trouble to escape to somewhere else, when they were perfectly happy where they were.

She told Jess they couldn't manage it.

"But you *can*," Jess insisted. "It's all about mindset." Since quitting her job the year before, she'd founded an online bookshop called Chloe & Olivia, which dealt in rare first editions by women authors, and now she spent her mornings doing yoga and meditation. Jess thought everything was possible. It never seemed to occur to her that such boundless-ness might be the exclusive purview of women whose husbands made six-figure salaries.

"Plus the car won't make it," Clara reminded Nick. Their car, fourth-hand, was mostly decorative, parked in the laneway out back. When her sister gave it to them, it was barely running. They kept it primarily to assure those who became unduly distressed at the idea of people with children who didn't own a car—"You'll see," people (Jess) kept telling Clara when she was pregnant with Lu, the same way they'd been so sure that she and Nick would need to make the baby sleep in another room, or else let her cry at night, which Clara never had and never would. Anyway, they didn't need a car. Everything they needed was within walking distance, and everything else was accessible by transit, and they never went anywhere anyway. Which was just fine; have you ever tried to leave the house with three babies?

But Jess refused to give in. Adam was going to be in the city working most of the summer, driving up on weekends, and he was willing to bring them and all their gear. "There will be room in the van," Jess said, and there would be, because they owned not one van but two, each large enough to transport an entire sports team. Clara had never been sure of the point of such vehicles, except perhaps to make it impossible for friends to decline invitations to the cottage.

"Well, good," said Nick, when Clara told him this. "Because maybe I don't want to decline. It's been ages since I had anything like a summer holiday." Clara thought about how sofas don't get summer holidays, how sofas are on duty all the time. Nick said, "Come on, it will do you good to get away." He knew that Clara was nervous, afraid of any change that might upset the careful arrangement of their domestic life. "We can do this," he said. And in those rare instances when Nick didn't take her side, he tended to be right. She'd follow his lead.

Jess sealed the deal with a promise: "We can go swimming again. Think of it—a cool lake just steps from the door."

But not once did she ever mention that those steps descended from a cliff edge. The cottage—which was in fact a six-bedroom house, far bigger than their place in the city—was perilously perched, offering awesome views of sunrises and night skies and glittering water, but those forty-seven steps down to the dock and the beach were forty-seven steps on a staircase that had seen better days and was its own kind of death trap. Never mind the cliff itself. Clara was now the mother of three mobile, danger-prone, impulsive children. Why hadn't it occurred to Jess that the edge of a cliff might not be the ideal location to bring them to?

The drive up went smoothly. The twins stayed asleep. Lu babbled happily in her car seat, Clara beside her, passing her toys and books and her sippy-cup, all of which she insisted on throwing on the floor and then demanded be returned to her.

Nick sat in the front with Adam and they talked, though Clara didn't know what about because the music was playing and she couldn't hear them. This had been annoying at first, but she let it go and tried to appreciate the scenes sweeping by outside. They were lucky, she knew this. They'd never had a family vacation before. She was trying to be positive, trying to feel she hadn't been coerced into this. She was still nervous about having all her children in the van, hurtling through space at such terrifying speed. There were so many upsides to never going anywhere.

But Adam was a safe driver, and the kids were fine. Clara kept handing Lu animal crackers, which seemed to keep her happy. They were going to stop for wild blueberries at a road-side stand just after the highway exit. Clara insisted that Nick pay for the blueberries, even though they were so expensive. Economics were different up here. But it was only for a week, and she would go with the flow.

"It's a bit much, I know," said Adam, as he parked out-side the three-car garage. They had bought the property in a foreclosure, construction finishing just before the bottom fell out of the economy again. Nobody had ever lived in the house, and now it belonged to Jess and Adam. They took no responsibility for the grandeur. Their bedroom had come with a whirlpool tub set in a bay window with dramatic lake views. Clara had watched an online slide show left over from the real estate sale.

The house was just visible up a path through the trees, and Clara heard a door slam. There were voices, and somebody running, and mosquitos buzzing already. The twins were start-ing to wake up now that the car had stopped and Clara waved the bugs away from them as she unbuckled Shadoe from her car seat. She'd peed through her diaper, Clara discovered, holding her on one hip anyway—thank goodness there was laundry here—as she released Pauly from the other seat. Nick was dealing with Lu and all their stuff. Jess had come out with her kids, everyone in their bathing suits.

Bella said, "Somebody smells like pee."

"It's me," said Clara, because now it was.

"I've been reading the news," said Jess, gathering up the bags and suitcases that Nick and Adam were unloading from the back of the van. "I have to say it's kind of ominous. They're appointing a new Supreme Court justice and his name is Brett."

"Brett?" Clara followed Jess up to the house, with its heaping window boxes and wraparound porch, complete with a swing. "Not *our* Brett." Clara was recalling the Drama Society director from so many years ago. Brett Bickford. One time on stage he'd stuck his tongue in her ear.

"I don't think there was much risk of our Brett becoming a Supreme Court justice," said Jess as she led them inside. The house was new and shiny and just understated enough that what was most striking was the scene through the huge windows lining the walls in every room.

"But how could anyone named Brett become a Supreme Court justice in the first place?" Clara asked. "I mean, I'm sure there are some fine Bretts out there, but that just doesn't seem appropriate." The kitchen was huge and it opened onto a deck that showed off the lake in dramatic fashion. The sun was shining, sparkling on the water, and there were wind-surfers and sailboats and you could hold the whole picture in a glance.

Clara's kids, meanwhile, were taken in by the open space and smooth wooden floors that were so good for sliding, dis-covering that they could stretch out their arms and touch nothing. Shadoe was lying on the floor and spinning around on her bum, which was wet now, Clara remembered. Not good news for hardwood, so she dug through the diaper bags to find supplies with which to change her.

"And he's pro-life," called Jess. "Another one."

"Of course he is," said Clara, polishing away the damp-ness on the floor with a clean onesie. It had been almost two years since the most devastating election, one that had upended so many standards and precedents and any adher-ence to general decency. Terrible people had been elevated to positions of power, and there was such a string of horrifying headlines that Clara had almost ceased to be outraged by it all. "Once upon a time, that would have been something to be embarrassed about."

"They're chipping away, little by little, bit by bit. All those things we took for granted." Jess sat down on the couch while Clara changed Shadoe's diaper. "I never thought it would come to this. Didn't even think it was a possibility."

Setting Shadoe back on her feet and watching her immediately set off, Clara said, "It wasn't until I finally had my kids that I really knew what the stakes were, what the choices I'd made really *meant*. How significant and pivotal they had been."

"We're going backwards," said Jess. "Such a slippery slope."

So this was exactly the image in Clara's mind as they joined the others on the deck and she realized how far down below them the lake was. Stone steps led down to a narrow expanse of lawn and there the world ended, dropping away to nothing.

There wasn't a fence or even a railing. Clara supposed that with their own children old enough to have mastered the basics of gravity and natural consequences, Jess and Adam didn't feel they needed one. But even if there had been a railing—how could anyone be so short-sighted as to buy a house on the edge of a cliff?

"They're a disaster," Jess admitted, pointing to the steps. "When we bought the place, the house itself was finished, but everything else was still in turmoil. We put the sod down, or else we'd be swimming in a sea of mud. But there's still a lot of work to be done. We're going to get new stairs built, but we've already spent so much on everything else. Anyway, we're in no hurry. These are admirably rustic." The family whose cottage had stood here before this house was built had made their way down the stairs for decades.

Clara wondered if the place had been sold because everyone had ended up in a pile of bodies at the bottom.

"Watch that one," Jess called out after treading carefully on another broken step. She looked over her shoulder to make sure Clara was getting down okay. Adam and Nick had stayed up at the house with the kids. Jess was wearing a bathing suit and nothing else, not even a sarong to cover her scary thighs, but Clara had forgotten that not all thighs were scary. Jess's were firm and strong, and they probably didn't meet at the top.

Jess turned around again. "What?" she called.

Clara had stopped. It had just occurred to her that as difficult as it was making her way down, she'd only have to climb back up again and that was going to be worse.

But Jess didn't notice the discomfort, gesturing toward the sparkling lake, the clear blue sky. "Isn't it glorious?" she asked. "Photos don't even do it justice."

"It's beautiful," said Clara, and it really was. The view was striking, the weather was perfect, and if they'd just install a funicular, it might be fine.

"Our own private beach," said Jess once they'd arrived at the bottom. "Get a load of that." A spread of golden sand, and a dock with a ladder. A boat was tied to the dock, covered with a tarpaulin. They only used it on the weekends when Adam was there; Jess didn't like to drive it. "See, I told you all this would be worth the trip."

"You told me," said Clara, weary. "So how's it going, anyway?" she asked. "Being up here all alone."

"Not so alone," said Jess. Nahlah had been up two weeks ago with her kids. Adam's brother's family too. They'd had a lot of company. Jess was able to keep up with her shop, working remotely. "It's pretty good, actually," she said. "And I certainly don't miss the heat of the city."

"The heat's not been *that* bad," said Clara. They had a small air conditioner in the window in their bedroom that dripped out onto the alley. They'd only had to turn it on a handful of times so far.

Jess sat down on the dock and dangled her feet in the water, gesturing for Clara to sit down beside her. "Hey, are we okay?" she asked.

The water wasn't even cold, and between that and the breeze and the warmth from the sun, all the elements were perfect. "What do you mean?" Clara asked. Because she'd made it to the bottom of the stairs—they were fine. Everything was fine. Right now, at least, all Bretts aside.

"Just a tension I'm picking up on," said Jess. "I had to fight to get you up here. Is something up?"

"No, it's fine."

"I don't believe you." Jess had become more direct and harder to distract since she'd left her job and stopped being tired all the time. "You're all *uneasy*."

Clara waited a moment. "Have I ever really been easy?" she asked with a smile.

"Fair," Jess conceded.

"And it is a lot to contend with," Clara admitted. "Being away from home, with little kids. You remember what it was like. It's overwhelming. And all this—" Pointing up at the house. "It's kind of opulent."

"You don't like it." Jess's voice was flat.

"No, I love it," Clara said. "But it's just, I don't know, highly irregular? For us, me and Nick, I mean. It's wonderful, and I'm so happy for you, and grateful for your generosity, but I really don't like knowing that I'm never going to be able to properly return the favour. You know that's hard for me."

"This is friendship, though," said Jess. "It's not a ledger sheet."

"Easy to say when you're not the one incurring debt."

"Are you kidding me?" Jess asked.

"You've opened up your home to us," Clara insisted. "And I'd offer to do the same in return, but we don't have enough chairs. You'd have to sit on the floor. Nick will bring you a drink, but probably in a juice glass."

"Nick's drinks are the best."

"I still don't think that makes us even."

"But it's not a contest," said Jess. "It isn't a race, and don't you remember how you opened up *the world* to me? Inviting me into your room all those years ago? You saved me, Clara. You even made me, I think. And if I have to start paying you back for that, then I'll never be done. Like, the opulence here is just a drop in the bucket."

Jess really meant this too, Clara knew. Maybe it was even true. Somehow in the end, would it all come out even? Could she actually just sit back and enjoy this? "I have no idea how we fit in that room," she finally said. "Both of us in that single bed."

"I loved that room," said Jess.

"Me too," said Clara. "But it was absolutely nowhere until you showed up."

"And I was such a mess," said Jess. "The bottom of the world had just fallen out, and there was no one to catch me. Until you."

"And an abortion," Clara reminded her.

"You and an abortion. Which is what all those Bretts just don't understand, the way it's always a beginning. That without abortion, there would be none of this." She gestured at the whole wide world. "Or us." She said, "We've been so lucky."

"And even when we weren't lucky, we were lucky," said Clara. "Isn't that the real luck? To have stayed together all through our lives?"

Jess recognized the reference. "Like 'Snow White and Rose Red.'"

"The only pair of girls in all of the Grimms. And where are all the rest of them, I wonder?" Clara asked.

"Out picking parsley, I guess."

Clara spoke after a moment. "You've got to know, you made me too."

And then they were quiet, listening to the sounds of seagulls, boats on the water, a door slam.

"You think we can hide down here forever?" Clara whispered.

"Maybe they've forgotten all about us."

"It's unlikely," said Clara, as somewhere up above, one of her children started to scream.

Someone was always screaming. "High needs" is what Jess called it when she was referring to the demands of Clara's children upon their mother's time. Lucinda, Paulina and Shadoe were all remarkably chilled-out kids singularly, but it was more a fact of culmination. If any of them had truly had high needs, Clara would have been in trouble. She was actually grateful for her children's patience and understanding, and the good thing was that they were usually only hysterical one at a time, and if it all added up to someone being hysterical all the time it wasn't their fault.

It was evening and they were inside instead of on the porch because Clara wanted to be able to hear the children if they called her—she didn't believe in baby monitors. Jess's kids had drifted off to sleep without ceremony, or maybe there had been a ceremony, but Clara hadn't noticed in the flurry of her own children's routine, which mainly constituted wrestling all of them into pyjamas and trying and failing to make them stay in bed.

"And I don't know that it's anyone's fault exactly," said Clara, Shadoe in her arms getting one last feed (Clara hoped it was the last) before bedtime. "It is what it is. What can you do?" A rhetorical question. She was so tired, and this was what she'd really been dreading about a week in somebody else's home: when the kids go to bed the day is expected to continue.

"The night is young," said Adam, taking four beers from the fridge, and Nick looked gleeful. He'd forgotten there was an option of a night having youth, other than the infantile kind that insisted on each waking up every hour.

Clara said, "None for me." You could drink while breast-feeding, true, all in moderation, but not while breastfeeding three. This was her reality and she'd made peace with it, glad that nobody gave her a hard time about it. Besides, Nick would drink enough for both of them.

From her seat in the big chair in the corner, Shadoe in her arms, Clara said, "It's weird to be at a cottage that's nicer than my house is."

"This cottage is nicer than everybody's house is," said Jess. "I'm not going to pretend it's normal."

"But we're going to make it cabin-chic," said Adam. "Hang a paddle on the wall. A moose head."

"We will not," said Jess. She took a drink of beer from a tall glass. "It was eleven years ago, can you believe it, when

Bella was a baby and we came up to that place you were staying at on Lake Simcoe."

"The map," said Adam. "Remember the map?"

"You don't draw maps anymore," said Nick to Clara. "I'd forgotten about that. You were a regular cartographer. All those details."

"Three babies, and you stop thinking about details," said Clara. "The world is officially out of my hands." Shadoe was done feeding. She held her out to Nick to take up to bed, even though the likelihood of her staying there was slim. Her three kids would all bunk in together, and even all the way downstairs Clara could hear Lu and Pauly squealing.

Jess said, "Amazing to think how far we've come. And all the people we've acquired."

"Summer accommodations have gone a bit upscale as well," said Clara.

"At least there's room for all of us," Jess said. "Might have been tricky to accommodate five kids in those bunkbeds."

"It was a nice place," said Adam. "I think. It was a thousand years ago. I can barely remember."

"We were babies," said Jess.

"And Bella was so little," said Clara. "You were a maniac. I had no idea."

"It ends," said Jess. "The mania. I thought it never would. I thought I'd be locked in that upside-down chaos, where day was night and the neediness was unrelenting. It really felt like life-or-death sometimes. And I thought it would stay like that forever."

"But one day they start sleeping," said Adam. "I have no idea how it happens, but they do, and there's no more diapers, and it all becomes more manageable. The problems themselves become more complicated, but you deal with it."

"It ends," Jess repeated.

Clara said, "But what if I don't want it to?" She sipped pink lemonade from a beer glass. "I don't know," she said. "It doesn't seem all that bad to me. Everything they need, I can give. It's so easy. It's never going to be so simple again."

"But you get yourself back," said Jess.

Nick returned now with Pauly in his arms and dumped her in Clara's lap. Case in point. "I've never been more myself in my entire life," Clara said, pulling up her shirt and opening the clasp on her nursing bra. The good thing about twins was that they kept things symmetrical.

"You'll see," said Jess. "When the girls are bigger. It's like discovering the world all over again. It's all out there, and you can suddenly do anything."

"Maybe," said Clara. "But I'm not ready yet." Nick took her glass and placed it on the table, because she was now immobile with the sucking toddler slung across her middle.

"How long are you planning to keep breastfeeding?" Jess asked, blunt now.

"We'll be finished when we're finished," Clara said. It was too easy to bait Jess.

"But like, not until they're in kindergarten. They're already old enough to walk up and just ask for it."

Clara said, "What's wrong with that?"

"It's weird." Jess shrugged.

"For whom?" Clara asked.

Adam said, "Now, now."

"It's honestly practical," Clara said. "I might not still be breastfeeding Lu if I didn't have the twins. But since I'm breastfeeding some of them, why not all of them?"

"But soon you'll be done with babies," said Jess.

And Clara said, "Maybe not?"

"Seriously?" Jess was flabbergasted.

"Sure," said Clara, smiling.

"No. Come on." Clara just shrugged, so Jess looked around the room. "Nick? Tell me she's kidding."

Nick just looked sheepish. He'd already finished one beer and was on his second. It had been years since he'd had this much fun. The poor guy didn't get out much.

Clara said, "Why should I be kidding?"

"Because there comes a point," said Jess, "when you know you're done."

"I've heard some people say that," said Clara.

"You have three kids already!"

Clara said, "Then what's another one?"

"Different strokes for different folks," said Adam, relaxed enough to really mean this.

"These aren't strokes, Adam," said Jess, who never relaxed. "This is lunacy. And last time, Clara, you almost died."

Clara sighed, and they all sat silently for a moment, sipping their drinks, comfortable enough not to be riled by the tension in the air. This is what happens when you've known each other forever.

"Is this what you want, Nick?" Jess was insistent. Clara wasn't sure what Nick was going to say, because they'd never really talked about it, because when would they have found the time in the tornado of the last few years? But it had been implied. All those years of wanting . . . it would be strange if it suddenly abated. The longing was still there, it was like a kind of habit.

Nick said, "I like babies." Nick was reliable. He, too, was happy in the whirlwind, and once in a while things settled down enough for that to be affirmed—a moment in which their eyes locked, the solid grasp of his hand in hers, the way he came home every night and took up the baton, keeping their family going. He would draw Clara a bath, and she'd retreat for the only part of the day she was ever alone, emerging restored, ready to go again. He loved it as much as she did, all of this. When Clara settled into bed at night for a brief rest between feeding one child or another, he'd curl up around her and whisper, half-asleep, "You, my darlin', are my home."

Jess said, "I'm just speaking in terms of practicality."

"I don't know," said Clara. "We don't think in those terms. Whatever happens happens. The universe has a plan."

"But you're allowed to make your own plan."

"All my own plans have only ever been overwritten," Clara said. "I'm not trying to drive you berserk, Jess. You asked, and this is how it is. Maybe we'll have another baby, I don't know. I don't even know if we can. But like Nick said, we like babies."

Jess said, "But everybody likes babies. That doesn't mean we have to welcome them indefinitely."

"I can think of worse things," Clara said.

"I like having babies," Nick said. "I like making babies."

"Now you're being gross," said Clara. "They don't want to hear that."

"Not really," said Adam.

"So you're just going to keep having babies and breast-feeding everybody forever," said Jess.

"Yes," said Clara. "That's exactly my plan. Forever, and everybody. Each and every one." Pauly was falling asleep on the nipple. "Can you get her?" she asked Nick. "If you carry her gently, she might stay asleep."

As Nick headed upstairs, Jess asked Clara, "Don't you ever get tired?" Her questioning was less confrontational this time; she was genuinely curious.

And Clara said, shifting in her chair and tucking her legs under her, "I'm tired all the time. But you get on with what you have to do."

"You don't have to do any of this," said Jess.

"But I *want* to," said Clara.

"It becomes so narrow," said Jess. "Life with a baby. That's how I remember it. The universe shrank to the size of a nut. Like being locked in the world's tiniest closet. With no windows."

Clara said, "I don't know. I remember having the whole wide world before I had babies, entire continents, swaths of land and so much limitlessness. And I was just lost and miserable."

"But you weren't," said Jess. "You did everything. I never could have done what you did. You were fearless, and you were awesome."

"I like to think she still is," said Nick, coming back into the room.

Jess said, "I'm not saying she's not."

Clara said, "But I was always sad. And now I'm not anymore, which is the best definition of success I can think of."

They were all quiet for a moment, until Jess said, "You're not *really* going to have another baby, right?"

"Well, not *now*," said Clara. "But I don't know. It's not really even up to me."

"But it is," said Jess, rubbing her forehead. Her glass was empty. "I mean, who else would it be up to?"

"You're making me want to turn the TV on," said Adam. "Do you want me to turn the TV on?"

"No. I'm sorry," Jess said, but not to anyone in particular. She got up and headed for the kitchen. "Anyone else need a drink?"

Clara said, "We're not going to be up much longer anyway. This is the latest we've been awake in such a long time."

They lasted fifteen more minutes. The drive had been tiring, and Clara had had no chance for the afternoon nap she usually took to help her through until the evening. She'd made it until 10 p.m., which was a triumph, but now she needed to get whatever sleep she could before one of the children woke up.

Clara and Nick's room was next to the one where the children were sleeping—for now. Nick and Clara hadn't spent a night unaccompanied by a baby or three since Lu's birth, and so it seemed luxurious to just walk in, flick the light on, and talk in audible tones. The carpet beneath Clara's bare feet was lush, and the bed was soft and king-sized. At home they made do with a double because nothing else would fit in their room, so this was a treat, exactly as Jess had told her it would be. Nighttime at home had become all about dim light, hushed voices, and babies' cries. But now here they were, Clara and her husband, who hadn't really had an actual conversation in two years.

They pulled down the weighted duvet and crawled into the big bed from separate sides, then moved towards each other from what felt like a long distance.

She said, "Here you are." She was so tired her eyes were closed already, but she wanted to be close to Nick, to savour this moment when it was just the two of them. Falling asleep straightaway would be a waste.

He moved away and she heard the click as he turned off the bedside lamp. It was warm under the duvet, which was nice because the AC was on full blast and the house was freezing. Nick was warm too, and he cuddled up close to her.

"So you want another baby," he said.

She shook him off a bit. "Not right now," she said.

"You were goading her."

"A bit," she said. She kissed his shoulder. "Do you?"

"Do I what?"

"Want another baby."

He was quiet. Then he said, "We don't even know if we could."

"But if it happened?"

"If it happened it would happen."

"It would be crazy."

"So you weren't just taking the piss."

"I was, a little," she said. She rolled onto her back. "I like having babies. I love it. I'd keep having them over and over so there was always at least one. Big kids are so much more complicated. Less portable."

"Especially when there are three."

She nodded. "It's not rational, I know," she said. "But what's rational about wanting a baby at all?"

"It's about survival, I guess," Nick said. "Perpetuating the species."

"But on a practical level," she said. "It's madness. And I kind of love the madness."

He kissed her on the forehead. "And I love you."

"Then you're mad," she said.

"Don't I know it." He said, "You're sure you don't want to make a baby tonight?"

She rolled away from him. "With a bed this big, we could sleep in different time zones."

He moved towards her. "I like our bed," he said. "Our bed where my feet hang off the end. That's madness too."

Clara put her arms around him and breathed him in. He'd be heading back to the city tomorrow night with Adam. Althea had been enlisted to fill the parenting gap, to ensure that Clara's week at the cottage was something like the holiday Jess had promised. Clara's chief concern in all of this was mostly sentimental; she and Nick had never spent a week apart. Even when she'd been in the hospital after the twins, he'd spent the nights trying to sleep on a chair beside her. She didn't want to be without him and didn't even know how to be.

She said, "Maybe we could go back with you tomorrow."

"And miss your holiday?"

"I'll miss you," she said.

"You should stay," he said.

"Won't you miss me?"

"Of course," he said. "But you'll have a good time, and then you'll be home again. It will be good for you."

"You'll be all alone." She said, "Promise you'll tell me what that's like. Take notes and answer my questions. What is quiet?"

"If you wanted the answer to that," he said, "you wouldn't want another baby."

"I want another baby," she said, trying out the sound of the words. "But what if I end up wanting babies forever? What if I do turn into that woman who lives in a shoe?"

"We couldn't afford a shoe," said Nick.

"Maybe we could all just move up here," said Clara. "We could take over a wing of this place, and they might not even notice."

"Live between the floors," said Nick. "Subsisting on table scraps and making furniture out of empty spools of thread. Dollhouse furniture."

"I'm going to miss you so much," she said, holding him close, trying to remember.

Finally, Clara confessed she was nervous about the kids being out on the lawn. Lu had been down there playing with Bella, and Althea had been watching them, but the problem wasn't supervision.

"All it takes is for someone to slip, or go after a ball. I can't, Jess," said Clara. "It really scares me."

And so Althea brought the kids back up to the deck, where they could block off the steps and everyone could play in relative safety. Bella was annoyed that her freedom was being curtailed, and Miles kept kicking his ball over the railing. Clara was in the kitchen giving the twins breakfast, and they were itching to go out into the sunshine.

"Well, hurry up and finish," Clara told them, picking up their spoons from the floor, where they had hurled them over and over. Clara had tied them to the kitchen chairs with hemp rope harnesses, a clever substitute for highchairs, but now apple sauce was smeared across the upholstered chair backs. And it was flavoured and coloured with raspberry, and so were their faces.

"Don't worry," called Jess, tossing Clara a wet cloth. "It will wipe clean." She was almost pathologically unwilling to be rattled. Clara found it kind of annoying. Maybe having a kitchen out of a television commercial turned you into a person from a television commercial, she reflected. Any minute Jess might start confessing her enthusiasm for yoghurt.

"Listen, I got you something," Jess said. "Don't get mad."

"You got me something?" Jess handed her a package wrapped in brown paper stamped with her shop's elegant C&O logo in fancy script. "It was just your birthday, and I didn't get you anything at all," said Clara.

"You did," said Jess. "You came here. And this something is almost nothing. It's just fun. A beach read."

"A beach read," said Clara. "There's a pipe dream. I haven't read anything in a hundred years."

"Well, you might be able to pull it off," said Jess. "Or you can come up again next summer, and you'll definitely be able to." She said, "'This time next year—' It's the only thought that got me through the baby days. And it was easier with Miles, because I knew we'd never have to go through it ever again."

The twins were almost finished eating. Clara wiped her hands on her dress and unwrapped the package: *Fried Green Tomatoes at the Whistle Stop Café*. "I remember this," said Clara. There'd been a movie too. It was one of the books she'd read when they first met. "Idgie Threadgoode," she recalled, unearthing the character's name. "This is a first edition?" she asked. Clara liked the idea behind Jess's shop, but it was not a place for bargain hunters.

Jess said, "Well, it's a first edition mass-market paperback. Feel free to break the spine or drop it off the side of the dock. No pressure. It's meant to be read."

"I'll try," said Clara. It was a thoughtful gift. "I'm just going to get these guys cleaned up," she said. It made no sense the way people went on about how demanding breastfeeding was when solid foods just led to one chore after another: preparing, defrosting, serving, cleaning.

"Take your time," Jess called over her shoulder as she loaded the dishwasher. "And then we'll head down to the beach." Those stairs again.

The thing about having forty-seven steps is that you only want to take one trip, so they had to bring everything all at once when they went down. Jess was laden with mini-coolers, towels, snacks, pool noodles, and other toys. Althea led Lu down, and Clara was holding the twins, one on her back in a carrier and the other on her hip. *Fried Green Tomatoes* was under her arm, wishful thinking.

It was a long journey, with Miles and Bella scampering ahead just fast enough that an onlooker would fear for their lives at the sight of their winged feet flying down the dilapidated staircase. Lu hampered their progress by periodically sitting down on her little bum and refusing to hold Althea's hand. Clara decided to simply trust her feet, one step after another.

Once they finally got to the bottom, the little ones were happy to play in the sand, digging into it with their fists and shovelling handfuls in their mouths. This made Jess so uneasy she looked at Clara with concern.

"Don't worry," said Clara, amused at her friend's expression. "It's what they came from anyway. Just imagine it's stardust."

Lu paddled in the water, still refusing to take Althea's hand, but the nanny stayed close, attentive. This meant that Clara could relax a little bit and let the babies enjoy the sand. Miles and Bella were jumping off the dock, creating terrific splashes. The sun was glorious, and the scrubby trees along the shore provided relief from its intensity. There was a light breeze. All this was okay. Clara still felt unbalanced for not having Nick close at hand, but it was okay. They were going to be fine. It was a beautiful day.

"Want to swim?" asked Jess. "The water is nice. And we can get away right now. Want to? While we've got the chance?"

Althea said she would watch the twins and call Clara back to shore if necessary, and Jess was right; there would never be a better moment to escape. Clara peeled off her oversized T-shirt, revealing her big body and pale skin.

"Move on, nothing to see here," she said to Jess, who was staring. "Just a lady's white, white bod." She wore a new suit, purchased to assuage some of her dread of this holiday. It was plain black, with gathering fabric across the stomach to hide any kind of unsightliness and legs that came partway down the thighs with old-fashioned glamour. It was the most expensive item of clothing she'd bought in years, but it was worth it for the confidence it gave her to walk down to the water with her friend, whose discovery of yoga had banished all evidence that her body had ever borne children.

They grabbed pool noodles and waded into the water. Their inclination would have been to jump off the dock too, but they wanted space from Miles and Bella. And so they had to ease their way in slowly, the worst way, feeling the shock of the water over and over.

"Don't stop moving," Jess called out, the pool noodle under her arms keeping her buoyant. "You'll get used to it."

And they did. They kicked and kicked, swimming out until the water was deep enough that even the weeds were far below and it was hard to see the details on the shore because of the way the sunlight sparkled on the water.

"We've lost our moorings," said Clara.

Jess said, "But doesn't it feel good?"

It did. It was wonderful to be floating, weightless, Clara on her back feeling the warm sun on her face. The water was invigorating. Possibilities were endless.

"This is what I wanted," said Jess. "For you to be here and for us to be doing something in the here and now. To have a conversation that doesn't necessarily start with, 'Remember when . . .'"

"But you do remember when," said Clara, treading water.

Jess said, "Of course I do. Sitting on the windowsill upstairs in your room, remember that? I remember everything."

"It's all kind of blurry for me," said Clara. "All of the days, and the way they run together. I never thought it would happen, that those days would seem far away."

"We were so young," said Jess. "We thought we'd just arrived . . ."

"But life is long," said Clara.

"And yet it all starts to go by so fast."

"We could have just floated away back then," said Clara. "That's what I remember, the freedom. But also so much wanting and longing."

"*So* much longing," agreed Jess. "One good thing about this march toward death is that you never ever have to be in your early twenties again."

A boat sped by and its wake sent them rolling up and down, waves splashing in their faces.

"They're okay?" Clara asked, looking to the shore, where the children were still absorbed in their pursuits. She couldn't see the twins now. This was the farthest away she'd ever been from them.

"They're fine," said Jess. "Althea's great. I told you."

"You told me," said Clara, on her back again. "Look at that sky. So vivid. So much *blue*. If I painted that, you'd tell me it couldn't be real."

"But I wouldn't," said Jess. "I've seen the sky."

"And the way it disappears, blending right into the horizon, the lake. How there's no real distinction between one thing and another."

A plane far overhead drew a line right in the centre.

"It's only us," said Jess. "And we're so small."

Clara agreed. "Miniscule."

ACKNOWLEDGEMENTS

The article about children locked in hot cars is the Pulitzer Prize–winning "Fatal Distraction" by Gene Weingarten, published in the *Washington Post* in 2009. Charlotte Nordstrom is not a real person, but Ursula Nordstrom was a legendary children's book editor whose collected letters, *Dear Genius*, is one of the best books I've ever read. The Charlotte Nordstrom Institute for Folk and Fairy Tales was inspired by the Osborne Collection of Early Children's Books at the Lillian H. Smith Library in Toronto, and while I made up its employees' petty grievances, the place is worth a visit. A trip to "Pompeii: In the Shadow of the Volcano" at the Royal Ontario Museum in 2015 gave me the spark of this tale. "The children you have make any other world impossible" is something Dr. Rebecca Dolgoy said to me many years ago, before she really knew. Thanks to Melissa Borg-Olivier for telling me about the edible qualities of tulip bulbs.

Being edited by Bhavna Chauhan (AGAIN!) is one of the great thrills of my life—thank you for believing in these characters and this story. I'm so grateful for that single thread of gold that tied me to you. And to Megan Kwan, whose engagement with this story has been so rich and insightful. I'm grateful also to everybody at Doubleday Canada and Penguin Random House Canada—Amy Black, Val Gow, Maria Golikova, Kaitlin Smith, Chalista Andadari, Lisa Jager, Kate Panek—for their hard work in bringing this book into the world. And to my agent, Samantha Haywood, and her colleagues at Transatlantic Literary Agency for being in my corner and doing it so well.

I owe a lot to writers and friends whose true and complicated stories of motherhood enabled me to imagine my way into heightened and essential scenes. This book also owes a debt to Margaret Atwood's *The Edible Woman*, whose depiction of a monstrously pregnant woman confined to a chaise longue has haunted me forever.

I would know nothing about long friendships were it not for the women to whom this book is dedicated—I feel like this book was born out of conversations we've been having for the last three decades—and so many others, including my cousin, Susannah Campbell, who is my oldest friend, and my sister, Christy Massey, who is my second-oldest. I'm so grateful to Rebecca Rosenblum, who read a painfully early draft of this book and provided valuable feedback. Thank you to Nathalie Foy, in whose company I began writing my very first draft during our writing dates at the Red Fish Blue Fish Creative Café. And to my Salonista and Coven friends, the very best colleagues in this writing life.

Because of Kiley Turner and Craig Riggs, I have the greatest job at 49thShelf.com. Because of Nurith and Eldad Jungreis, I have a wonderful home (and the best neighbours). I am ever grateful to my parents for all their love and support, to my children for the lucky fact of their existence, and to Stuart Lawler, my partner in all things, not least for always knowing that if he wanted to be my lover, he had to get with my friends.

1. Jess and Clara have very different approaches to life, love, motherhood, but they manage to be friends anyway. What do you think makes them so compatible? What makes their friendship endure? Do you think they will remain friends for life?

2. Which of the characters did you connect most strongly to in this novel and why? Who did you relate to the least?

3. Did Jess and Clara's friendship call to mind a certain friend in your life, past or present? In what ways is that relationship similar to theirs? How is it different?

4. How would you describe Jess and Clara's individual experiences of motherhood? Did you find one more relatable over the other?

5. One of Kerry Clare's favourite lines in the book is, "That night she would fall asleep in her clothes, waking in the morning with that delicious kind of ache and regret that

affirms that, while your life might be ridiculous, at least you're actually alive." (p. 35) Describe a time you had a similar feeling, choosing to do something you might regret later. What line or moment in the novel has stuck most with you?

6. Describe the arcs of Jess and Clara's characters from the beginning of the novel to its end. Did your opinion of either of them change as the story unfolded?

7. Who would you cast in the movie adaptation of *Asking for a Friend*?

8. Kerry Clare incorporates the theme of fairytales throughout. Did any of the earlier versions of tales surprise you? What's your favourite fairy tale?

9. How do the ways Clara and Jess cope with loss and grief differ from each other? How are they similar?

10. Like the author, Clara and Jess often turn to tea and swimming throughout the novel when seeking comfort and calm. What are some of the things or practices that you turn to in times of unrest?

11. Clara realizes that "she'd come to depend on Jess during their years together, a fact that drove her to put distance between them just to prove that she could." (p. 87) Discuss the themes of independence and co-dependence as they are explored throughout the different stages of Jess and Clara's friendship. Describe a point in your life where you felt moved to test your independence.

12. The author has woven several cultural references to the late nineties and early aughts into the story. If you, like Jess and Clara, grew up during these years, what were some of your favourite nods to these times?

13. At one point, Jess thinks, "Surely it was time she became the pilot of her life?" (p. 79) What are your thoughts on leaving matters up to fate versus taking destiny into your own hands? Do you think, up until that point, that Jess was just a passenger in her life? Why or why not?

© Stuart Lawler

KERRY CLARE is the author of novels *Waiting for a Star to Fall* and *Mitzi Bytes*, and editor of *The M Word: Conversations About Motherhood*. A National Magazine Award–nominated essayist, and editor of Canadian books website 49thShelf.com, she writes about books and reading at her long-time blog, Pickle Me This. She lives in Toronto with her family.

 @kerryreads